THE

CHOSEN

ONE

a novel by

T. B. MARKINSON

Published by T. B. Markinson

Visit T. B. Markinson's official website at

tbmarkinson.wordpress.com for the latest news, book details,

and other information.

Copyright © T. B. Markinson, 2015

Cover Design by Erin Dameron-Hill / EDHGraphics

Edited by Jeri Walker and Karin Cox

Proofread by Kelly Hashway

CHAPTER
one

ALL I COULD THINK WAS *va-va-voom*. At ten minutes to eight in the morning on the second Monday in September, I hadn't expected to meet the girl of my dreams. Yet when she had arrived, I barely registered her presence.

Moments before, I had entered a lecture room at Whitlock University and chosen the third row by the door. I claimed a metal ergonomic chair on wheels, which looked more like a torture device. Each row was slightly higher than the one before it, with long tables configured at an awkward oval shape, conducive for discussion, not comfort.

I studied the room. On the far side, the floor-to-ceiling windows overlooked the Charles River. The room had recently been remodeled and still smelled of fresh paint and new carpet. The ivy-covered red brick and white columns on the exterior maintained the charm of the year it was built, 1743.

Even when dream girl stood next to me and asked whether the seat to the immediate left was taken, I didn't peek in her direction. I shrugged without glancing up, too busy doodling on the first page of my Massachusetts history notepad and twirling ginger hair around one finger. I shifted focus, scanning *Politico* headlines on my iPad. Politics was a personal obsession that had started as a forced family obligation. I could spout the names of all the presidents and first ladies before I mastered the alphabet. By the age of ten, I was drinking the Kool-Aid.

But when the girl continued to stand next to me, a weird tingling sensation zipped through my body, compelling me to look at the source of the voice.

She smiled nervously, and that was when I noticed her soft blue-gray eyes. Such startling eyes — more gray than blue.

That was when *va-va-voom* invaded my mind. I'd never been girl-crazy before, although by the age of fourteen I knew I was into chicks. My political ambition had ruled everything out, until this morning. Avoiding scandal was the name of the game. Tick all the right boxes. Attend a top-ten college. Rack up years of dedicated volunteer service, internships, et cetera. It was all for the goal: the top prize in American politics.

Girls were a risk I didn't need. Until now, except for a small but disastrous blip, I had stayed the course. My urges were satiated by countless lesbian romance novels and films. The safest relationships were those in my head. I could live with that.

Or so I thought.

Never before had I been turned on by someone's eyes, but hers … *Oh my.*

Prior to this September day, gray had seemed like such a blah color. Insignificant. Now it defined everything. Her gray eyes were inquisitive, alive, sweet, and smoking hot — not to mention completely unusual for someone with darker skin. The throbbing intensified, and I shifted in my seat to smother the fire down below.

The girl cautiously slid into the vacant seat, and I pretended to stifle a yawn with my palm and peered around the room, all the while checking out the gray-eyed bombshell sitting so close I could feel her body heat. She wore a plain black T-shirt — not too tight, although it showed plenty — dark skinny jeans, and black Nikes. Her spiky, short pixie cut was a silky dark chestnut.

Her posture wasn't slack or upright, suggesting she didn't want to be noticed. But those bewitching eyes with lush lashes were way too noticeable, hypnotic even.

She resembled someone, but who? I peeped again. Her full lips reminded me of Rosario Dawson — a girl I'd had a crush on since seeing her sing "Out Tonight" in *Rent*. Rosario had been one of my first imaginary girlfriends when I was fourteen. For a brief moment, I imagined the girl sitting next to me dancing in a strip club, a la Rosario, in a shiny black bra, panties, and long black boots.

The warmth in my panties spread. Would there be a wet spot on the back of my dress if I stood?

I fidgeted in my seat and coughed nervously. Surely no one in the classroom sensed my longing. Crossing my legs, I leaned on the table with both arms. Then I closed my eyes and mentally chanted, *Just don't think about her* ten times.

Okay, Ainsley, I think the leaky situation is under control. My eyes popped open, and I couldn't stop myself from taking another sneak peek at those wonderful eyes.

The unquenchable throbbing returned with a vengeance.

I needed a new game plan, an image that would kill all illicit thoughts.

Think, Ains.

Grandmother.

The image of my thin, ninety-one-year-old Carmichael matriarch standing on the front porch, leaning on her cane, watching and commanding the family from afar, haunted my every action and thought.

For a moment, I forgot all about Gray Eyes.

Damn, did I just give her a nickname?

A few more students straggled in and took their seats. The room buzzed with tension, like we were waiting for a pep talk from our coach before starting a championship game. However, this wasn't a game. Not for me, at least. It was a step. Grandmother was grooming me to become the youngest female president of the

United States.

No joke.

One minute to go before the first class of my first semester at Whitlock University commenced.

I glanced at Gray Eyes. It seemed to be her first time as well. She had pen and paper ready. Not many of the other students had bothered to open their bags, let alone drag out materials to take notes. A few had powered up their laptops, but I think they were catching up with social media, not prepping for a lecture. The girl in front of me updated her Facebook status to "Starting another semester. Can't wait to graduate this May." I stifled a laugh. She had waited three years to take a freshman-level course. *What an amateur.*

My mind wandered back to Gray Eyes, and I wanted her to turn toward me so I could feast on those eyes. From stolen glimpses, I sensed roiling emotions ranging from angry to scared to cocky. Seeing all those feelings crammed into one pair of eyes was simultaneously disconcerting and comforting. I hungered for a better chance to detect the range of her emotions, but immediately started up the "no-relationships" mantra in my head again. As Grandma repeatedly said, "You were put on this earth to be president. Nothing else." I believed it.

A woman in her late fifties paraded in, set a black leather briefcase next to the lectern, and wrote her name on the whiteboard. She gripped the pen with meaty fingers, as if she wanted to snap it in half. Her name, Dr. Gingas, appeared with the final stroke of the marker, but I already knew it.

Rustling filled the lecture hall as everyone waited for the professor to begin. The portly woman, stuffed into a nondescript black skirt and blazer, didn't seem to be in a hurry. Instead, Dr. Gingas momentarily locked eyes with each student — roughly forty-five pupils. Her beady eyes, set behind a long, sharp nose and puffy cheeks, conjured up some nasty similarities in my mind, the most apropos being a comparison to Genghis Khan, the cruel Mongol conqueror of the 1200s. I had a hunch that Dr. Gingas had experienced a difficult childhood and now repeatedly sought revenge on her unsuspecting students.

I sized up Gray Eyes in her dark clothes, took a gander at Dr. Gingas, and then stared down at my outfit. My pink sundress stood out like a flamingo in Alaska, which brought a smile to my face. My mother had always insisted I should never wear pink, stating it didn't suit the curly red locks I wore swept back in a ponytail most days. Unless I spent an ample amount of time in the morning taming the unruliness, my tight curls sprang in every direction like weeds in a hanging flower basket. I was an early riser, however, I preferred to cram every waking moment with working out, reading political tomes and blogs, studying history, scouring newspapers, absorbing the daily briefing reports I received from Grandmother's goons, listening to political podcasts, volunteering, and so much more than styling my hair. Wearing pink wasn't a blatant attempt to throw off my parental shackles, though. It had been my favorite color ever since preschool, when I'd had to forego carrying my pink Beanie Baby sock monkey everywhere. And I didn't give a damn if the color clashed with my Scottish heritage.

"Good morning, class. From the looks of it, some of your colleagues decided to skip the first day, thinking we'd only go over the syllabus." The professor smirked, happy to rain on people's parade.

I glanced around the room, noticing a few empty seats but not enough to warrant the statement. Something told me Dr. Gingas didn't like being dissed, period.

"That's a shame, since I like to jump right in. Everyone take out a piece of paper. Don't forget to write your name in the upper right-hand corner, along with your student ID number. This will count for your attendance today."

She waited behind the podium while everyone followed her directions. Her fingers glommed the edges, whitening her knuckles. Was she always this uptight, or was she trying to scare the crapola out of me? Either way, it was working.

"Here's the first of many pop quizzes."

Several groans came from the audience.

She put a palm up to silence the protests. "You aren't in high school anymore. I'm not here to hold your hand. Trust me, the real world is a fucking bitch. It's best you learn that now." From the glint in her eyes, she took great pleasure in teaching us that lesson. It was something I'd already learned. Before I was born, my eldest brother died from leukemia, and my father was killed in a car accident the day before my birth.

Dr. Gingas ignored the gasps and busied herself by flipping on a projector and firing up a PowerPoint presentation. A list of ten ridiculously simple questions appeared on the whiteboard. "Who is the current governor of Massachusetts? What year did Massachusetts become a state? What was its nickname(s)?" It was hard not to laugh as I scanned them before quickly jotting down the answers.

Several minutes ticked by. Some students stared at the questions and then down at their papers, lost. *Really?* Okay, some of these jokers might be from a different state, but the questions were child's play. Just keeping up with the local news and blogs would answer half of them. This entry-level class wasn't mandatory unless a student planned to pursue a career in politics. Everyone knew that. At least, I thought so. I viewed this class as the first step in my presidential quest.

It sounded preposterous, but my family had been involved in politics since before the Revolutionary War.

I could practically hear my grandmother's monologue about the Carmichael scion in my head: *The Carmichael drive to succeed on American soil started back in the mid-1600s, Ainsley. Our first Scottish ancestor didn't immigrate to America by choice. He was captured during the Battle of Dunbar in Scotland, which took place on September 3, 1650. English forces under Oliver Cromwell defeated a Scottish army, who supported King Charles II. The Scots were soundly beaten and hundreds died on the battlefield. The prisoners of war were forced to march south, toward England. Hundreds, if not thousands, perished. The survivors arrived at Durham Cathedral, where they were imprisoned. The remaining prisoners were eventually shipped to the colonies in New England, Virginia, and the Caribbean as* convict *laborers.*

Usually, she whispered the word "convict."

George Carmichael had landed in Massachusetts stripped of his freedom. When he had stepped off the boat nearly 365 years ago, his ignoble start on American soil had needled him as much as it continued to infuriate Grandmother today.

Me, I didn't care too much about the origins of the Carmichaels — not that I would ever say so to Grandmother, who had an unpleasant and finite way of dealing with insubordination. I cared about the future. My future. But I was wise enough to know George Carmichael's past played a key role in my political biography. Every good politician needed an inspiring narrative.

"Time's up! Pass your papers forward." Dr. Gingas motioned to hurry and not waste time.

The crinkling of papers being shuffled forward and students grumbling permeated the air.

Dr. Gingas rifled through the papers, scanning the answers. I was amazed by her speed, considering there were roughly forty-something quizzes. She pulled two papers out of the pile and compared them to the one at the top of the stack.

"Where is Ainsley Carmichael?"

I raised my arm. Dr. Gingas nodded crisply in my direction. I couldn't tell whether she was satisfied or not with my quiz, although I was fairly certain I had answered the questions correctly — not that I would argue with Genghis.

Some murmuring arose, and a few people turned to eyeball me — the daughter of the senior Massachusetts senator, niece of the Democratic Leader in the House of Representatives. A decade ago, another family member had been governor of the Bay State.

"Maya Chandler?"

Gray Eyes raised her hand but kept her eyes locked on the notepad. Dr. Gingas didn't acknowledge that Maya refused to look at her. However, my intuition pinged loudly. There was no way Dr. Gingas didn't notice. I wouldn't want to play poker with Professor Khan. She probably preferred Russian roulette anyway.

"And Susie Quillian?"

Susie?

How had I missed her entrance? I'd been so entranced by Gray Eyes that I'd forgotten the first rule of politics: know your adversary.

I honed in on my blonde nemesis since kindergarten. Per usual, she sat in the front row, smack-dab in the center. Her father, Reginald Quillian, had been the Republican governor of Massachusetts back before I wore big-girl pants. The Carmichaels were staunch Democrats. In 2008, Reggie tried to win my mother's senate seat. To be fair, the election was much closer than anticipated.

The day Susie's father had lost was the exact day Susie declared all-out war. Susie didn't dream about being president, unlike me, but politics coursed through her veins all the same. While I idolized Honest Abe, Susie aspired to be a controversial Ann Coulter, the conservative political commentator. In high school, Susie started a blog. By the time she was a junior, she'd launched her YouTube channel: *Susie Q's Tattler*, where she highlighted all the "misdeeds" of politicians. Her broad stroke target was Democrats, but most of her venom was directed at my family, and I took the brunt of the abuse. The divide between the truth and Susie Q was wider and deeper than the Grand Canyon.

"The three of you get an A for today." Dr. Gingas set the papers down on the table and walked to the lectern. She advanced to the next PowerPoint slide, casually stating, "The rest of you get an F." A hint of glee resided in her frown.

Someone laughed but stopped immediately when Dr. Gingas snapped her head up to locate the offender. "There will be ten pop quizzes this semester. You'll be allowed to drop your lowest grade."

"But that's not fair," whined a male voice from the back of the room.

The professor's eyes twinkled. "My class, my rules."

"What is this? A dictatorship?" challenged another student.

"Very good. You do know something about history and

government. I was starting to wonder if I'd wandered into the wrong classroom." Dr. Gingas grinned. I waited for her to start shouting, "Off with their heads."

Maya the Gray squirmed in her seat, keeping her head down. *Shoot! Did I just give her another nickname?*

Dr. Gingas began her lecture, telling us how pilgrims lived in 1620. Maya's pen furiously scribbled notes on environmentally friendly paper. Was she transcribing every single word?

The remaining thirty minutes flew by. When Dr. Gingas stopped speaking, I was surprised to find I had taken three full pages of notes, front and back.

"I didn't bother printing out the syllabus, since the department is cutting back on expenses," said Dr. Gingas. "When you log into your student account, you'll find it. If you checked yesterday, you probably would have noticed the warning about the pop quiz today. Actually, all of the questions were posted, although I'm assuming only three of you bothered to check." She thrust her double chin at me, followed by Maya, who didn't notice Dr. Gingas's stare, and finally at Susie. Several students closed their notebooks and laptops angrily.

"It is imperative that you check your account every day for messages and assignments. Welcome to Whitlock University, folks." With that, she plucked her thumb drive from the podium computer, smooshed the quiz papers into her briefcase, and stormed out of the room.

Students rushed out after her, swearing under their breath. I took my time putting my notebook and tablet away. Maya was still writing in her notebook, and I wanted to see her face again. A few students stared at me like they wanted to toss me in front of the next train on the Red Line. They glared at Maya the Gray too, to no avail. She had only looked up for the quiz and to occasionally check the PowerPoint slides.

Susie flashed a malicious grin as she passed, snapping a photo of me on her iPhone. "Well, well, well, Piglet," she said. "I would say congrats, but I don't like to encourage cheaters."

"How does knowing the answers equate to cheating? You passed as well. Does that mean you cheated?" I asked, ignoring the nickname I'd earned at sixteen in an incident that irrevocably shaped my opinion on trusting girls, even childhood friends.

Susie put a finger to her chin and cocked her head. "Please, we both know who's smarter. And your family history screams the truth. Carmichaels love to discover the questions ahead of time. Like mother, like daughter."

"I didn't know the questions were available." I sensed my face was starting to match my hair. Reggie Quillian had accused my mother of cheating during the senatorial debates by bribing people for the questions ahead of time.

"Yeah, right. You Carmichaels are all alike." She triumphantly sashayed out, her hips swaying from side to side. I had to admit she had a nice ass. Not that I would ever pursue such an evil bitch, not even for an imagined romance.

Aghast by her accusation, I fumed silently. The only person within hearing distance was Maya, and she was lost in her note-taking. Her pen never stilled during the brief confrontation. Was she deaf? No, that couldn't be; she had raised her hand when prompted. Maybe she had a photographic memory and was literally transcribing the PowerPoint slides. Was this part of her study routine? Repetition?

I pretended to peruse my cell phone for e-mails, stalling to catch one more glimpse of those eyes. Soon, it was just the two of us in the room. I cleared my throat, but Maya continued to scribble even as students for the next class filtered in.

It was probably for the best, anyway. It wasn't like I would consider dropping my no-girls rule, not even for Gray Eyes.

CHAPTER *two*

I WANDERED TO THE COFFEE shop in the student union and logged into my student account on my iPad. I hadn't checked my university account yet, so I was curious to see whether Dr. Gingas was fibbing. Sure enough, there was the syllabus and the pop quiz warning, along with all the questions. My next class wasn't until eleven, so I opened up the syllabus and scanned the breakdown of assignments.

My eyes zeroed in on the words "group project." Just great. Every such project I had worked on in high school had been a complete failure. Not that I failed. No, I did all the work, and everyone received an A due to my diligence.

I checked my e-mail and saw one from Mother. The subject line read, "What's the nickname of Massachusetts?"

I dashed out of the building. She answered on the first ring, laughing.

"You knew?" I asked.

"You still haven't answered. What's the nickname?"

"The Bay State," I said through gritted teeth. "Or the Baked Bean State."

She stopped laughing briefly. "Don't forget the Old Colony State and the Pilgrim State."

"You could have warned me."

My mother, the senator, knew every history and political science professor at Whitlock.

"Now that would be cheating. I believe today's lesson is 'always be prepared, even when you don't think you need to be.'" I could feel her slimy politician smile over the phone. "What's the first rule in politics?"

"Know your adversary." I grunted.

I could hear someone talking to her, and the rustle of her hand covering the phone's speaker. And then she was back. "If I'm not mistaken, your next class is at eleven. I hope you're prepared this time." She ended the call.

My next class was an introduction to Shakespeare, and I knew full well she didn't know the professor. Mom was purposefully trying to scare me, and it wasn't working. Not completely.

CHAPTER
three

AROUND FIVE, I FINISHED UP my final class for the day. I packed classes in on Mondays, Wednesdays, and Fridays, leaving Tuesdays and Thursdays to continue my volunteer and political work. This semester, I was to intern for Paulette Murray, a member of the Massachusetts senate, every Tuesday. On Thursdays, I was scheduled to help out at a homeless shelter for teens and a community center. My cousins teased that I was a do-gooder poser, which was better than what my peers said. Most accused me of wanting to pad my resume solely to get elected in the future. Volunteering was never an option in my family, but unlike most of my family members, I actually enjoyed community work. Making a difference in the lives of ordinary folks was hard to explain, except to say that it powered me through the rest of my obligations. Yes, my ultimate drive was to be president, but I wanted to be a president who would help change the lives of those in need. My motto was "Be like Abe." He abolished slavery. I wanted to be as transformative, if not more.

I walked through Harvard Square to meet my cousin Fiona for dinner. Several street musicians were camped out, guitar cases open for collecting tips. University students, tourists, and locals crammed the sidewalks, making it difficult to walk without bumping into someone or something.

A thin woman in her twenties placed a paper in my palm. "Read," she instructed. I couldn't stop staring at her frizzy hair and bugged-out eyes. The crazy person tapped the paper again. "You must read."

"Me?" I tapped my chest.

"It's for you. Read," she commanded.

I held it up and read aloud, "'The winds and waves are always on the side of the ablest navigators.'" I glanced up. "What the?" But the woman was gone. My eyes searched for her to no avail; the crowd gobbled her up, denying me a chance to ask questions. "Freak," I muttered under my breath, tucking the paper into my bag.

Twenty feet away I spied a girl in a black T-shirt and jeans rounding the corner of Brattle Street toward Mt. Auburn Street. She disappeared quickly, and I wasn't entirely certain it was Gray Eyes, but my body was tingling like it had earlier. All thoughts of the mad woman who had accosted me seconds before faded from my brain.

I wavered, trying to decide whether to head in the opposite direction to the restaurant so I wouldn't be late meeting Fiona, or to chase after some girl who might not even be the mysterious Maya the Gray. Even if it was her, what was my plan? Slam her against a wall, say, "Hey, we're going to be friends whether you want to or not," and follow up by tossing an arm around her shoulder?

Why the compulsion to chase after a girl I had no intention of seeking a relationship with?

Screw it. I chased after Maya. If I found her, I'd go from there. I was fairly sure my initial plan would only get me arrested. I needed to channel suaveness. Think JFK.

The black shirt disappeared into a trendy Parisian café called La Creperie. Perfect. I texted my cousin to meet me there, claiming I was in dire need of a caffeine fix and I'd heard through the family grapevine that this joint had the best java and crepes. As Fiona was a coffee junkie, I knew she wouldn't complain.

I stalled outside, scanning articles on *HuffPo* and praying Gray Eyes wasn't getting her order to go. I glanced at my watch. Six minutes had passed. Surely she'd already ordered, and it was safe for me to venture inside.

Think JFK.

I opened the door.

Maya stood to the side of the register, waiting.

I strode to the counter like I owned the place. "Hi! Was your day as long as mine?" I asked the female employee, who sported nose, eyebrow, and lip piercings. Yikes. She would never be elected to any office with those, not even dogcatcher. I dropped my school bag down on the tiled floor.

The woman behind the counter stared at me like I was the biggest fool in the world. Of course her day had been long; she'd probably manned the counter for hours, on her feet, making thin pancakes and fancy cups of coffee for spoiled brats who considered a full day of classes backbreaking work.

I worried the heat emanating from my cheeks would set off the fire alarm. Instead of JFK, I'd come across as a grade-A jackass.

"What can I get you?" the woman said with as much cheer as possible, considering she looked like she wanted to tell me to go eff myself.

I couldn't blame her. "Coffee, please." I really wanted something with a wow factor, but I could feel Maya studying me, and I didn't think ordering a froufrou drink would impress her at all.

"For here or to go?"

I wasn't positive, but it sounded like the pierced woman stressed the words *to go*, implying I wasn't welcome to stay.

"Here, please," I responded cheerily. "I'm meeting someone." I better justify why I wasn't taking her not-so-subtle hint.

"Right." The woman stared off to my right as if she thought I was the type to have imaginary friends. I didn't, of course, just imaginary sex flings, but it was probably best to keep that to myself.

Luckily, Fiona, who lived a few blocks from the restaurant, rushed in at that point. "Ainsley, darling!" she squealed as if it had been years since we'd seen each other. In actuality, it had only been a couple of days, and we had spent the entire summer together at the Cape. Fiona wrapped her arms around me. "I've missed you." She planted a sloppy kiss on each cheek.

We looked like lovers, not cousins. It was the first time she had ever greeted me in this fashion, and talk about awful timing — worse than awful.

It dawned on me that my mouth was open in shock. "I-I missed you too," I stammered.

Not noticing my discomfort, Fiona spun around to order. This couldn't have gone any worse if I had planned it. Maya was still waiting for her order with an expression that was hard to read: amusement or disgust? Maybe both.

Shit! Do something, Ainsley.

"Uh, you're in my class, aren't you?"

"Your class?" Maya quirked an eyebrow. Her sultry voice matched my Rosario Dawson *Rent* imaginings. Va-va-voom!

"History of Massachusetts," I clarified, trying to ignore the sensation zipping through my body while worrying I was grinning like a fool.

"Yes, I'm in that class." Her eyes pulled me in.

I put a hand out. "I'm Ainsley."

"Maya." Several rough calluses pressed into my palm. After one resolute up-and-down motion she broke contact, leaving me wanting more.

Fiona draped an arm around my shoulders. "So, do you feel like a woman now?"

I nearly dropped my coffee cup. "W-what?"

Maya the Gray tilted her head ever so slightly, as if curious, but it was hard to read her thoughts. She'd give Dr. Gingas a run for her money in the poker-face department.

"Now that you're officially a college student, of course. What did you think I meant?" Fiona's towering, broad-shouldered frame stepped in front of me, and she bent her head over mine, as if she couldn't hear little me standing there at five three. "Did you finally pop — ?"

I cut her off. "No! Of course not!"

Feet shuffled behind us, and I was absolutely mortified that Maya had overheard Fee asking whether I was still a virgin. How could I explain my countless imaginary conquests?

Fiona laughed her boisterous laugh, which always reminded me of Teddy Roosevelt, and I half-expected her to belt out, "Dee-lighted!"

Gray Eyes finally received her savory crepe. It smelled of cheese and ham, and she moved to the back of the shop to sit at a secluded table mostly hidden by a column covered in vintage French movie posters. Thank God for her need for privacy; who knew what calamity would strike next?

"Your drink." Pierced-girl half-heartedly motioned to Fee's latte. We took a seat near the counter. My eyes searched for Maya, but the column kept her out of sight, although obviously not out of mind. What was wrong with me today?

"So tell me. How was your day?" Fiona asked.

"Fine," I muttered, sipping at my lackluster coffee. I hated to admit it, but I was the type who needed coffee with frills or an abundance of flavor — preferably both.

Fiona eyed me over her hazelnut latte. "What's up your bum?"

"Nothing. Why?" I stared intently at the place where Maya's head would be, even though all I could see was a poster of Audrey Hepburn and Fred Astaire in *Drôle de Frimousse*.

"Because you're acting like a spoiled brat. What gives?"

"Guess who's in my Mass history class?"

"Roughly forty Massholes."

"True. But also the biggest Masshole: Susie Quillian."

"Really?" Fee's voice was operatic. "How is Bottlenose?" Fiona's nickname for Susie referred to bottlenose dolphins, one of

17

the cutest but deadliest of animals. It wasn't unusual for them to kill another porpoise just to play with the lifeless body.

"She accused me of cheating on today's pop quiz."

Fee smiled. "So, just as deadly." She tapped her cell phone. "Or not. No story about you on her blog today, just another condemnation of Obamacare."

"Oh please! Susie wouldn't know the truth if it bit her in that perfectly round caboose."

"Ainsley Carmichael!" Fee slapped the top of the table. "Do you have the hots for Susie Q?" She waggled her strawberry blonde eyebrows and leaned closer. "Scandalous! You two could be like the married Democratic commentator James Carville and Republican consultant Mary Matalin. Grandmother would blow her stack!"

"What? No. Not a chance in hell!" I sat back in my chair.

"Methinks the lady doth protest too much. And I wouldn't fault you. I'd sleep with her." Fiona waved a hand.

"Oh my God! Oh my God!" I rubbed my face with a palm. "Must erase that image from my mind!"

She laughed. "Seriously, what's bugging you? I don't believe Susie Q is the source, unless she really does get you all hot and bothered. There's a first time for everything, my dear cousin."

"What does that mean?"

"Google 'uptight asexual girl excessively focused on her future political career' and your pic pops up."

"That's not true." Fee knew me better than most, but even she didn't know about the racy lesbian romance novels I devoured nightly.

"Yeah?" Fiona punched some keys on her phone before handing it over to me.

Right there on Susie Q's blog was an article about me titled "The Sexless Ice Princess."

"When did she publish this?"

"Right before your high school graduation."

"That bitch! And after the Cassidy situation — how could she?" I continued to scrutinize Fee's phone as if I was expecting the truth to magically appear.

"Please. You aren't suggesting Susie is rational or sticks to one narrative, are you? Ains, you know better than most that media hacks will write anything and everything to keep their name in the who's who. Besides, scandals are short-lived for most involved."

"Not for Grandmother. She never forgets." I set the phone, screen side down, on the tabletop. Out of sight but not out of mind.

"True."

"What else has she said about my sex life?"

Fee crossed her arms. "I wasn't aware you had one."

I glared as she mimed fanning flames.

"So sensitive!" Fee said. "She also claims you're a repressed lesbian."

"I am not!"

"Lesbian or repressed?" Fiona cackled.

"I'm out and proud! Marched in the parade last year." I thumped the table. When I was fifteen, I'd come out to my mother and grandmother. The news was treated like every other milestone in the family. A conference of the Carmichael brain trust was called to determine whether I should stay in the closet or announce it to all the world. Grandmother's minions polled millennials to determine my lesbian fate: be out and proud or keep it under wraps. Turned out, people my age didn't care about sexuality, so we decided to embrace it from the outset, otherwise I would risk being viewed as a flip-flopper — deadly for politicians, just ask failed presidential wannabe Mitt Romney.

"Prove it! Kiss a girl. One measly kiss. Come on, baby, step your way out of the sexually repressed darkness and into the mind-blowing light that only happens via fornication." Fee nearly glowed.

"Via fornication." I had to chuckle. She was so passionate about *it* that I feared I'd blab about the stirrings Gray Eyes caused. "I … oh, I don't know what to say."

"Not all experiences will end up like — "

I cleared my throat. "Let's not talk about her. She's dead to me."

"Not true. Cassidy is alive and well on Susie's *Tattler*. I love that Susie has die-hard goons dedicated to her cause. Look out Roger Ailes and Rupert Murdoch." Fiona's smile dared me to take the bait.

In my junior year, I had momentarily let my guard down and attempted to date a lesbian named Cassidy, who also happened to be on Susie Q's payroll. I was still reeling from the fallout. The humiliation solidified one thing: my desire to become president. It seemed a more obtainable goal than finding someone I could trust completely. The Cassidy Incident made it even more obvious that we Carmichaels had a target on our backs in today's media environment.

"Wait." I remembered the weird quote, pulled it out of my bag, and flattened the crumpled flyer. "Read this."

Fee scanned it, scrunching her face. "Where'd you get this?"

"Some lunatic handed it to me on my way here."

"The crazies keep on getting crazier. Such a random quote to hand out." She set the crinkled paper on the table.

I tapped it with my forefinger. "Here's the thing. I didn't see her with a stack of papers. She only handed this to me."

Fee scratched the tip of her nose. "Susie accused you of cheating today?"

"Yeah, but how does that relate to this?" I wasn't liking where this was heading.

"How does she think you cheated?" Fee sipped her drink.

"Knowing the questions to a pop quiz ahead of time."

"It kinda fits. You navigated your way to an A." Fiona's squished face implied it was a stretch at best.

"I didn't cheat!" I slapped the tabletop.

"Doesn't matter. That's how it's been framed. Maybe Susie, if she was even involved, is trying to freak you out more than normal. Did you recognize the person?" She narrowed her eyes.

"No. She looked like a drugged-out homeless person." I

shrugged.

"Cambridge isn't short on those types. But why?"

"Why what?"

Fee straightened in her chair. "Bottlenose has always been after you, but what's triggering the full court press? Paying someone to give you a random quote, which is ambiguous at best, what's the reasoning for that?"

"Good God, I don't even want to contemplate that. Besides, trying to figure out Susie's motives is useless. She changes direction every time a new scandal erupts."

"That could be the meaning. She'll out-navigate you." Fiona reread the quote, shook her head, and shoved the paper to the corner of the table. Fee hoisted a shoulder, giving up on figuring out the vindictive motive. "Honestly, I don't think the two are connected. You" — she extended a finger, aiming at my chest — "have watched too many episodes of *Scandal*."

"Me? You're the one who got me into the show. And *House of Cards* — even the British version."

"How was I supposed to know watching those shows would turn you into a paranoid loon who craved even more attention?"

"Craving attention! I try to stay under the radar."

While I aspired to be president, Fiona wanted to be a presidential scholar along the lines of Doris Kearns Goodwin, the historian who won the Pulitzer for *No Ordinary Time: Franklin and Eleanor Roosevelt*. Fiona already dressed like a professor. Her purple blazer and white scoop-necked shirt were accented with a floral silk scarf. She added a twist by wearing jeans with a tear, not that she bought them that way; no Carmichael would buy torn jeans. Fee had ripped hers during our attempt to break into Susie Q's house, after I learned Cassidy had recorded me. I still couldn't think of that day without experiencing mind-numbing vertigo. That clip had destroyed my hopes of ever finding love. We failed to locate any trace of the video, and Fee had fallen out of a tree, breaking her wrist and tearing her jeans.

I patted Fee's hand. Time to change the subject. "How's

Hahvard?" I drawled.

"Smashing. Just smashing," Fiona answered.

I burst into giggles, relieved to shove the Susie weirdness out of my mind momentarily.

My cousin bent forward conspiratorially. "Did you meet any gorgeous women today?"

I couldn't control myself. I glanced toward Maya and nearly toppled out of my chair when she approached the counter, wearing an apron. She worked here? That made my poor first impression earlier a hundred times worse. Oh, and what would she think of Fiona and her airs?

I wanted to die.

"Uh," was all I could say.

Fiona eyed Maya and smiled surreptitiously — not because she knew my secret but because that was how she always smiled. Gray Eyes glanced at me and then at Fiona, her expression frozen, and then took up her station behind the register, going out of her way to keep me out of her direct line of sight.

"You have to jump back on the horse, Ains. Don't let the Cassidy incident keep you out of the game. That's not how Carmichaels do it."

"Puh-lease. Carmichaels are doing it too much. I'm not going to fall victim to unnecessary scandal. I have one goal in life." I stabbed the air with a finger.

Fee sighed dramatically. "Here it comes."

"Here *what* comes?" I stiffened in my seat.

"How you are Grandmother's 'Chosen One' to become the first Carmichael to win the White House." She rolled her eyes and made air quotes.

"Whatever." I laughed. "You're just jealous I'm the Chosen One." I stuck my tongue out.

"That'll be the day. I plan on having as many lovers as possible. Besides, being Grandmother's little Mini-Me is creepy."

"I'm not her Mini-Me!"

"No? You receive daily debriefing e-mails from her political goons, and you both use the same makeup artists, hair peeps, and personal shoppers — even if I'm certain you picked out today's outfit." She eyed my pink dress with a smirk and continued listing our similarities, ending with the coup de grace, "She even gave you her name, Ains." Fiona slurped the rest of her coffee. "I'm famished. Let's scram." She pointed to the coffee I'd barely touched. "Clearly you aren't impressed with this joint. Too bad. I'd love to come back for the praline and Cointreau crepe I've heard about."

Luckily, I had turned back around in my chair and couldn't see Gray Eyes. I didn't have the guts to rubberneck over my shoulder to assess the damage either. Of course, Maya would have had to be deaf to have missed my earlier insult, and Fiona was anything but a quiet talker, so she probably also caught the tail end of our conversation. Considering my luck so far, her ears had eaten up everything, word for word, and a simple web search would unearth the dreaded video on Susie Q's blog as soon as I was out of sight.

CHAPTER
four

WEDNESDAY MORNING ARRIVED MUCH SOONER than I wanted. After the La Creperie fiasco, I dreaded seeing Maya. I stood outside the classroom, digging deep to find the motivation to move, but my legs refused to budge. It was like I was trapped in the same nightmare I'd had since I was eight. An axe murderer was running toward me, but I couldn't move. It was as if my legs were encased in wet cement that hardened faster than the charging lunatic, who looked a lot like Rush Limbaugh. Right as he raised his axe, I screamed, waking myself up.

Someone tapped my shoulder, and I jumped.

A female laughed. "I'm sorry. I didn't mean to startle you."

I turned ever so slowly to see Maya the Gray.

Her poker face was firmly in place, but softness resided in her eyes, and the corners of her lips twisted up a smidgeon.

"Oh, hi," I said, like a bumbling fool who had never spoken to a beautiful girl before. Not in real life, at least.

"Class starts in a couple of minutes. You better hurry." Without another word, she strutted into the room and sat in the same seat she had occupied on Monday.

I took the seat next to her, racking my brain for a witty

comment to salvage a morsel of my dignity. I swiveled in the metal chair, and my thigh rubbed against it, emitting the loudest farting sound in history. Why had I worn a skirt today?

Dr. Gingas walked in right as the entire class broke into a fit of childish giggles. Susie Q flipped around and gawked, open-mouthed. If she hadn't previously realized it was me, the steam gushing out of my every pore immediately ratted me out. She snapped a photo with her cell.

"I wasn't expecting this kind of welcome after Monday." Dr. Gingas nodded in my direction, indicating she understood the source of the amusement.

To say I wanted to die was an understatement. I wanted to go back in time and erase my entire existence. Stop my parents from marrying. No wait, I wanted to go way back, change the outcome of the Battle of Dunbar, and completely obliterate the American Carmichael branch.

Luckily, Dr. Gingas skipped the pre-lecture formalities and got right to work. When only ten minutes remained, she mentioned the group project and gave us the remaining time to find a partner.

Everyone rushed about to hookup with a friend or with someone they thought looked nerdy enough to do all the work for them. No one approached me, and I was still too mortified by Fart-Gate to ask anyone. Most people my age loved social media; I fucking hated it. Our family had always lived under a microscope, but the technological changes of the previous five years made being famous even more unbearable.

Maya didn't move from her seat. She continued to jot down notes until some dude who looked like he spent hours in front of a mirror turned in his chair and said, "What d'you say? Shall we join forces?" His leer implied he wanted to join in several different ways and positions.

Maya didn't bother to look at him. Instead, she jabbed a thumb in my direction. "Thanks, but I'm hooking up with her."

The guy squinted at me, smiled in a not-so-friendly manner, and then tapped the shoulder of the girl in front of him, asking her to join the dark side. The foolish girl accepted, and he immediately started to give her a suggestive shoulder rub.

I leaned over, carefully this time so as not to make the obnoxious sound again, and whispered, "Thank you."

"I'd be a fool to deny the Chosen One." Her voice was barely audible, but her grin was loud and clear. She thought I was cute — an ass probably too, given the conversation she'd overheard, but I still sensed she was drawn to me.

"I'm so sorry about the other night," I babbled.

Maya set her pen down and studied me. "According to the syllabus, we have to give a presentation on a person or event that was a major influence at the time. Can you control your nerves, or should we do a recording? We don't want you going off script," she teased.

I placed a hand on her arm. "Oh, I'm very good when it comes to that."

Maya's gray eyes traveled from my hand on her arm to my eyes. "You're very good at what?"

I steadied my nerves. "Giving speeches, for one thing."

"What else?" Maya leaned back in the chair and crossed her arms.

"Time's up!" shouted Dr. Gingas.

Maya laughed. "Safe, for now." She picked up her pen again. "If you can stomach another horrible cup of coffee," she said, winking, "meet me at the coffee shop tonight. I'd like to get a jumpstart on the project."

I wanted to jump her bones. *No, Ainsley. Never going to happen. Remember Cassidy.*

I nodded. "What time?"

"Eight-ish?"

I nodded again. Knowing she wouldn't stop writing to shoot the shit, I bolted out of the room to text Fiona.

After several texts explaining what had happened, Fiona agreed to meet me for dinner before my study date with Maya. *Not date — appointment. Must keep a clear head.*

By the time I walked into the Mexican restaurant, I had managed to tamp down my embarrassment level some, but by the way random people stopped to whisper as I walked by, I figured Susie's *Tattler* had already blown Fart-Gate completely out of the water. I had to control the urge to tell everyone I was innocent. It was the chair.

The imaginary newscaster in my head, one hand gripping a microphone, blared, "Well, Phil, Ainsley Carmichael has been taken to the psychiatric unit at Mass General after telling every stranger she passed of her complete innocence. That it was the chair. One witness said she was babbling, 'The chair, the chair, the chair' as attendants in white coats whisked her into the ambulance."

I imagined this newscaster a lot, giving the play-by-play of my stupidity in life. The first time it occurred, I was in the second grade. I ran out of the room, crying after I flubbed a presentation on how to pot a geranium for show and tell. Not only did I drop the clay pot on my foot, but I also dumped the entire bag of soil all over the carpet.

I scanned the crowd in the restaurant, easily locating Fee's towering frame.

"Ainsley, darling. How was your day?" Fiona's lips curled up into a shit-eating grin. "Oh, that's right. You had a rip-roaring good time."

"Fee-own-a! This is not the time to be you. I need a friend."

"Of course it is. It's always the time to be myself. I would never curb your personality. Sounds like you don't either. You just let things go."

I blew out a rush of angry air. She laughed at my expense and looped her arm through mine, pulling me to the bar to wait for a table to clear. "I need a drink. What'll ya have?"

She didn't wait for my response but ordered a Diet Coke for me and a white wine for herself. She'd recently turned twenty-one, but no one had ever carded her before. Her professorial stature aided and abetted her underage drinking, and had done so since age sixteen. Before our drinks arrived, a table cleared, and my cousin shoved me over to stake our claim. This place had the best enchiladas in town, but the seating policy was democratic — or in the immortal words of Abraham Lincoln, "of the people, by the people, and for the people."

Fiona hoisted our drinks above her strawberry blonde head and pirouetted over to the table without spilling a drop.

"I ordered our food at the bar." She nodded toward the bartender, who flashed a thumbs-up and then turned to a coworker and made a farting gesture with his armpit. He pointed to me, grinning like a five-year-old boy.

I pretended not to notice.

We always selected the enchilada special, which included cheese, chicken, and beef with black beans and rice.

"So, how bad was it?" Fiona sipped her wine, trying hard not to laugh at my expense.

"Horrendous. I'm surprised you couldn't hear it." Heat rose to my cheeks.

"I did hear something, but I thought it was a plane breaking the sound barrier. It was quite the crack!" She hooted.

"Oh, so funny." I plunged my straw into the glass and stirred the ice cubes, enjoying the soda's fizzy coolness in contrast with my burning face.

My cousin placed a hand on my arm. "I'm sure it wasn't that bad."

"Trust me, it was. People have been gawking all day."

"Do you mean …?" Fiona reached for her phone. "Oh, Ainsley!" She slapped her thigh. "That Susie sure has your number."

"I don't want to know the headline. Please shut it off." I snapped my eyelids together just in case Fiona didn't heed my command.

An epic sound that brought to mind an elephant farting was proof positive Fiona was watching the *Tattler* on YouTube.

"Seriously, Fee. Put it away or I'm leaving."

"Fine. I'll watch it later. I wonder if I can use the fart sound for your ringtone?"

I made a face.

My phone vibrated. A text flashed across the screen: *Revenge is profitable; gratitude is expensive.*

"Speak of the devil." I spun the phone around for Fee to read.

"What the?" Her face twisted up. "Who sent this?"

"Unknown number, but come on … This is the work of one person: Susie Q."

Fee stared at the screen. "I don't know. I've been thinking about the other quote since Monday. Seems too intellectual for her. What does this mean, really?"

"Who knows? Maybe she wants money to back off."

"She wants you to act thankful for her ridicule? That doesn't make any sense."

"Please. Sense and Susie are never in the same hemisphere."

"If it is her, she's getting weirder. Be careful. Have you thought about mentioning this to Grandmother?"

"What? No?" I leaned back in my chair, stretching my arms behind me and accidentally bumping into someone's chair. I glanced over my shoulder half-expecting to see Susie or Cassidy. "Sorry," I mumbled to a professor type in his fifties.

"It's bad enough Susie is tormenting me," I said, turning back to Fiona. "I don't need Grandmother coming to my rescue. She already controls ninety percent of my life. Do I want to hand over the remaining ten percent?"

Fee studied my face with understanding eyes. "Just be careful. If you keep getting," she paused to mull over her words, "unconventional quotes, I really think you should loop in the big guns."

"I promise," I lied. Susie was a pain, but I could handle her. Besides, I was convinced the best method was to ignore people like Susie. Attention only gave her the power she desired.

Fiona brushed it off and launched into a story about one of her classmates who'd confused Teddy and Franklin Roosevelt. She tossed both arms in the air. "I mean, seriously. Who does that?"

I had to laugh that Fiona considered this *faux pas* worse than my alleged fart.

"It's a wonder she ever got into Harvard," she said.

"I know!" I agreed, relieved the punch line wasn't at my expense.

Our meals arrived. Without skipping a beat, Fiona dug her fork in. Around bites, she continued telling me about her day. "During our discussion of a letter by John Adams to his wife, this guy who hasn't said a peep in the three classes we've taken together over the past two years raised his hand and asked, 'What does saucy mean?'" Fiona let forth a gale of laughter.

I chewed the inside of my cheek to obliterate all thoughts of saucy positions with Maya.

Fiona grew serious, set her fork down, and said, "You know, Ainsley, as your future presidential biographer, I'm going to have to tell the truth." She pinned me with shimmering emerald eyes and continued. "The whole truth. Including your flatulence."

"Fee!"

She put a palm up. "I'm serious, inquiring minds want to know." Merriment danced across her face, forcing all the serious-ness to the side. "It will be painful to write about this incident, but I have a feeling this moment will shape your future. I'm positive." She winked and motioned for me to get up. "Let's go to that coffee shop. We have time to squeeze in a cup before your study date. I'm dying for one of their lattes. When I woke up this morning, my first thought was *I want one*."

Odd, my first thought was I wanted to kiss Maya. Not that I'd ever tell anyone. I could just picture Grandmother's minions polling focus groups about their thoughts on interracial lesbian relationships.

Maya manned the cash register. I hadn't contemplated she'd be working tonight, even though she had suggested the shop. I did my best to push aside any trace of guilt from my expression. I'd been volunteering since I was fourteen, but I hadn't ever worked for a paycheck, mainly because I didn't need to earn money. Not ever. That's what the trust fund was for.

We arrived at twenty minutes to eight, and Maya glanced at her watch.

"Sorry, I'm early — "

"But I've been dying for a latte all day," Fiona interrupted.

Maya motioned for us to order.

Fiona barked her order in the clipped Carmichael tone.

I smiled, completely unsure what I should try. "Uh, coffee."

"Just coffee?" Maya hitched up one eyebrow. My insides went deliciously gooey.

I nodded, knowing I probably appeared as flummoxed as a first-time skydiver.

Maya relaxed her facial features — not into a smile per se, but not her stern poker face either. "I'll make you something. Trust me."

I prayed she'd wink at me, but she didn't. Without saying another word, she wheeled about. Fiona studied my face with a wide-eyed expression I hadn't seen before.

When we took our seats, Fiona whispered. "You like her, don't you?"

"W-what?" I stammered without peeling my eyes off Maya the Gray.

"Oh my God! You actually like her." Fiona slapped the table. Everyone but Maya turned to gawk. I frantically gestured for her to zip it.

"This is huge!" Fiona ignored my efforts, although she did lower her voice as much as she was capable of. "Your first college crush." She patted my arm like I'd just taken my first step.

Maya approached and placed her special brew in front of me. "If this doesn't win you over, I don't know what will." She turned on her heel like a soldier and marched back to her post.

Fiona nudged my arm. "Go ahead. Sample her *love* potion."

I rolled my eyes before taking a sip. "Oh my God!"

Maya jerked her head in my direction. I nodded appreciatively, and she raised a thin eyebrow. I shivered.

"That good, huh?" Fiona sipped her latte. "Damn, mine's better this time. If you don't sleep with this woman so we can have a lifetime supply, I will."

"Shush!" I shook my head. "I can't believe you said that." I spoke into my cup. I couldn't stop drinking Maya's brew either.

Fiona leaned across the table. "You're going to have to pop your cherry at some point, Ainsley darling. People won't vote for a woman who can't get laid."

I peered around Fiona's massive mound of hair to see if Maya had overheard.

"I don't even know if she's into chicks," I said, even though my gaydar had been buzzing since I'd first locked eyes with Maya.

My cousin not-so-discreetly eyed Maya and bobbed her head. The way she ogled her made it seem like she was the one who wanted to get her naked. "Oh, yeah. She's a carpet muncher."

"Fiona!" I slapped her arm.

"God, you're the youngest old maid I've ever met." She raised the coffee cup to her mouth, took a sip, and licked her lips. "Don't let this opportunity pass you by like the last one."

"The last one?" I squinted.

"The cheerleader."

"Whatever. Tina only wanted to sleep with me because the football team dared her to."

"Not seeing the problem." Fiona took another swig. "Damn, this stuff is like crack. I'm hooked!"

I ignored her histrionics. "The cheerleader wasn't even gay."

"So? I wasn't gay when I slept with Mary, and trust me, I don't regret it. Not for a second. Join the twenty-first century — sexuality is fluid." She wiggled her eyebrows to emphasize the point.

"You slept with Mary?" I whispered into my palm.

She shrugged like it was no big deal.

"Catholic Mary from school?" I pushed.

"Yep, that's the one. I've slept with a few Catholics. Let me tell you; they go all out to make the guilt worth it. Is your girl Catholic?" Her hopeful eyes darted in Maya's direction.

"I don't know," I said. "I don't know anything about her, really."

"Ah, that's your problem." Fiona set her cup down hard, stressing her point.

"Really? Tell me what my problem is." I playfully crossed my arms.

"You can't get the Cassidy monkey off your back. You want to vet a person before even holding hands. Trust your gut. Be like George W."

"And start two unwinnable wars?"

Fiona set her cup down. "Not what I was going for. Dubya is the kind of guy people want to have a beer with. You're channeling Hillary. No one wants to have a beer with her. Get my drift?" She quirked both eyebrows.

"I'm frigid." It wasn't the first time Fee had told me this.

"You can be around people you don't know." Fiona avoided my eyes. "You're eighteen. Act like it."

"By fornicating?" I joked.

"Exactly!" she said in all seriousness. "If you only learn one thing from me, I hope it's this: Love is a fabrication. Now sex, that's real. And once you start, you won't want to stop."

I shook my head. From what I'd seen, sex was the quickest way to destroy a political future. This nation was too puritanical; any digression was cause for social media outrage. But I didn't want to get into that with Fiona. Instead, I diverted by asking, "Would you have sex with Dubya?"

"Maybe if he was thirty years younger. Never Hillary. Shit, even Bill doesn't. I bet they had to do artificial insemination for Chelsea."

I covered my mouth so I wouldn't spew coffee everywhere. "I never know what's going to come out of your mouth."

"That's why you like hanging out with me."

"'Tis true. You make me laugh. And you never put any videos

on the Web."

My eyes wandered to Maya, who was removing her apron, and warmth oozed through my body. I removed my cardigan, leaving just my tank and jeans.

Fiona picked up on the change in my body language. "Oh, you got it bad, Cuz."

Maya approached the table with a book bag and a chocolate crepe on a plate, but she didn't say anything. I envisioned licking chocolate off her body.

Snap out of it, Ainsley. Stop acting like a character in a romance novel. That shit ain't real, and even if it were, it isn't in the cards.

Fiona looked back and forth a couple of times and chuckled to herself. "Well, then. Don't let me get in the way." I kicked her shin under the table, which only made her smirk.

"I'll let you two get to it, then. Studying, that is," she added to rile me even more, before slamming the rest of her drink, placing a hand on Maya's shoulder, and motioning for her to take her seat.

Maya nodded. She seemed a bit flushed, but I assumed it was due to her just finishing work, rather than a reaction to Fiona's lewd smile.

The awkwardness remained even after Fee left.

"I'm sorry. Fiona can be a bit much." I wasn't entirely sure why I was apologizing; maybe because Maya was sitting across from me and not saying a word. I had no idea how to get the ball rolling.

She started to respond but resorted to a shrug.

"Okay, then …" I failed to think of anything else to add.

"Do you like chocolate?"

"Is Obama a Democrat?"

She smiled and set the crepe in front of me.

"Is she a *friend* of yours?" Maya thrust her chin in the direction of the door Fiona had just departed through.

Did she emphasize friend as a way to suss out whether I was gay?

"Fiona?" I almost toppled out of my chair. Maya the Gray

was fishing for dirt. "Yes. Well, she's my cousin to be exact."

"Are you always exact?" Maya's tongue darted out to wet her lips, and I caught myself staring at the moisture.

I returned a tight-lipped smile, and Maya locked her mysterious gray eyes onto mine.

"D-do you have any ideas in mind for our project?" I scratched my eyebrow with a pen in an attempt to snap out of the hypnotic gray-eyed trance.

"*Little Women*," she stated without showing a trace of emotion.

I stroked my chin. "I'm sorry."

"*Little Women.*"

I leaned closer and whispered, "What about them?" Was she referring to midgets?

Maya the Gray smiled her first full smile. "The novel by Louisa May Alcott."

"Oh!" I palmed the top of my head. "Yes, yes." I bobbled my head up and down, feeling like a hula girl on a car dashboard. "I must confess — "

Her smile turned seductive, which knocked the rest of the words right out of my head.

"You must confess …" She motioned for me to continue.

"I must confess …" I paused, unsure, but then blurted, "I don't know much about *Little Women* — the book or the author." I rushed the words, wondering whether she was able to parse that the reason for my nervous chatter was I was attracted to her. Uncontrollably attracted to Maya the Gray. Dammit!

"I find her fascinating." Maya leaned back in her chair, completely at ease.

"The author?" Why wasn't Fiona here to ask the questions I really wanted answered: Was Maya into women? Was she speaking in code or innuendo? Or was I just used to Fiona and her antics? And surely if Maya were speaking in code, she'd come up with a better clue than the unsettling and slightly pervy *Little Women* line. Wait, did that make me a perv by reading too much into it?

"Yes, the author." She winked, giving me the illusion she understood what I meant. I blinked, and her face was suddenly devoid of any emotion, leaving me to wonder whether I'd imagined the wink.

Or had she put something in my coffee in the hope I'd do or say something crazy and she could upload a video on YouTube and make a killing? Had Susie Q already gotten to Maya as well? Apparently homeless chicks were on her payroll.

I took a deep breath and massaged my eyelids, clueless as to what we were even talking about. Was I being overly paranoid?

"What angle are you thinking of for the research project?" I asked.

"How Louisa was able to succeed in a man's world, especially since her own father failed miserably."

"Oh, Fiona would love this topic."

"You don't?" she asked in a tone that wasn't overly concerned.

"What? Oh no, of course I love it. I was just saying … Oh, never mind." I waved a hand. "It's a great topic, and I think our professor will appreciate it." God, did she think I was a suck-up now? Why did I bring up Dr. Gingas?

"Do you have a car?" she asked.

I turned my head to the right, trying to detect some hidden meaning in the change of conversation. "Yes. Yes, I do."

"Good. We should go to her house this weekend."

"Her house?" The crepe called to me, and I could no longer resist. My gut told me Maya hadn't spiked it. I bit into it. "This is wonderful. Just like Paris. Thank you." I shoveled in another bite, not caring what she thought about my gluttony. Besides, it was probably best if I didn't speak too much.

She raised a palm, acknowledging the thank-you. "Alcott's house. It's in Concord. Have you been?" Her face remained expressionless, but her eyes sparked with curiosity. Why was she so mysterious? Surely she understood the effect she had on me.

I swallowed, and spoke behind my hand. "That sounds great. I've always wanted to go but never seemed to find the time."

"Are you free all day Saturday? There's so much to see. Walden Pond, Sleepy Hollow Cemetery, the Old Manse, and the North Bridge." She put her palm up. "I know that's associated with the American Revolution, but I've always wanted to see the bridge."

"Have you ever been to Concord or Lexington?"

She shook her head. "I've read about them and seen photos, of course. Google Earth is amazing."

I sat there, stunned. All of the words flew out of her mouth, and even though her demeanor didn't show any emotion, her voice did. She was excited, thrilled even. History and historical sites ignited her passions. I never truly appreciated living in such a historical place until that moment. I imagined ripping off her clothes on the North Bridge.

"We can go wherever you want. I'll take you anywhere." I prayed my face wasn't betraying me. Was I batting my eyelids, looking like a vapid girl with a high-school crush?

Maya dipped her head slightly, staring off to the right, lost in her own secretive world. Would I ever get a glimpse?

Then she handed over a sheet of paper with a list printed in elegant script. "Here are some biographies I recommend. The one by Reisen is pretty good, and *Eden's Outcasts* won a Pulitzer. Did you know Alcott's novels sold more copies than Herman Melville's and Henry James's combined?"

"I didn't. Not surprised though. I prefer *Little Women* over *Moby Dick*."

"I thought you said you didn't read *Little Women*."

I hadn't read *Moby Dick* either. "What? Oh, I did, years ago, I think," I lied. "Is that your favorite book?"

"One of them. What's yours?"

"Anything by David McCullough."

"The historian?" She perked up in her seat.

"Yes."

"I read *1776*," she said. "My mom is a history nut."

"Really? I recommend *John Adams*, *Truman*, *The Great Bridge*,

Mornings on Horseback — oh, anything by him, really. I haven't read his latest, *The Wright Brothers,* yet."

"I didn't know he released a new one. My mom's birthday is next week." Maya jotted a note. "What do you think of Dr. Gingas?"

Her habit of changing the conversation reminded me of Fiona. "I wouldn't want to get on her bad side."

Maya shifted in her seat. "True. She knows her stuff, though. I admire that."

"My mother speaks highly of her." I wanted to kick myself for mentioning the senator.

"Has she been teaching that long?"

"Oh no. They're friends."

"Ah, you have inside information. Don't let Susie Q know."

"So you overheard that conversation as well? The one when she accused me of cheating?" I kept my tone light.

"Hard not to. It happened right in front of me." She smirked. "Why does she hate you so much?"

"Do you read her blog?" I asked as breezily as possible.

"She has a blog?" Maya's pen scratched, and I prayed she wasn't making a note about that.

"So I've been told. I don't have time to read it." I waved my hand in a *la de da* way. "To answer your question, Susie and I have been going to the same school since kindergarten. We're kinda competitive."

"Is that what you call it? Seemed more cutthroat."

"She takes it seriously."

"Her blog or not liking you?" The corners of Maya's eyes crinkled.

"Both, I think."

"Her loss." Maya tapped her pen on a notebook. "Right. Let's brainstorm some ideas."

We batted around concepts. Actually, Maya supplied key facts about Alcott while I asked questions.

"Did you know she eschewed getting married? She thought

women of her day were seeking marriage for money. She claimed she preferred autonomy and liberation to indulgences." Maya tugged at a string on a flimsy leather bracelet. From its looks, it had been tied around her left wrist for years.

"I can relate."

"You don't want to marry?" Maya still fidgeted with the string, but she focused solely on my answer.

"Not really."

"What about relationships?"

"They seem like they're more trouble than they're worth," I blurted.

"Do you ever see yourself in a relationship?"

"Well ..." Why was I hedging? The answer was never. "I hate to say never." I was aghast this had come out of my trap.

"Such a diplomatic answer." She grinned. "I have to agree with you about never saying never."

"You just did. Twice."

She smiled, and I gestured for her to continue.

"I will admit independence is the word I live by."

Hearing her claim that was oddly unsettling, even if I wholeheartedly agreed, so I steered us back to Louisa May Alcott. Fiona would love the sick twist of fate: finding the one who didn't want to be found.

Maya stifled a yawn. "I'm sorry. I've been up since four."

"Wow. I thought I was an early riser." I tapped a finger on her list. "I'll pick these up. You look like you need some rest."

"Not in the near future. Not yet, at least." She motioned to her book bag.

"Oh, okay. I won't keep you from studying. See ya on Friday," I said, sensing I should run before I got to know more about her. Having a crush on someone was one thing; developing feelings was simply out of the question. "We can discuss what time to meet on Saturday. Thanks for the crepe."

She cocked her head and leveled her eyes on mine as if she knew the effect they had. "Sounds good. I'm looking forward to it." Again enthusiasm tinged her voice, but besides those marvelous eyes, the rest of her face was devoid of emotion. How did she do that? Was she always this controlled? This guarded? She was like my soul mate — a non-relationship-seeking soul mate.

CHAPTER
five

FIONA WOULD BE NEARBY, WANTING to hear the scuttlebutt. Not that I had any. Nor would I share — not the real scuttlebutt — not even to Fiona, the person I trusted the most.

Fiona responded to my text, informing me she was in the bookstore a couple of blocks away. I raced over to buy some Concord travel guides, *Little Women*, and the biographies on the list before the store closed. I planned to skim the travel guides before the weekend. It'd been years since I'd visited Concord, and that had been for a school field trip.

Fiona found me in the travel section. "What are you doing? They're closing." She tugged my arms, which were laden with Alcott books and guides.

"I need travel guides for Concord."

"Concord! You know that's here in Mass. You don't really need a guide. Just get in your car and go. Live on the edge. Besides, you can find most things on the Internet these days." She tsked at my bookish ways.

I grabbed two more guides and rushed to the register.

"Wait, you forgot one," Fiona shouted. She placed the *Literary Trail of Greater Boston* on top of the stack.

"Oh, Fee, I could kiss you right now."

"Would that make us kissing cousins?" She studied the low-hanging ceiling, lost in thought. Someone had switched off the lights in the back of the store to let customers know it was time to scram.

The clerk reddened, rushing through the transaction, much to my amusement. Fiona never tried to shock people, but her frankness had that effect. I hefted the shopping bag over my shoulder. "Let's go to your apartment and start sifting through these babies."

Fiona hooked her arm through mine. "Do you plan on telling me what's going on? Why the mad dash?"

It started to rain, but the drops were more of a nuisance than anything. Besides, her apartment was only a couple of blocks from Harvard Square. We walked down a side street on a bricked sidewalk encased on one side by an ivy-covered brick wall leading south toward the Charles River. A lone cab passed us on the narrow street.

"Maya wants to go to Concord with me this Saturday for our research project."

"Research?" She tugged on my arm, teasing.

"Yes, for our history project." I rolled my eyes, even though she couldn't see.

"I see. And you want to impress the hell out of the coffee-goddess." The steady trickle of rain transformed into water daggers stabbing our skin, and she clutched my arm. "Come on!"

We dashed across Mt. Auburn Street and broke into a full sprint, laughing all the way to her building.

Moments later, Fiona was dressed in a robe with a towel wrapped around her head. She put a teakettle on as I sat at the table in her spacious kitchen, towel-drying my curls, which *boinged* more than usual. I wore a pair of Fee's crimson sweats and a gray Harvard T-shirt.

She cracked the window by the table, leaving the curtains drawn. A breeze made them billow, letting in sprinkles of rain. Fee lit a cigarette with her Zippo, which displayed an image of Ulysses

S. Grant in his Civil War uniform. I pulled a face at the cigarette, not Grant, even though his presidency was riddled with scandals.

She ignored me and flipped through one of the books. "Hey, listen to this. Henry James referred to Concord as 'the biggest little place in America.'" Blowing the smoke over her shoulder, she said, "I didn't know that, or I forgot. Throw a pebble in this state and you're bound to hit at least one historical marker." She stared at the red tip of the cigarette between her fingers.

I pulled a small leather notebook out and jotted down the quote.

"Emerson, Hawthorne, Alcott, Thoreau … all these minds in one tiny place. This is jolly good stuff. How did I forget all this?"

"Too busy studying presidents." I shrugged.

The teakettle whistled. With the cigarette dangling from her bottom lip, Fiona poured two cups of tea, all while still reading one of the guides. She only stopped to grab an Irish whiskey bottle from the cabinet above, proof that her on-again, off-again boyfriend was back in the picture.

"No thanks," I mumbled, engrossed in reading about Concord on my tablet. "Hey, did you know Doris Kearns Goodwin lives there?"

Fiona ripped the iPad out of my hand and greedily read the words. The towel around her head loosened, and she set it aside. Wet, strawberry blonde locks dangled around her face as she said, "I seem to remember a professor saying something about her living there." She gave the tablet back and blew into her tea. "Maybe I'll tag along with you two in the hope we can bump into her."

"You will not!"

"I can act as your personal historian." She lifted the cup to her lips. "Now that would impress the coffee-goddess."

"No presidents are from there. That's your specialty."

Fiona smacked her lips and flipped the pages of another travel guide. "I can cram it all in. I don't have any classes tomorrow."

I briefly considered the proposition. "No. But can you help me cram it into my head?"

Feigning hurt, Fiona said, "Of course, darling. Wouldn't it be grand if you popped your cherry at Walden Pond? What would Thoreau's ghost say about that?"

"Such a one-track mind." I groaned. "I can't risk an affair. Remember the failed presidential runs of Gary Hart and John Edwards?"

"News flash! You have to be in a relationship in order to have an affair. And you're a college freshman. No one expects you not to date. Why don't you just admit the truth?" She crossed her arms, grinning.

Oh God, did she know I was falling for Maya?

"Which is?"

"You're girl-shy after Cassidy."

I plugged both ears with my fingers. "Don't mention that name. She's dead to me."

Fee yanked my hands away from my head. "You can't live in a protective, presidential bubble all your life. That's not living, dear cousin. Stop being afraid."

CHAPTER
six

MAYA WAS STANDING OUTSIDE WHEN I pulled up. Her long-sleeved, pale purple-gray shirt and loose fit boyfriend-cut jeans surprised me. I'd only seen her in a crisp black T-shirt and dark jeans, but I started to wonder whether she only wore that on the days she worked, which was every day I'd seen her. When did she find time to study? I liked seeing the laidback Maya.

"I picked up some bagels." She hoisted a brown lunch sack and gently wiggled it. "And I made coffee." Maya whipped out a steel thermos that looked older than both of us put together. "Enough to get us through the entire day."

She must have noticed me eye it, because she added, "Used to belong to my granddad. Is it okay if I pour you a cup in here?" She motioned to my car, which was spotless and still had a new-car smell. "I promise not to spill."

"Sure. I'm dying for your special brew." I watched her meticulously pour the drink into a travel cup, not wasting a drop. Nearly finished, she licked her lips, and I had to fight the impulse to kiss her.

I needed to nip my sexual urges in the bud. I was the sexless Ice Princess, after all. *Remember John Edwards, and the trouble he got into.*

Maya handed me the mug.

"Thanks." I took a sip. "Oh my God! You have to share your trick."

She sank into the eco-friendly cloth seat, gripping her coffee with both hands, her eyes on the road ahead. "What do you mean?"

"You make the best coffee. Even Fiona thinks so, and she's the biggest coffee snob you'll ever meet."

A satisfied nod conveyed my compliment pleased her.

"Sorry, can't tell ya. Industry secret." Her voice was softer today, more relaxed. "Is Fiona a snob about everything?"

Technically, the answer was yes, but Fiona didn't realize she was, and she didn't do it to act superior. She was a perfectionist who demanded everyone and everything else should be perfect as well.

"A snob? No, I wouldn't say that. I would say she wants things her way, and she's not afraid to voice her opinion when disappointed. But I wouldn't classify her as a snob. She's just Fiona." I tapped the steering wheel, cursing myself for rambling.

"What about you?" she asked.

"What? Am I a snob?" I peeked at her, and she nodded. "No!" I slapped her leg playfully, surprised I had dared to touch her and equally shocked she hadn't attempted to jump out of the car. Her protective shield was still up, but not as strong. White-knuckling the leather-wrapped gearshift in order to control my desire to stroke her leg, I slipped the car into third and eased into the left lane. Traffic was light. Maya had insisted we get an early start. I hadn't slept much the night before, thanks to preparing for today, and then good old-fashioned nerves had kicked in as soon as my head hit the pillow.

The GPS voice instructed me to take a slight right onto US-3. I did. Maya remained quiet, shifting in her seat.

"You okay?" I asked.

"Yeah. Just looking." She said it so innocently that it dawned on me she might not leave the city much.

The GPS voice chimed, "At the next roundabout, take the

first exit onto MA-2 west."

"Did you leave your car back home? Parking in the city can be a bitch."

She shook her head. "Never had a car."

What was that like? I was on my second new car after receiving a Ford Focus Electric for my high school graduation. "Do you have a driver's license?"

"Yep."

"Where did you grow up?"

"Wyoming."

"Oh. I've never been. Is it nice there?"

"It's brown." She motioned to the scenery. "It still shocks me how green it gets here."

It was mid-September, and the leaves hadn't yet started to turn. We had until the first week of December to finish our project.

"Did you move for school?" I hoped I wasn't coming across like I was fishing.

"Nah. My mom and I moved here when I was in the third grade."

She wasn't overly specific, but I didn't want to pry. I hated people prying into my life.

"I've always lived in Boston. My mother is — "

"A senator." She threw it out there as if it was an everyday thing. Too many people sucked up to me in the hope of gaining access to Mother. Besides the Cassidy incident, it was another reason I had never dated in high school — the posers who wanted to use me. Some wanted internships or recommendations. One girl even asked whether my mother could get rid of her cousin's parking violations. "Hey, babe, want to catch a movie? And can your mom fix Vinny's parking tickets?"

Fiona experienced the same, which was one of the reasons we stuck together. But Maya didn't come across as a manipulator.

"Is your father still in Wyoming?"

She hitched up a shoulder in the universal "don't know" gesture.

Without thinking, I'd crashed into a sensitive subject and I needed to do damage control. "Are you close with your mom?"

Maya nodded. "Thick as thieves." She faced the front. "We were always more like sisters, really. What about you? Are you close with your mom?"

"Um, sure. It's hard sometimes with her job. She's always traveling." I stared at the road, unsure whether to continue. "My dad died before I was born."

"I'm sorry." Her voice was soft and full of understanding.

I hardly ever mentioned my dad to people outside of the family, and on the rare occasions I did, it was usually a conversation killer.

She tapped a finger on the lid of her travel mug. "Do you think it'll rain?"

I sensed Maya understood my pain of not having a father figure. "Probably." I ducked my head to get a better view of the clouds that hugged the horizon. "Hopefully just sprinkles, though." Afraid we would drift into silence, I blurted, "Do you have any siblings?"

"Nope. You?"

"A brother and a sister." I didn't bring up my dead brother, Craig. There was enough sadness hanging over our heads. And no one ever brought up Uncle Liam, who'd been missing since 2002.

"Has your family always lived in Boston?" she asked.

"Yep. We go way back. Have you ever heard of the Battle of Dunbar?" I glanced at her.

"Can't say I have? Was it during the Revolutionary War?" She looked at me, interested.

"Nah. It was in Scotland, way back in the 1600s. One of my ancestors was captured by the English and got sent to the colonies as an indentured servant."

Maya turned her upper body to face me, clearly interested. "Really? So you come from slaves?"

"Kinda." I almost asked her whether she did as well, but stopped myself.

"My mom's Puerto Rican. For a school project, I researched our family tree and found out that ancestors on her father's side were African slaves. We think so, anyway. Records are hard to track down, obviously." She added the last bit as if she'd sensed my train of thought.

I racked my brain for facts on Puerto Rico, not coming up with much. "English and Spanish are the official languages, right?"

She nodded.

"Do you speak Spanish?"

"*Sí*. I'm not fluent, though. Mom is fluent. When she's mad, Spanish flies out of her mouth like projectile vomit."

I laughed. "Can you teach me some key words? I know a bit of French after living there one summer a couple of years ago."

"I wondered about that. You said the crepe was as good as the ones in Paris." She refreshed my cup of coffee. "Spanish should come easily for you. I'd be more than happy to be your personal Spanish tutor." She grinned and patted my thigh, implying "and then some."

I smiled back, unsure how to respond.

Another silence descended, and I turned up the volume on the radio. I bobbed my head to Taylor Swift's song, "Wildest Dreams." Maya didn't react. Something told me she wasn't a Swiftie.

"Bang Bang" came on next. I almost laughed. Maya raked a hand through her spiky hair, obviously disliking the song, and when Ed Sheeran's "Don't" started, I switched radio stations.

Her head bobbed slightly to Florence + The Machine's "Dog Days are Over" — one of my absolute favorite songs — and when I started to sing along, she arched one eyebrow, impressed. Maya the Gray got into the song, swaying in her seat. Her shoulders relaxed. Those wonderful gray eyes beamed. By the end of the song, both of us were belting out the lyrics, drowning out Florence. I didn't want the magical experience to end.

"I didn't know you were a Florence fan," I said. I suspected she'd reply with a nod, so I hit the button on the steering wheel to stream, "Shake it Out." Maya knew all the words. I only knew the chorus, but when it was time, I sang my heart out. Maya laughed. She actually laughed. If it weren't uber-creepy, I'd have silenced the music to listen to her melodious laugh. Usually, she was controlled, but not when she laughed.

We listened to Florence's ghostly vocals in the next song "What the Water Gave Me" in quiet contemplation. I hadn't planned the song, but given it was about the loss of loved ones and overwhelming struggles in life, it fit the mood.

Walden Pond was the first stop of the day. Maya led the way on the dirt path that skirted the water's edge.

She glanced back over her shoulder at me, right as I tripped over a tree branch and toppled into the brush headfirst.

"You okay?" She helped me to my feet.

"Totally fine, unless you count my ego." I brushed off my jeans.

"Tell you what, I won't tell anyone." She removed a sprig from my hair.

"How much will your silence cost?" I joked.

She shook her head, amused. "Free this time. But if you keep it up, I may have to start charging you. Whitlock ain't cheap." She winked, and I sensed a frisson of excitement. Was I the cause? Maya turned to the water. "This pond is a wonderful example of a kettle hole. Do you know what that is?"

I shook my head.

"Thousands of years ago, when the glaciers were retreating, meltwater drained here." She formed her hands into a cone shape. "It's fifty to sixty feet deep."

Maya glanced back at me, and we shared another moment before she motioned for us to continue down the path.

On the far side of the pond, away from the parking lot and road, we stumbled upon the site of Thoreau's cabin. Not much remained. A reconstruction stood near the visitor center, but the demarcation of the real thing had a bigger impact on Maya. She stood reverently, soaking in the quiet, her eyes scanning the trees. Slowly, she turned and studied the water. Across the way, a lone man paddled a canoe. Reflections of the foliage rippled along the water's surface, compounding the sensation of green all around us.

"Can you imagine?" she asked.

"What?" I whispered, fearful I'd ruin the serenity or the growing connection between us.

"Living here, away from it all. No Google, no advertisements, no tourists …" She sat on a log.

I glanced at my watch. "It's not even nine. I imagine busloads of tourists will be arriving soon."

She grinned at me like I was a child who missed the big picture. "I know. I was trying to envision it during his time."

My cheeks prickled with warmth. "Of course. I for one wouldn't miss the likes of Susie Q."

She laughed. "You really don't like her."

"She makes my life hell."

Maya straddled the log and placed a hand on each of her knees. "How?"

"Do you know what it's like to have everything you do splashed for all the world to see?"

Maya shook her head. "I stick to myself, mostly."

"You're lucky. I feel like a zoo creature ninety percent of the time." I sighed. "It wouldn't be so bad if Susie Q stuck to the facts, but — "

"I saw the bit about the … fart." She stared at an ant crawling along the log.

"You read her blog?" I placed a hand on my heart.

"Only that one article. I was curious after you mentioned her last time." She hitched up an apologetic shoulder.

"I didn't fart." I tore a leaf in half.

"I know. It was the chair."

"The rest of that day, wherever I went, I swore people were staring at me or laughing. I know it sounds silly, but you have no idea what it's like being famous because your mother is the senior senator of Massachusetts. I've seen people in classes, coffee shops, or wherever, googling me. One person asked me to sign his iPad. Some assume they know me because they've read my Wikipedia page." I sucked in some air. "Susie made high school hell." I locked eyes on Maya. "Please, don't ever read or watch her reports from high school. I wouldn't be able to stand it."

"If I were to read your Wiki page, what would I find?" She leaned back, gripping the log.

"You haven't googled me?" I was dumbfounded.

She shook her head, amused. "Why would I? You're right here."

"Just the Carmichael highlights. We've had a member in the Senate and House since the founding of the US. Two governors of Massachusetts. Three mayors of Boston." I ticked each one off on a finger.

"Any mention of your father?" She lowered her eyes.

"It briefly mentions his death and how my mother was elected to his senate seat."

"Anything about you?"

I scrunched my face. "Not much. Just the schools I attended, my charity work, and I think it's been updated to say I'm currently enrolled in Whitlock."

She whistled. "Do you update the page?"

"Oh no. We have people."

"Right. People. Well, Miss Carmichael, if you don't mind, I'd like to get to know the real you. Not the created you."

"Not the created me — I like that."

"Thoreau wrote, 'The language of friendship is not words, but meanings.' I've always liked how he put it. Sometimes I wonder whether friendships can exist in today's meaningless world."

I laughed. "You have a worse opinion of society than I have."

"Is that good or bad?" She smirked.

"It's good in my book." I stared up at her with hooded eyes.

"Did you know Thoreau used to take children on hikes through the woods here? One day, he pointed out a cobweb to a young Louisa May Alcott and told her it wasn't a cobweb but a handkerchief left by a fairy."

"Oh, that's sweet, but ..."

"But what?" Maya's soft eyes were alluring.

"I'm not sure I would have believed it. Not even as a child."

"And I'm the cynic." She hooted.

"We can be cynics together."

A chipmunk scrounged through fallen leaves nearby, unafraid. Maya watched with a wisp of a smile. "Maybe we should move here. Get away from it all. You can escape the family dynasty, and I can ..." Sadness made her shoulders sag. I wondered what she wanted to escape, but I feared asking. *Quid pro quo* was a bitch. "Maybe then, we'd believe in fairies."

"It might take years to get to that point."

"I'm game. Can you live in a tent?" she teased.

I scrunched my face. "Uh, maybe."

Her knowing smile made it crystal clear I hadn't been convincing about my "roughing it" abilities. I was not Teddy Roosevelt. A wicked glint appeared in her eyes. "What would Thoreau say about Susie Q?"

Relieved that she let me off the camping hook, I snorted. "God, I think he would hate her."

"That settles it." She put a palm on my thigh. "I won't ever read anything by Susie Q."

"You promise?"

"I promise, Ainsley." She nudged my foot with hers. "I can't stand people like Susie: the type who use others to make a name for themselves. Private lives are just that, private. Although, it's getting harder and harder for people to maintain them, even nobodies like me."

"You aren't a nobody." I smacked her arm.

"Hey, I want to be a nobody. I strive to be a nobody." She put both palms in the air and smiled. "It makes me free."

"That may be the case, but you aren't a nobody to me."

She seemed to study me quite frankly, and I thought I detected a glimmer of longing in her eyes. I wanted to lean in, but I couldn't — Cassidy and Susie Q had ruined that for me.

"What's our next stop?" I hopped up.

We wandered along the brick pathway leading to Bronson Alcott's Concord School of Philosophy. We'd just completed the tour of Orchard House, and the school, while on the property, wasn't officially part of the tour. The ugly, dirty-brown building surrounded by grass and trees looked out of place.

Maya peered through the window. "Did you know Louisa helped pay for the school? Bronson was brilliant — a true idealist — but he could never channel his ideas into making money, not like his daughter."

I glanced over my shoulder at Orchard House. "It's really beautiful here. So quiet."

Maya laughed. "Too quiet for Louisa. She loved city life. The theater. She acted some." Maya turned back to the school. "Emerson said when Bronson sat down to write, his intellect left him."

"I feel like that sometimes when I have to write a paper."

She nudged my side. "Does that mean I'll write the paper and you'll do the presentation in class?"

"Maybe. I'm good at research, though." I leaned against the building, somewhat surprised the worn boards held my weight. "Did they get along?"

"Bronson and Louisa?"

I nodded.

"Yes and no. They were a lot alike, so naturally they butted heads. There were differences, important differences. His principles ranked higher than taking care of his family." Maya crossed her arms and rested a shoulder on the wall. "That must have rankled Louisa some. She had to work so hard to pay off the family's debt, and her father … well, he always had his head in the clouds. The father was supposed to be the breadwinner, not the daughter. I admire that she was."

Maya stared at the horizon, lost in thought, and I wondered whether she was thinking of her father. Was he like Bronson? Too self-involved? Idealistic? Yet Louisa was able to overcome the obstacles and make a name for herself. Where Bronson failed, his daughter succeeded. Is that the narrative Maya wanted for herself?

"I don't agree with her, though. I'd love to live here." She spread out both arms, twirling. "Away from the city."

"It's so green here." My eyes scanned all four directions. "Green, green, green, green."

"Exactly." She seemed pleased I'd remembered her comment from the car. "Can you imagine living here when she did, surrounded by so many great minds, the thinkers of the time? It's hard for me to believe she wasn't happy here."

"Sometimes you don't know what you have until it's too late."

Maya nodded thoughtfully. "Too true. And sometimes we covet things we can't have. Ever."

After visiting many of the sites, we popped into a tavern in downtown Lexington for a late lunch. The restaurant was new but was situated in a building that dated back centuries. Only a half-dozen tables filled the open floor plan, set up family style with old-fashioned wooden chairs. A roaring fire in the corner combated the damp air. A storm brewed outside, reflected within Maya's eyes.

"How come you haven't visited Concord much?" Maya dipped a spoon into a bowl of clam chowder.

"I think when you live here, you take a lot for granted. I remember visiting on a school trip, but my main memory consists of John Briggs pantsing Kevin Spade in the Walden Pond parking lot, shouting 'How do you like them apples, Thoreau?'"

Maya laughed, and the tension in her shoulder's eased.

"Did your school visit?" I asked, cracking pepper over my chowder.

She looked down at her soup. "I could never afford school trips. They never cost much, but ..."

I nodded. I'd never considered that.

"That's why I waited two years to apply to Whitlock, and then deferred a year when I was accepted. My momma always told me paying one's own way is the greatest gift I can give myself."

I quickly did the math. It meant Maya was at least twenty-one. "Have you applied for scholarships? My mother — "

She tsked playfully. "Remember, I'm not Susie. I like you, Ainsley. Half the time I forget your last name."

"Only half the time?"

"It's hard to forget when the tour guide at the Alcott house kept saying, 'Miss Carmichael, you might find this interesting.'"

My face sizzled at egg-frying temperature. "That was so embarrassing," I whispered.

"You're very recognizable, your face and your hair." She smiled bashfully. "A lot of women would kill for your hair."

"Not you?"

"Not sure it would suit my complexion." She rubbed her chin thoughtfully. "Besides, it looks way better on you."

I smiled.

"To answer your question, though, I did score a couple of small scholarships. Also, I've held so many part-time jobs I don't think I've slept much since high school. Started my first business when I was nine."

"What business?" I dumped more crackers into my soup.

"Dog walking." She reached into her canvas bag and pulled out a business card.

"You still walk dogs?"

"Not as much, but I have some steady clients. I house-sit as well. My goal is to line up enough house-sitting jobs next year that I don't have to pay rent at all."

"Give me some cards. I know people who are always in need." I put a palm out.

She hesitated, but her stiffness melted. "Really? That'd be great." She handed me three.

I laughed. "More."

Maya fished out an additional five. "Let me know if you need more."

"I might." I deposited the stack in my wallet. "What's been the craziest part-time job?"

"Craziest?" She buttered a piece of roll. "Not sure it was the craziest, but I worked at a call center that cold-called people for opinion polls. You learn a lot about human nature when you interrupt people during the dinner hour to ask what they think about the current state of the economy." She popped the roll into her mouth.

"I bet."

Maya washed the bread down with water. "One lady described miniature aliens that were climbing out of her kitchen cupboard."

I burst into laughter and covered my mouth. "Really?"

"I think she was seeing ants, but I didn't say anything. It's sad really." She smiled, letting me off the hook for laughing.

"The saddest calls were with the elderly. One woman who'd just lost her husband of fifty-three years would keep me on the phone just to chat. The first time we spoke, I accidentally entered the wrong data into the system. On my next shift, I had to call back to clarify. After that, I made a habit of messing up her calls. My supervisor caught on, and I actually got fired." She grinned. "But I still call Florence occasionally, just to check in."

"Is she in Boston?"

"Yes." The look she gave me suggested she was questioning my motive.

"I volunteer at the community center. It has a program for seniors who want to make friends. They go on bi-monthly outings, and we're starting a computer class so they can connect online with friends and family members who are out of state."

"Really? Flo would love the outings. Not sure she has a computer, though." Maya scratched the side of her forehead.

"No worries. I'll get her one." I clamped down on my bottom lip.

"You'd do that?" Maya's eyes narrowed.

"Not me. It's part of the program, but I'll help her fill out all the forms and speak with the director of the group. It's a new program, and we want it to succeed."

"So not everyone in the program gets a computer?" The twinkle in her eyes dimmed.

"Unfortunately, the budget is too small." I made the universal *what can you do?* gesture, palms in the air. "But we're hoping to grow it. We need enthusiastic seniors like Flo to help us spread the word."

Maya leaned back. "Oh, she's enthusiastic, all right. I'll give her a ring. Do you volunteer a lot?"

"Yep, since middle school. That's my favorite part — " I cut myself off, before I could say it was my favorite part of the Carmichael presidential quest. That tidbit was never mentioned outside of Carmichael circles.

"About being rich," she ribbed me. To soften the blow, she placed a hand on my thigh and gave it a squeeze.

"No! It's my favorite part of planning my career in politics."

"You want to be a senator, like your mom?" There wasn't a trace of condescension on her face.

"Not sure about senator. I like helping people. I want to help as many people as possible." I didn't add *by being President of the United States.*

"That's my dream — to be a community organizer. I know what it's like to feel all alone in this big, bad, scary world." Her grin didn't reach her eyes.

"Me too." I stirred my soup with a spoon.

I expected Maya to jeer, but her soft intake of breath conveyed how well she understood. "It's strange. There are millions of people on this planet, but most of us feel like no one understands or cares. It doesn't take much to change that. Imagine if everyone you saw simply said hello. You might feel less like an outsider."

Outsider.

With one word, she'd described my life to a T. If I succeeded and became president, would I be even lonelier than I was now? Would I ever be able to meet another Maya?

"Of course, now people only write *hello* — they don't say it." Maya stopped and studied my face to see if I understood.

I planted a smile. "You mean they hashtag hello."

A mist enveloped the grounds of Sleepy Hollow Cemetery moments after we arrived, as if the ghosts of Emerson, Hawthorne, Thoreau, and Alcott were making their presence known. We'd spent the past forty-five minutes stumbling along muddy paths, locating the graves of the most famous residents. Their final resting place was park-like with slight hills and trees. The effect was beautiful and peaceful: no doubt the designer's intent.

We left Louisa May Alcott's grave for last. Rain flecked our faces, prompting me to pop open an umbrella to protect us. Maya hadn't noticed. Her eyes were glued to Alcott's grave, and her body was motionless. Was she in a trance or tapping into some unknown reservoir of knowledge? It was a privilege to witness the connection. A frisson of attraction between us had been building all day. During lunch, Maya had rested a hand on my thigh and left it there for three and a half minutes, according to the clock on the wall behind the bar. It was the best 210 seconds of my life — so far.

The pitter-patter of raindrops increased, pulling Maya out of her daze. She peered into my eyes and smiled, like she was letting me in on a secret. My lips puckered and the umbrella slipped in my hand, exposing us to the elements. A huge drop of rain splashed on my nose, startling me. Her grin widened as she brushed off the droplet, and then she rested her hand on my cheek. I closed my eyes, nuzzling into her touch.

That was when it happened. Her lips were soft, like cashmere, and I instinctively opened my mouth to prompt her tongue to enter. The umbrella tumbled completely from my hand as I wrapped one arm around her waist and cupped the back of Maya's head with the other, pulling her closer, my desire to become one intensifying. I fisted her hair, and she responded by deepening the kiss.

I don't think I'd understood the power of locking mouths until that moment. The sensuality. The longing. What had I been missing?

Maya's hand slipped under my shirt, and its iciness against my bare skin made me shiver. She pulled her hand and lips away. "I'm sorry. You're freezing." Resting her forehead against mine, she gazed intently into my eyes.

"I don't care," I whispered.

She smiled, and our lips joined again.

We continued kissing for what seemed like forever, blowing the 210-second record out of the water. Her hand slipped back under my cream Ralph Lauren tunic top, her fingertips trailing up and down my back.

When her hand cupped my bra, my eyes snapped open.

Was I going to pop my cherry in the Sleepy Hollow Cemetery? I couldn't decide whether it was creepy or cool, given the setting.

As if in tune with my thought, she put the brakes on.

But she still gazed at me with a terrifying intensity as she trailed a finger down the side of my face. "Ainsley, I'm sorry." Her voice brimmed with uncharacteristic emotion. "This … this isn't a good idea."

"What isn't? This?" I motioned to the grounds and almost offered to check us into a hotel.

She clasped her rain-soaked hands around mine. "I want to be with you. I really do, but …" She stared up at the sky, at a loss for words. "You don't know me, really."

I let out a nervous chuckle. "But I want to. I want to know everything about you, Maya Chandler."

"About Maya Chandler, right? That's impossible for you, of all people."

"Why?"

"Ains, we come from two different worlds."

That was the point where she decided to give me a nickname, just as she was pulling the rug out from underneath me.

"But we don't have to live by two different rules." *Does that sound as lame to her as it does to me?*

She sighed, dropped my hands, and turned her back on me, with an air of finality.

"I'm not good at letting people in, giving them a chance," she said over her shoulder. For a brief moment, she paused, and I thought she might turn around and rush back toward me. She didn't.

I wanted to scream at her to come back. My mouth opened, but no words came out. I stood unprotected in the rain, miserable, alone.

Seconds that seemed like a lifetime passed before I came to my senses. I plucked the umbrella off the muddy path, shook loose the leaves and dirt, and followed Maya's tracks to my car. I unlocked the doors and we both slid inside, not speaking. Her teeth chattered, and I kicked up the heat to dry us off.

Maya sat motionless in her seat. I didn't put the car into gear. Instead, I waited for her to elaborate, to say anything.

Only silence filled the car. The most unbearable silence pervaded my ears.

CHAPTER
seven

MY FIST POUNDED ON FIONA'S door.

"Hold your horses, will ya?" Fee shouted.

When she opened the door, I fell into her arms, sobbing, "We kissed."

Fiona's arms encircled me. "What'd you do? Bite her tongue off or something?"

"No," I wailed. "But I might as well have. She ran away."

"Right," was all Fiona said as she shoved me inside. "Sit. I'm going to get you a change of clothes and make some tea. Did you walk all the way back in the rain?"

After I'd dropped Maya off, I'd parked my car near my dorm and walked the two miles to Fiona's apartment across the Charles. I had hoped the rain would wash away the pain and bring clarity. Neither had happened.

"Tell me again. Her words exactly," Fiona said.

"She said she wanted to be with me, but it wasn't a good idea," I responded, holding back a sob. Our first kiss had been better than perfect, but the feeling didn't last. "And when I said I wanted to get to know her, she said that wasn't possible for me."

I sank into Fiona's plush couch cushions, feeling no comfort. Fee's Boston terrier, Grover, was spending the day with her, instead of at Fiona's mom's. Grover sat on my lap, resting his head on his front paws and staring up at me with mournful eyes. I scratched his ear.

"For you specifically?"

I shrugged. "I didn't think to clarify."

Fiona tapped her cigarette against the ashtray, deep in thought.

"And she didn't say another word in the car?" she asked.

"She thanked me for driving when I pulled up in front of her building." I sat up on the couch. Grover snorted his disgust at being jostled. "Sorry, Grover." I stroked his head. "There was a moment when I thought she was going to say more, but she clammed up and said she'd see me Monday."

"Monday?" Fiona's eyes widened with hope.

I squashed it. "We have class together."

Grover sighed. I sank into the couch, and he settled on my lap again.

"Right." Fiona leaned back against the sofa, taking a long, dramatic drag on her cigarette.

I pulled the hood of the sweatshirt over my head and tightened the strings. "Do you think it happened again?"

"I don't see Maya doing something like that. She's not Cassidy, and she's nothing like Bottlenose."

Just to be sure, Fiona checked out Susie's blog. No updates since last night. If she had footage of me crashing and burning, it would be up already.

"But who is she?"

"Good question. Who is Maya the Gray? Have you googled her?"

I shook my head. "I hate when people google me."

Fiona nodded. "I know, but …"

"But we want to know. I want to know." I yanked off the hood.

Grover barked his approval.

Fee laughed at her dog. "Well, that settles it. We have to find out who she is. I didn't peg her as the theatrical type, but …"

"That's just it. She isn't your typical teenage drama queen. Hell, she's not even a teenager anymore. And I don't think she's playing hard to get. It's bigger than you and I can imagine, I suspect."

Fiona flipped her laptop open. "What's her last name?"

"Chandler."

"Maya Chandler," Fiona parroted as she typed the name into the search bar. "There aren't too many on Facebook, actually." She scrolled down. None of the pictures matched. "Does she have a middle name? Maybe she goes by Maya Ann or something."

"I don't know. But earlier today she mentioned people's private lives should remain private."

"Okay, so not the social media type. Do you have a photo? Maybe we'll find something she doesn't even know is out there. The Web is worse than Big Brother."

I had snapped a photo earlier in the day when Maya wasn't looking. I e-mailed it to Fiona.

Annoyed by the commotion, Grover jumped off the couch and settled on his bed with a bone big enough for a Doberman.

"This is how they do it on *Catfish*." She opened a Google browser page, clicked on "images" and then on the camera icon in the search bar and uploaded Maya's photo. No exact matches. None of the suggested possibilities bore any resemblance.

"Phone number?" Fiona's attempt not to sound desperate was admirable. How many people our age, besides us, didn't have any social media accounts?

I shook my head. "Only her school e-mail."

We stared at the MacBook, crestfallen.

"That's it!" Fiona slapped her thigh. "Chuck."

"Chuck?"

"My buddy, Chuck. He's like the computer whiz Garcia on *Criminal Minds*. If there's information out there, he'll find it."

"Oh, I don't know, Fee. She was adamant this morning that private lives are off-limits. I just don't know." I palmed the top of my head with both hands, smoothing my curly locks.

Fee gripped her cell phone. "It's not you digging. It's me."

"But ..."

"Another Cassidy is not going to happen on my watch." Before I could stop her, Fiona was e-mailing Chuck, giving him all the details, which didn't include much. Her name, Puerto Rican heritage, Wyoming, the class we had together, and the street I picked her up on. It didn't strike me as odd until Fiona asked me her address. Maya had never provided a physical address. Instead, she'd said she'd meet me on the corner of Commonwealth and Massachusetts Avenue. When she'd suggested the location, it made perfect sense. Parking in the city was like finding a polar bear in the Arctic: not impossible, but difficult, frustrating, and a time suck.

While we waited, Fee popped off the couch. "Going to put a load of laundry in. Want me to toss in your wet clothes?"

"Yeah, thanks."

She hummed the *Snow White and the Seven Dwarfs* song "Whistle While You Work." Halfway through the song she stopped. "Ainsley," she called out from the laundry room behind the kitchen.

"What?" I shouted from the couch.

Fiona entered the room. "Did you fall down on your date?" She held up my jeans with dirt smears on the knees. "Maybe this is the reason."

"What are you saying? She doesn't like me because I'm accident-prone?"

Fee laughed.

I rolled my eyes. "Don't pile on more fears, please."

"Oh, you're no fun." She about-faced and returned to the laundry room.

The chime on my phone alerted me I had a text. Hopeful it was from Maya, I pounced, but as my eyes scanned the text, all my optimism was squashed.

History is little more than the register of the crimes, follies, and misfortunes of mankind.

The message came from an unknown number again, but it wasn't difficult to guess the sender. "Give it a rest, Susie!" I tossed the phone into the far corner of the couch.

Fiona's phone buzzed forty-five minutes later. She tapped the e-mail app on her cell and quickly scanned Chuck's message. "Yeah … okay … Dorchester … Mattapan?" Fiona covered half her mouth with a palm to hide her shock. She mumbled "Sorry" through her fingers.

Back in the nineties, Mattapan became infamous for its crime, and many referred to it as Murdapan. It had cleaned up some since then, but few visited the area unless absolutely necessary.

"How does being from Mattapan make a difference?" I mused out loud. Grover cocked his head, doing his best to follow the conversation. I tossed a tennis ball down the hallway, and he gave chase.

Fiona pushed a button, blackening the screen, but didn't say anything.

"Tell me everything in the e-mail!" I shook her arm up and down.

She laughed. "Okay, but don't get your hopes up. It seems your Maya Chandler is still a mystery for the most part. She and her mom moved into a house in Mattapan in 2003, and that's the first bit of information Chuck could find. There are no birth records for Maya or her mother. It's like they magically appeared in 2003 in Murdapan, of all places. Her mom is a waitress, according to her taxes."

"Taxes?"

"I told you Chuck was good."

"But how? If she filed taxes, she must have a social security number. Surely Maya does as well. Hard to believe La Creperie would hire her on the sly."

"She does make the best coffee."

"Fiona." I flashed an admonishing glance to silence her. "Why isn't there a record of them before 2003?" I sighed. "What does that mean? Witness protection?"

"Did she say anything about Wyoming?"

"All she said was that it was brown."

"Brown?" Fiona scratched her chin.

"She said she was just a kid when they moved."

"That's not much to go on. Who is this chick?"

"So much for being like Dubya," I said.

Fee lit another cigarette. "What?"

"You told me to follow my gut. Look where that got me — ditched in a cemetery by a girl who doesn't seem to exist."

CHAPTER eight

AT 7:55 A.M. ON MONDAY MORNING, I briefly considered skipping class for the first time in my life. I was probably the only person in my high school who had never ditched a class — not one. Many people claimed I was too uptight; that wasn't it, not entirely. I'd just never wanted to. Not all of my classes rocked my world, of course, but I didn't loathe any either. The truth: ditching wasn't in my genetic code. Carmichael's never dodged a commitment — never ever.

Yet the mere thought of seeing Maya first thing made my stomach twist in knots, like that time I had *E. coli* after eating a salad in Mexico. When I woke this morning, the cramps in my belly screamed, "the squirts are coming, the squirts are coming" like a demented Paul Revere.

I placed the back of my hand on my forehead, and I swore my temperature hovered around one hundred or higher. Maybe I did have food poisoning; surely that was an acceptable excuse for missing class. Or was I simply worked up about seeing Maya?

Dr. Gingas wobbled down the corridor, conjuring an image of a wounded, two-legged rhinoceros. Wounded or not, she was still intent on going in for the kill.

There was no way in hell this woman would excuse any absence, no matter what. Even death wouldn't be acceptable. According to the syllabus, we were allotted three absences. After that, each absence lowered our grade by one letter, but I suspected Dr. Gingas would consider failing someone for missing a single class.

"You feeling all right, Ms. Carmichael?"

"What? Yes, I'm fine." I smoothed my V-neck T-shirt.

"Glad to hear it. Now stop your dillydallying and get your keister in your seat, pronto." She stretched out a stubby finger and stabbed it at the door.

Did she sense I was acting like an attention-seeking prima donna, or did she just not give a damn enough to notice anything except that the class was about to start? More than likely, it was the latter.

Maya was in her usual seat, and I knew I had to sit next to her or Susie Q would take note. Most assuredly Maya would, too, and I didn't want to give either that satisfaction.

Maya adjusted in her seat when I sat down, but she didn't acknowledge my presence, not that I had time to opine. Our dictatorial professor started lecturing as soon as she was halfway into the classroom. She held her briefcase like she was guarding missile launch codes.

I whipped out my notebook and got down to business.

The fifty minutes flew by, and before I had settled into a groove, everyone was cramming their belongings into book bags. Maya continued to jot down notes. Before I had the chance to stand, the scratch of her pen stopped. Curious, I turned to her.

She paled when we locked eyes, and I wondered whether the entire school was infected with *E. coli*. Her usual bright gray eyes looked more like three-day-old snow in the gutter.

"Would you like to grab a cup of coffee?" she asked.

I scrutinized her face, trying to determine whether I was experiencing fever-induced delusions and hearing voices. Maya's lips had moved, but still. She was talking to me … on campus. And after the incident.

"Uh, sure."

"If you don't have time …" She stopped without any interruption on my part.

I laughed awkwardly, sounding a bit like a hyena who didn't understand the punch line.

Maya actually smiled at that and seemed to recover her usual composure: paradoxically cocky, scared, and alluring. Who was Maya the Gray? What was she? And why couldn't I know?

Several other students stared at me as if I was a special case or something. A brilliant autistic student, perhaps, who knew a million and one facts about Massachusetts but not how to interact with humans. People exiting the room gave me a wide berth, which was a feat, considering I blocked most of the pathway to freedom. Every single person wore a sympathetic smile that suggested, "I think it's great the institution lets you out for classes."

Maya nudged my arm. "You ready?"

I didn't think she was really asking, just forcing me to get my hiney moving and out of everyone's way.

I blew out some air, and a loose strand of hair from my ponytail poked me in the eye. I yelped. Why had that hurt so much? Like a razor blade slicing through an eyeball?

Maya suppressed a smile, put a hand on my arm, and asked, "Are you okay?"

I glanced down at her hand, and she promptly yanked it away.

"Yeah, just determined to make a spectacle out of myself in front of you every chance I get," I said, not caring how she or anyone else took it. I was sick and tired of living in a fishbowl.

"You do have a knack for it." Her smile was genuine, which irked me.

"Like you can talk," I snapped. I slugged my bag over my shoulder and headed toward the exit.

Screw coffee. I wanted to be alone.

I didn't get ten yards from the building before someone tugged on my arm. Whipping around ready for a fight, I found

Maya with mournful, downcast eyes.

"At least let me buy you a cup of coffee, after …" Words failed her again.

"Fine. I have time before English," I said, much more brusquely than intended. She looked miserable, and I didn't understand why I couldn't tell her it was okay. I was being that girl I despised: the overly dramatic and insufferable scorned teenage girl — the type in movies. So we kissed and then she shot me down. *Not the end of the world, Ainsley.*

So why did I feel that way? I hated her for it. And I hated myself for letting it happen. Again.

We trudged to a coffee cart inside the entrance of the Student Union. Was she as uncomfortable as I was? Her slumped shoulders said yes. Could everyone read on my face that Maya had rejected me after rocking my world with her lips? I didn't need a scarlet A, just a big, fat, cherry-red L for Loser. Or LL for Lesbian Loser. I was waiting for Maya to deliver the breakup *coup de grace*: it's not you, it's me.

Coffees in hand, neither of us knew what to do.

Maya motioned to the glass door etched with the university's initials, WU, and its sunray logo. "Would you like to find a quiet spot?"

I nodded like a child who had just recovered from a tantrum, minus the snot-smeared face.

Several large trees surrounded a bench on the side of the building. It was a lovers' paradise. *Flipping fantastic!*

Maya sat with her legs slightly open, elbows on each thigh, and fiddled with the plastic lid on her coffee. I noticed she wasn't wearing her work clothes.

Perched in the corner with my legs primly crossed, I kept my eyes forward.

"I'm really sorry about — "

"Don't worry about it." I cut her off. "It happens …" What was I going to say? It happens to me all the time? Could I be any more awkward?

"No, please. Let me explain." She shuffled her feet in the dirt. "I like you. I do. The kiss … and you're absolutely adorable, even when you're trying to be tough, but … it's just that, well, what kind of future could we have?" She peered into the distance.

"What do you mean?"

"Your mom is a senator."

"Huh?" I still wasn't getting it.

"And I'm a poor kid from Mattapan."

Chuck was dead-on with that one. "And?"

"Oh, come on, Ainsley. You know what I mean?"

I shook my head.

"We both have ancestors who were slaves, but you don't look it, and I do," she whispered. "Not to mention you're filthy rich and I'm poorer than poor."

I tapped the top of the plastic coffee lid. "You think I'm elitist and racist."

"What? No! It's not that. It's just …"

"It's just what?" I pushed. There was so much more to this story. Like how come there wasn't a record of Maya or her mom before 2003?

"My own family doesn't talk to me …"

"Because you're not white or because you're poor?"

Was her father white? Rich? I was desperate to fill in the blanks.

She nodded halfheartedly, not confirming which. Maybe both reasons mattered somehow.

Ostracized by her family, being a minority and gay in Wyoming, moving to Mattapan under suspicious circumstances — she had life experiences I would never be able to relate to. Maya wouldn't be able to relate to mine either. Did that matter, though? Taylor Swift's "Love Story" started to play in my head.

"And then I kissed a prominent white senator's daughter." She smirked. "Back home, I'd get shot for that." Her expression showed she wasn't teasing.

I let out a slow breath, trying to take everything in.

"It's not like that here." I nearly choked on the untruth. Massachusetts was a lot more liberal than the rest of the US, but only certain chunks of it. Ignorance and hate lurked in every corner of America.

"Okay, it's not perfect here, but it has to be better than Wyoming. I mean, nothing against your home state; it's just you don't have to be so afraid here."

"Says the girl who's never had to deal with discrimination. Ever hear of Ferguson, Sandra Bland, Trayvon Martin, Oscar Grant, or Freddie Gray …?" She motioned she could go on.

"And you think that'll happen if you're seen with me?" I placed a hand on my heart.

"Because you plan on being seen with me all the time? Out in the open?" She motioned to the safety provided by the trees.

"Hey, that's not fair! *You* suggested this place."

"But you tend to drift to secluded places. You hardly talk to anyone in class."

"Neither do you! That's one of the things I like about you."

"That I know my place?"

I blinked. "I would never say or think such a thing. What I meant is that you're one of the few people I've met who seems real, not someone who's filling space on social media to show how cool and important they are. I love your authenticity. What happened to being cynics together?" I tried to spark the feelings we'd shared at Walden Pond.

"And how can I maintain my authenticity if I'm with one of the most recognizable girls on campus? I don't want my picture splashed all over the Internet, or to appear in the social pages."

I groaned. "You can't have it both ways, Maya. First you say I want to keep you hidden, and now you're saying you don't want to be seen with me. Which is it?"

She covered her eyes with both hands. "I don't know. I just don't know if this" — she motioned to us — "can work. Ever. We're so different."

"But we aren't — not inside. We both just want to be left

alone."

The tightness in her facial muscles confused me. Was she angry? Or about to give in?

"You have no idea what it's like being from Mattapan and attending Whitlock. Being a minority, fatherless, struggling to keep a roof over my head, and alone."

"You have no idea what it's like to be me. Everyone has treated me differently because of my last name. I thought you were different," I said without thinking. "I'm not a person; I'm a Carmichael. That's all anyone sees."

She flinched but quickly recovered. "Must be such a hardship. How do you get out of bed every day?"

The conversation had taken a massive wrong turn. "I can't change who I am," I said through gritted teeth. "I'm sorry you had it so rough while I was born with a silver spoon in my mouth, but you aren't the only one who's fatherless." I stood up in a huff, but I didn't rush off. I wanted her to stop me. I wanted her to say she was sorry, to say "to hell with it; let's give it a go."

She didn't. Maya continued to stare at her feet. Clearly she had no intention of continuing the conversation. That was that. I was the rich white girl. She was the poor minority. And in her world, that still mattered. I knew it mattered in my world, too, but at least I was willing to give us a chance.

"And that's all she said?" Fiona rubbed one of her earlobes. "No major bomb, just that she's poor and her mother was born in Puerto Rico?"

"Thank you!" I slapped the kitchen table.

"She has beautiful skin. You say her family goes back to the slave trade." Fiona grabbed a silver and red can from the fridge, popped the top of the Diet Coke, and handed it to me. "From the color of her skin, I'd say she was mixed, and damn, she inherited all the best genes from Africa, Europe, and America."

"Really, Fee. That's what you want to talk about?" I sipped my drink. "Can we get back to the matter at hand? It wasn't like she'd dropped a bombshell. I already knew she was a minority. I just don't think it's a big deal." Fiona's perky yellow walls oozed happiness, while I slowly perished from a broken heart.

Fiona shrugged. "For us, maybe. But what would your mother say, Ains? Her first thought would be your political ambition. And Grandmother would have a conniption." She eyed me knowingly. "Maya probably doesn't want to get hurt. Why fall for you when there's no chance? Not to mention she's hiding something. Why else wouldn't there be records? Think of how that'll look …"

"Don't say during my presidential campaign," I groaned. "Fuck my career. I'm not even out of college. I'm so sick and tired of making all of my decisions based on something that probably won't happen. Not to mention being hounded by Susie Q, who's bent on destroying any chance of happiness."

"Have you received anymore random texts?"

I swatted the air. "No." My right eye twitched uncontrollably. Rubbing it, I continued to keep Fee off the trail of quotes. "How many presidents have there been? Forty-something?"

"Forty-four. You know the number." Fiona poured another cup of tea from the pot and plopped in two sugar cubes, splashing tea onto the table. She swiped it away with her fingers.

"In over two hundred years, only forty-four individuals have held that office. And no woman has been elected so far, let alone a lesbian!" I let out an angry puff of air. "I'm tired of making all my decisions based on a long shot."

At eighteen, I was starting to realize I was constantly wracked with worry about my presidential quest. I would be judged on everything I did, not only as a senator's daughter, but as a future president. I avoided Facebook, Twitter, blogs, and any type of social media. Even Goodreads was out of the question, because what if I rated a book that could potentially become a scandal thirty years from now?

Scandal.

All my life had been devoted to dodging scandals so I wouldn't become a footnote in American history. Being with Maya might not be scandalous on a huge scale, but it could cause ripples — and I didn't give a damn. Not when I kissed her and not now. Fuck living in fear, because that wasn't living.

I was a late bloomer for everything. I was the last to lose my first tooth and the last to start my period. I still hadn't grown any boobs to speak of. A virgin. I never rebelled. None of this stuff had mattered months ago. Hell, it hadn't mattered weeks ago.

Fuck twenty years from now. I wanted to live in the moment.

How did this happen? How did Maya worm her way into my life and turn everything upside down?

Fiona snapped her fingers in my face. "Earth to Ainsley. You're doing that thing again."

"What thing?"

"Spacing out. Probably stewing about all the wrongs in the world."

"Close. All the wrongs in my life."

"That's not very presidential." Fiona placed an exaggerated hand on her chest, feigning bewilderment, and laughed. She sipped her tea and immediately scrunched up her face. "I wish we could go to La Creperie. That place has ruined me for all other hot beverages."

I perked up. "Why can't we?"

She sucked her lower lip into her mouth. "Won't that be awkward or come across as desperate?"

I waved her concerns away. "Maya wasn't wearing her black shirt today. I'm pretty sure she's not working."

Without waiting for me to continue, Fiona yanked her purse off the side table and shoved me toward the door. Outside, her arm encircled my waist and I leaned my head against her shoulder as we walked in silence past the John F. Kennedy School of Government.

Outside the entrance of La Creperie, Fiona asked, "Are you sure she's not here?"

"Of course." I still didn't know who Maya was, but I did know one thing: she was predictable, mostly. I brusquely tugged Fee's arm, taking her by surprise and causing us to stumble inside. We weren't making a grand entrance; we were making a spectacle.

"Grace isn't your thing, is it?" Fiona arched an eyebrow and straightened her blazer.

"It's hard to believe I took six years of ballet and tap lessons." Not flummoxed, I marched to the counter to order. Right when I reached the register, Maya stepped out from the back to relieve the person at the counter. Grace and timing weren't my strong suits, apparently.

Maya, stone-faced, waited for me to order. Fiona shuffled her feet, and I sensed she wanted to belt out, "Awkward!"

The overhead lights seemed unusually bright, and I simultaneously covered my eyes and squinted.

"Hello, we're back for your wonderful brews." Fiona came to my rescue. "I'm addicted to the hazelnut latte, so I dragged my dear cousin here kicking and screaming."

Some rescue.

Maya punched a few keys on the register and busied herself making our drinks.

Fiona dug a ten and three ones out of her Woodrow Wilson wallet, which she'd been carrying since she was twelve.

"I can bring them to your table if you like." Maya glanced over her shoulder at the customer behind us, dismissing us with a curt nod.

"That would be marvelous." Fiona jostled me toward a table in the rear — the same one behind the column where Maya had hidden that first night. There was no denying Fiona was relishing my mortification. "You're more entertaining than all the John Hughes' flicks put together."

I scowled at her. "Glad someone is finding this funny."

"I asked you, and you were so sure." She waved a haughty hand in the air.

I put a finger to my lips to silence her. The last thing I needed was to have Maya overhear. My plan was to bolt down our coffee and make a quick, and hopefully refined, exit.

"Oh, did I tell you, darling, that we've been summoned to a family dinner this weekend?" Fiona's sweet façade was a cover. Not that dinner with our family was horrible — draining was more like it.

"Everyone?"

"As far as I can tell. Mom told me to make sure you're there. Your mother is in California, fundraising for one of the senators — I can't remember which one." She tapped her nose with a finger.

"Why did your mom say I had to be there? Why single me out?"

"I dunno. A surprise, maybe."

"Sounds ominous. Do you remember the last family surprise?" I cringed.

Fiona looked away. "Yes. Yes, I do."

"Fiona … I'm sorry. That was stupid of me." I rested my hand on her arm.

The last family bombshell was the announcement that her parents would be living apart — permanently, although we were never to speak of it in public. Divorce wasn't an option, considering her father was an esteemed member in the House of Representatives. Fee's mom had put up with a lot, but when her husband had been caught with yet another staffer — actually two staffers, and one was male — she'd called it quits. That, of course, wasn't mentioned at the family estate either, but it was hard to avoid scintillating news reports about the male staffer on the evening news cycle for several days. Susie Q had a field day on the *Tattler*. Somehow, she managed to get her grubby paws on blurry photos that showed Fee's dad giving the dude a BJ.

Fiona, being the sexually fluid type, wasn't bothered that her father was comfortable being with men and women. Her anger stemmed from two sources: that her father was stupid enough to get caught and that it hurt her mom.

That meeting had been called to inform all of us to circle the wagons tighter than ever before. Fiona was whisked off to public events with her loving father, to show he was a family man. She played her role to perfection: smiling for the camera, planting kisses on her father's cheek, and acting like nothing was out of the ordinary. Fee's mom made a few appearances. When she did, they all held hands, with Fiona in the middle, a la the Clintons after the Lewinski brouhaha.

Duty.

Carmichaels believed in family duty, no matter what. Until recently, I believed it was akin to breathing — that it had to be done to survive.

"I need to use the bathroom." I stood up abruptly, turned, and crashed right into Maya, who was holding a coffee cup in each hand. One cup flew into the air and hung there for a split second before spiraling down like a shooting star, leaving a trail of brown. The crash was deafening.

I shrieked.

Maya set the other cup on a nearby table and reached for my hand. "Are you okay? You aren't burned, are you?"

I looked down at the floor. The cup had shattered like Humpty Dumpty. Maya's apron was sprayed with coffee, and my hand dripped with searing liquid, but I wasn't in pain. My brain could only comprehend that Maya was holding my hand, inspecting the faint red splotches. I was aware of her touch, nothing more.

It didn't last. She released my hand, letting it crash to my side. Maya marched to the back of the store, reappearing moments later with a bowl of cool water, which she plunged my hand into.

Neither of us spoke, but I noticed Fiona scrutinizing the situation.

"Does it hurt?" Maya asked.

I shook my head, unable to register whether she was annoyed or not. Was she worried about a lawsuit?

"Are you?" I asked. Her splattered apron revealed she had taken the brunt of the collision.

"I'm fine." She looked at Fiona. "You might want to take her to a doctor."

Fiona slapped the table. "Pat." Not saying anything else, she hopped up to make a call.

"Pat?" Maya queried.

"A doctor friend. We try to avoid making a fuss, to stay out of the news." I explained, feeling like a pompous fool.

"That must be hard for you." She smirked, avoiding my eyes.

I laughed. "I'm usually not this bad, I swear."

The shop was deserted, considering it was close to ten and the stress of classes hadn't kicked into full gear. Two weeks from now, I imagined the place would be filled with students in dire need of a caffeine fix to stay awake cramming into the wee hours.

"Are you working the rest of the night?"

She nodded. "We close at midnight."

"Alone?"

"Nah. Josh is on his dinner break. Allison had a family emergency and asked me to cover the rest of her shift."

Fiona returned with a mop and bucket. "Found this by the bathroom."

Maya jumped out of her seat. "Here, let me do that!"

"Pffft, I can handle it. Take care of her." She gestured to me, and Maya looked at the bucket and then back at me. Having a customer clean up a spill probably went completely against her moral fiber. However, considering who we were, she may have considered it an order. Secretly, I also wanted Maya to take care of me.

Maya retook her seat and lifted my hand out of the water to inspect the damage. It wasn't that bad, really, just red. It was hard to determine whether that was from the coffee or from the frigid water.

Fiona took great delight in mopping up the mess, whistling like a sailor swabbing the deck.

"There. Good as new." Fiona scooted the yellow bucket behind the counter. "All right, Pat's meeting us at my place." She shook Maya's hand. "We should have you over for dinner some night next week. Will Tuesday work?"

Speechless, Maya nodded.

"Good. Ainsley will give you my address."

With that, Fiona ushered me out.

Mission accomplished.

CHAPTER
nine

"I'M TELLING YOU THAT GIRL is gaga over you." Fiona tapped cigarette ash into a ceramic Richard Nixon tray. She sat in the window of the front room with one curtain partially pulled to the side to allow the smoke to escape.

Pat examined my hand. "What girl?" he asked in his thick Boston-Irish brogue. "Do tell." He fumbled through his black medical kit on the table in front of the couch.

"Not much to tell," I said through gritted teeth. The pain was starting to set in, not to mention the embarrassment.

"Not much to tell. Yeah, right. Our little Ainsley's in love." Fee stood up, gripped both of my shoulders, and leaned down to my level. "Our rigid girl has finally found someone to break down her wannabe presidential ice walls. Oh, this will make a splendid chapter in your bio. A horrific accident leaving you scarred for life, and your future wife ignoring her own pain to attend to you. Of course, it was at that moment you both knew you were destined to be together, no matter the odds."

"Oh, Fee. You should write fiction, because that's the biggest load of crap." Pat wrapped a sterile cloth around my hand, even though he had assured me the burn was nothing to be concerned about.

"Ouch!" I squirmed.

"Too tight?" Pat quirked an eyebrow.

Fiona burst into a fit of laughter. "Boy, have you got that right, mister."

Pat joined in at my expense.

"Yuck it up, you two. I'll get my revenge."

Unperturbed by my threat, Fee added, "Ainsley may be the first person to woo her beloved by farting."

"Farting?" Pat's dark-chocolate eyes left mine in search of Fiona's emerald ones. "You can't be serious."

"I am." Fiona tittered. "Not only that, she belted it out in front of her entire class."

Pat covered his mouth. I wasn't sure why he bothered, since he was already laughing uncontrollably.

"It was my chair! It squeaked!"

"That was no squeak. They heard your gas explosion in Hong Kong."

Pat grew serious. "Wait, was this last week at 1:17 p.m.?" He howled with laughter, rubbing tears of mirth from his eyes with the hem of his shirt. The light flickered off his shorn yellow hair. The top of his head resembled a fuzzy tennis ball that had seen better days. Regaining some of his composure, he added, "I didn't think you Carmichaels ever farted or took a dump, just in case someone was recording you."

"Only Ainsley," Fiona said matter-of-factly. She lit a joint and handed it to Pat. "Besides, Grandmother's minions sweep our places for bugs once a week."

"You're kidding." Pat lowered himself to the floor, sitting with his back against the couch, and stretched out his tree-trunk legs.

Fiona winked. The goons did do a sweep, but I sensed Fee knew she had said too much.

She handed him the roach, and he took a hit. After holding the smoke in, he handed it to me. "It'll help with the pain." He smiled like he actually believed he was giving out sound medical advice.

I shook my head.

Fiona took the joint and settled on the floor next to him, her legs almost as long as Pat's. "Don't bother. Ainsley is determined not to make Clinton's mistake."

Pat's face twisted.

"She doesn't want to have to explain that she never actually inhaled." Fiona stood and grabbed some whiskey from the bureau on the far side of the front room. "This should do the trick." She poured me a hefty dose, taking a sip before handing over the tumbler.

"But drinking is okay?" asked Pat.

"Hell, you can't be a politician and not drink. And we're Scottish. We've been in training since we were babes."

Pat shook his head at Fiona's logic.

"Our moms used to rub brandy on our gums when we were teething, or if we were acting up. Only the cheap shit, though." Fiona laughed. "I still can't stand the swill they used for medicinal purposes." She scrunched her nose.

Pat motioned for me to hand him the whiskey.

"Only if you promise not to mention the girl, or this, to anyone?" I raised my bandaged paw.

"Please. I'm a fourth-generation Irish-American from Southie. I know keeping my trap shut isn't just good manners; it's the difference between life and death." He smiled, but there was certainty in his squared shoulders. I wasn't positive, but I suspected some of his family members were connected to the mob.

Fiona rested her head on Pat's shoulder.

My phone vibrated. Ignoring the chemistry between Fee and Pat, I checked the message and groaned.

"What?" Fiona switched from light-hearted to deadly serious in less than a millisecond.

I read the text from my brother. "'Be prepared.' It's from Ham."

Fiona grabbed the phone. Squinting, she reread the two words before shaking the phone, as if trying to force it to elaborate. "That's it? 'Be prepared'? That could mean anything," she said in a nasal tone.

"Understatement of the year. In our family, anything goes," I said.

"How is one-eyed Hammie? I haven't seen that bastard in months." Pat took another hit of the joint, resting his head against the couch while pulling Fee closer with his other arm.

"One-eyed Hammie? You're awful." I threw a James Madison pillow at him.

He caught it and bonked my legs with it. "That's what we used to call him at school."

"Why are you getting your panties in a bunch? It's only because of Ham's firecracker incident and his damaged eye that your mom and dad went back to the drawing board for an heir, and ta-da, here you are." Fee sipped the communal whiskey glass.

"What?" Pat asked.

"After that firecracker exploded in Ham's face ..."

Pat nodded as if he understood. "Considering what happened, the damage didn't turn out that bad. Some scarring on the face — "

"And the bad eye. It's unnerving when you aren't expecting it." Fee raised the glass in the air and swirled the golden liquid.

"But how does that explain little Ainsley?" Pat batted his surprisingly long lashes at me.

"After Craig died, Ham became the heir apparent. But once he got disfigured, they needed to create another baby to take over the Carmichael reins. Ains was destined to be the Chosen One before she was even in the womb," Fiona elaborated.

"The Chosen One?" Pat craned his neck to peer into Fee's eyes.

"To become president."

"Fee!" I shouted.

"What? It's Pat — he's practically family." She handed the

glass to Pat.

They ignored my indignation. People outside of the family weren't supposed to know my purpose, although considering the political leanings of our family, it wasn't that much of a secret. Ever since kindergarten, kids had called me Madame President.

"What about Kylie?" Pat asked.

"Please. She has zero personality." Fiona's tone held no malice, just brutal honesty. Kylie would be the first to agree.

Pat stroked her leg. "What about you?"

"I'm freakishly tall and I have linebacker shoulders. Grandmother passed on me years ago."

"Shit. Your grandmother is a piece of work." Pat furrowed his brow and shook his head.

"Don't worry about me," Fee said. "The last thing I want is to be the Chosen One, and Kylie has her heart set on being a judge. Ham, though, he craves real power."

This piqued Pat's curiosity. "Does he want to be president?"

Fiona snorted. "Hell, no. He wants to control the president. Ham is like Geppetto." She mimed a puppet on strings. "He can be cold, calculating, and a son of a bitch. But he doesn't want to be in front of the cameras. He wants all the power."

"How?"

"Be the president's chief of staff."

My brother was convinced the president actually possessed little clout. In his opinion, the White House Chief of Staff held all the cards, and more than likely he was spot-on. President was a title, first and foremost. Still, most people recognized the names of former presidents. How many recognized their chiefs of staff?

Ham had landed a job in the White House two years ago, but it would take years for him to reach his coveted spot. Carmichaels always prepared for the long game.

"At least this weekend won't be boring. Pat, would you like to come along and enjoy the show?" Fiona asked.

"Are you bringing the new girl, Ainsley?" Pat didn't bother focusing his blurry eyes on me, keeping them on Fee.

"Nope," Fiona answered. "The Chosen One got shot down."

"Shot down how?"

"Right after they kissed for the first time, Maya — the girl — said it wouldn't work."

"Do I need to write you out a script for halitosis?" Pat chortled. "Farting, bad breath — you aren't the typical Carmichael, are you? And here I thought all these years you were the perfect one." He cleared his throat. "Oh, excuse me, the Chosen One."

"I've got a plan in motion to help my dear cousin out." Fee covered her mouth and whispered in Pat's ear.

He nodded.

I groaned. Now that Pat was involved in the Maya plot, my chances were slipping away faster than Sarah Palin's vice-presidential bid.

CHAPTER
Ten

FRIDAY EVENING, WE PICKED PAT up in my car. Before heading to the Cape, we stopped at Fiona's mom's house in Chestnut Hill to pick up Fee's beloved Grover.

"How come he doesn't live with you, Fee?" Pat scratched the Boston terrier's ears, not that Grover noticed. The dog stood on Pat's legs, stretching out his scrawny white neck to get a better look out the back window. Grover and car rides went together like peanut butter and jelly. To be fair, the dog loved just about everything. Boston terriers were renowned for being happy dogs, and Grover was living proof.

"Can't have pets in my building. I tried sneaking him in last year, but the landlord found out. Grover hates trash trucks, so every Friday he barked like mad and my bitch of a neighbor turned me in." Half of Fiona's body was in the back seat as she tried to get the dog's attention. Even she couldn't tempt Grover's eyes away from the window.

"Oh, please. Grover is at your place more than at your mom's." I adjusted the rearview mirror.

"*No pets* is a stupid rule if you ask me." She shrugged.

"And you haven't bribed your neighbor at all?" I shifted into third gear and gunned the Focus onto the highway.

"Bribed? Not really. Just had a heart-to-heart."

Grover barked at a tailgating Mercedes. The driver pulled into the emergency lane to pass me, flipping me the bird as he flew by. I rolled my eyes and maintained the speed limit.

"You haven't bribed or — "

"I'm not like Grandmother if that's what you're thinking." She waggled her eyebrows at me and turned back around.

Pat stretched out in the back seat, resting one of his feet on the back of the center console.

"I hope you brought shoes besides the flip-flops you're wearing," I told him, glancing in the rearview mirror to see a sly smile creep across his face.

"Nope!" He crossed his arms and nodded as if he had solved some ancient riddle. "No tennis for me."

Fiona sat back in her seat and eyed me. Then we burst into laughter. "Nice try. But it won't work."

Our family was nutty about tennis. Every time we got together, we held a competition. One word described it: fierce. Even guests had to participate. No excuses. Once, Grandmother made Fee's brother Rory play with a broken knee. She allowed him to use a wheelchair, and to make it fair, his able-bodied opponent had to be in a chair as well.

"I hate tennis. Why can't we play flag football or something?"

"What, and bruise our pretty faces?" Fiona said in a mocking tone. "We're a tennis family. We'll partner you with Ham. He can carry you. Ains will have to play with her burnt hand."

"As her doctor, I can write a note." He kept his hairy arms crossed, but the confident, sly smile was rapidly diminishing.

"Ha! Like Grandmother will respect a doctor's note."

"Fine! I'll hide in the guesthouse and sleep in. Playing tennis before eight is a crime."

"Morning reveille will wake you, and if you want to eat, you better play."

"Who's the honorary bugler this time?" I asked. Reveille was considered a privilege in our family, and a rite of passage that went back generations.

Fiona scrunched her brow. "I think it's Leah. Golly, we're running out of young ones. How long until we start getting pushed into having kids?" Fiona snorted.

"Ham's the most likely candidate. That's if he ever settles down," I said.

Pat let out a bark of laughter. "Ham settle down? Not bloody likely. He's a scamp, through and through."

"Not everyone wants to settle down like you, buster." Fee shook a finger at Pat. "Love is a Hallmark fabrication."

Pat guffawed. "Keep telling yourself that. Maybe someday you'll actually believe it."

"I do believe it." Fee whacked Pat's knee.

"That's not what you say when — "

"Irish!"

I turned the radio up so I wouldn't have to hear about their sex life. Fiona turned it back down.

"Don't you dare use that against me." She stabbed the air with an accusatory finger.

Pat leaned forward. "Just admit it; you love me. Every time we break up, you come crawling back."

"I have never come crawling back. You always plead with me and I feel sorry for you." Her lips curved into a genuine smile.

"If that makes you feel better, fine." Pat leaned closer and kissed her cheek. "Just think though, we could move in with each other. Travel the world. Skip having kids. Just enjoy life together."

I was too busy watching the road to see Fee's expression, but from the softening of her shoulders I suspected Pat was winning the love battle.

He fell back into his seat, victorious. "I don't see why you're fighting it so much. Just admit you love me."

"You know it's not that simple." She gripped the headrest and eyed Pat.

"Right. The monogamy gambit." He leaned forward again

until his face was an inch from hers. "I'm not ruling out the occasional threesome, if that'll make you happy."

"For Christ's sake." I couldn't turn the radio up fast enough or loud enough.

Ham was standing outside on the circular drive when we pulled up in front of the ten-bedroom clapboard house, originally constructed in 1907. Over the years, it'd been expanded as the family grew. Fee's dad owned a seven-bedroom house down the street, and my mom had the smallest, around the corner. Mom's was referred to as The Cottage, or the mini-big house, since it was a near-copy, minus four bedrooms.

Two of my young cousins chased each other around the flagpole that stood smack-dab in the drive — the original had stood for over a hundred years, but had been demolished two years earlier when Rory crashed into it on the Fourth of July. Fee had loved the irony of her brother proclaiming his independence on the Fourth by creaming the symbol of control on the estate.

Ham, wearing Stevie Wonder glasses to hide his damaged eye, shook Pat's hand, grinning like a little boy who'd just slipped a frog into the salad bowl. "Irish, so good to see you. How's the hospital treating you?"

"Kicking my ass, Hammie boy. Kicking my ass." Pat thumped Ham on the back and laughed.

Grover zipped around our feet, yapping. After being cooped up in the car for more than two hours, he wanted to play fetch.

"Come on, Grover, let's get your ball launcher." I popped the trunk of the Focus so Fee could grab Grover's toy. Fiona gave Ham a quick one-armed hug, and trotted off with her psycho, but adorable, terrier to play on the beach.

Four other dogs ran after them, all different sizes and breeds. Pat loped along after us as best he could in his flip-flops.

Ham watched the two of them, dogs in tow as they made their way to the beach.

As he watched them, I studied my brother. Something was

different. His shoulders looked manlier, his six-three frame straighter. Ham had always exuded confidence and charm; now he was exuding something else, too, but I couldn't put my finger on it.

Flashing his genuine politician's smile, Ham said, "So, you're a college student now. How does it feel, little sis?" He wrapped his arms around me and squeezed tighter than normal. Was he feeling old now that the baby of the family was no longer a child? More than ten years divided us, and Ham had done his best to fill Dad's shoes, acting like a father more than brother.

I ignored his diversion and asked, "What's the big news?" We climbed the seven steps up to the wrap-around porch.

When he ripped off his Stevie Wonder sunglasses, I noticed his good eye twinkled. "I'd like you to meet someone."

Someone? Did that mean what I thought it meant? Was that the difference I'd seen in him? Had my fiercely independent older brother fallen in love? If so, it was going to blow Fiona's lid.

Soft footsteps padded behind me, and I turned to see a stunning Asian woman with a beguiling smile that would make most men crumple to their knees. Hell, *I* almost crumpled! The ocean breeze moved through her silky, long black hair.

"Hello," she said, extending her hand. I shook it slowly, trying to comprehend everything in a flash.

"Hello." Did Grandmother know yet?

"Ainsley, I'd like you to meet Mei." Ham turned to the woman. "Mei, this is my baby sister." He squeezed my shoulder and kissed the top of my head.

"It's lovely to meet you, Mei."

Four dogs crashed past us, pursuing an errant tennis ball that nearly took out a window, their nails clawing to gain purchase on the deck. Grover followed them, and then Fiona and Pat, laughing.

"Sorry! Mr. Dog Lover is the worst when it comes to playing fetch. Can't aim for shit!" Fiona boisterously slapped Pat's back.

"The launcher is defective," Pat defended, flashing his *I'm busted* smile. Fiona and Pat noticed Mei at the same time and fell quiet.

I tugged on the back of Fiona's shirt to break her trance. "I'd like you to meet Mei."

Realizing her rudeness, Fee burst into a smile and tightly shook Mei's hand with both of her own. I feared Mei's arm would grow sore from being rigorously jiggled up and down. "How wonderful to meet you, Mei. Dee-lighted!"

Mei stared at Fiona, clearly trying to figure out whether Fiona was fucking with her. It usually took people some time to get used to Fiona's animated ways.

"Don't break her arm off, Fee. She's not a water pump." Ham laughed, easing the tension.

"Is this the big news, then?" Fiona was never known for beating around the bush. She nudged Ham's shoulder. "You've never brought a woman home before."

Mei's laughter sounded like raindrops: soft and comforting.

"So you automatically assume marriage?" Ham poked her in the side with his index finger.

The three of us nodded.

Ham glanced at Mei. "It's hard to get away with anything in this family." He laced his fingers through hers. "Yes. This is the big news." His grin was genuine, not his typical politician's rictus.

"When's the big day?" I asked.

"Not 'til June, so we can get married here." He pointed to the sprawling private beach.

"Are we the last to know, then?" Fiona arched one eyebrow in a show of displeasure. She'd always been closer to Ham and me than she was to her only sibling.

"The first, actually. Mei and I only arrived a few minutes ago, and we haven't run into any family yet. Grandmother is taking an afternoon siesta." He said the last sentence gravely. Grandmother was nearing ninety-two, and whenever her name came up in conversation, it was with an air of impending bad news. I was sure every major news outlet would have her obituary prepared and raring to go as soon as the announcement was made.

Not that Grandmother was feeble. For a woman in her

nineties, she had all of her mental capacities and was quite spry. She was the last surviving child of the great Alistair Carmichael, former governor of Massachusetts. When he died, at the age of 101, Grandmother became the head of the family. My mother had married into the family, but it was rumored she would be the one left in charge. Grandmother always said Mom was the daughter she had always wanted, which really irked Grandmother's daughter by birth, Bridget, who always attended these events but was about as sociable as wallpaper.

Grandfather, who'd had to change his last name to Carmichael, died ten years earlier, leaving a gaping hole in our family tree. Grandmother wouldn't speak about him for the first year. She missed him, but she was mostly angry he'd died without her permission. No one in our family did anything without Grandmother's stamp of approval, and that included kicking the bucket.

"Have you spoken to Grandmother …" I hesitated, selecting my next words carefully. "About June?" I perched on the arm of a teak Adirondack.

Ham nodded crisply. "We flew in from DC last weekend." His eyes skimmed the water before meeting mine again, and their seriousness vanished as if a crashing wave had just swept away anything important. "Right. So girls against the boys this weekend?"

He was referring to the tennis tournament, of course. "Don't you boys get tired of losing?" I asked.

"Want to put your money where your mouth is?" Fiona added.

Ham and Fee squared off like boxers before he finally cracked. "It's good to see you." He wrapped Fee up in a bear hug.

"What are you doing? Going soft?" Fiona slapped his back, but she didn't wiggle out of the hug.

Twenty-two Carmichaels, including the grown children of our missing Uncle Liam, sat at the table in the sparse dining room, flanked by Mother and Grandmother at the foot and head of the table, respectively. The room was dominated by the custom-made banquet table for thirty, leaving little room for frivolous décor or bric-a-brac. The curtains were pulled back, the bay window overlooking the Atlantic. Photographers wouldn't be able to spy on the family from here without a Hubble-like telescopic lens on a boat. The youngsters were tucked away in a room off the kitchen, where staff members could keep an eye on them.

My sister, Kylie, who was studying law at Princeton, arrived an hour before dinner, and after Grandmother gave her the nod, she rose, her black judge's robe swallowing her petite frame, and tapped a gavel on the table. "Ladies and gentlemen, I call the proceedings to order."

Ever since she'd been a toddler, Kylie had initiated every meal, toast, or whatnot with a judge's gavel that William Howard Taft had used many years ago. Ironically, Grandmother had tracked down the gavel that had belonged to the twenty-seventh president, arguably one of the worst leaders in American history. Years after leaving office, Taft became the tenth Chief Justice of the United States — the job he'd always coveted. Even if Grandmother had gently attempted to break the news to my only sister that she wouldn't be part of the presidential quest, Kylie wouldn't have cared. The tedium of court decisions and precedents got my sister's blood pumping. Ever since I could remember, she had aspired to sit on the bench.

Ham stood and cleared his throat.

"Some of you may not have heard the news yet, but we have a serious matter to discuss this evening." It looked like Ham was fighting to keep his lips from curving into a smile. "Ains, would you stand up please? Carefully." He motioned for me not to rush.

I thought he had been about to break the news of his engagement. Why did I have to stand? Confused, I complied.

"I first learned of the gravity of this situation from Susie Q's *Tattler*."

Some family members tittered. My cheeks burned. I had no clue what he was about to say, but I had no doubt I'd be displeased, not to mention utterly humiliated.

He tossed me a wrapped gift. "Go on. Open it."

I ripped off the paper, revealing a bottle of Beano. Channeling my anger, I focused a glare at Ham that had all the intent of striking him dead.

"As much as I liked Susie Q's headline 'The Fart Heard Around the World,' I think we need to nip your problem in the butt … I mean bud."

"Hear, hear," Rory rapped his knuckles on the table. "Giving the family a bad name."

That was rich coming from Rory.

"No, don't encourage her," Fiona countered.

Witnessing Fee side with her despised sibling hurt even more than Ham's sabotage.

Everyone chuckled. Uncle Hugh laughed enthusiastically, his bald head turning redder than a raspberry.

"It was the chair!" I exclaimed.

Everyone howled.

"I'll get you for this," I mouthed to Ham.

He shrugged and raised his wineglass. "To Ainsley, who's never afraid to make a statement."

Grandmother nodded at my mother, and I sensed neither was enjoying the knowledge that I'd made another ignoble appearance on Susie's blog. Before the end of the night, I'd get the "everything you do in public will be scrutinized" lecture.

Grandmother cleared her throat.

Ham duly noted the command. He put a hand out for Mei to stand next to him. "Some of you may be wondering why we are gathered here this weekend." He encircled Mei's waist. "It's to welcome Mei to the Carmichael clan. We're tying the knot this June." Ham kissed the top of her head, and she wrapped loving arms around his waist.

"It's about damn time," Rory boomed.

Even though none of us met Mei before today, it wasn't all that surprising to me or the rest of the clan, I assumed. Ham always kept his private life out of the news, which meant keeping it from family members as well. Did he agonize over asking Mei to marry him? Keeping a girlfriend out of the spotlight wasn't easy, but a wife would be nearly impossible. Part of me wondered about his motives. Ham was many things, calculating most of all.

Mother proudly smiled. She looked thin in her Lilly Pulitzer cashmere wrap cardigan, but everything else was perfect: her hair, makeup, and posture.

I used to be proud of her, but I was starting to realize it was all an image: a carefully constructed political narrative. She was always on point, and unlike me, gaffe resistant. She hadn't remarried, and even though it was never spoken aloud, it was assumed she never would. She would maintain her widow status — voters gobbled that shit up.

Was this the life I wanted: public orchestration even behind closed doors? Or did I want to be free?

Looking at Ham and Mei, I realized what I really wanted was Maya.

Later that night, after dinner, most of the younger generations were on the beach. It was fairly dark, but light from the full moon danced on the waters, providing some illumination. More importantly, it reminded me why I loved the family's private beach. I could watch and listen to the ocean for hours on end. And the best part — Susie Q couldn't get to me here.

Fiona was streaming music on her iPad, and she and Pat were dancing on the sand, or Pat was trying to dance. Oddly, Fiona, who was a fabulous tennis player, had never mastered dancing, probably because she made a competition out of it. When Pat zigged, she zagged, constantly forcing him to follow. Grover yapped at their feet, making an odd threesome.

Rory joined in too, much to Grover's delight. Fee's brother had recently finished another stint in rehab, and he looked pale and thin, a ghost of the man everyone expected him to be. He put on a brave face, nevertheless.

"Do you think he'll kick the habit for good?" I asked Ham.

"It's nice to think he will, but …"

It's been said that heroin is the most addictive narcotic, but it wasn't just that, although Ham and I understood. As if he knew we were talking about him, Rory crashed onto the sand between us.

"So you're really going to do it?" Rory asked.

"Get married?" Ham clarified.

"No. Fly to Mars. Of course I mean get married. That's why we're here, right?" Rory leaned back on his elbows.

"I am. What about you? What are your plans?"

"Lie low. Dad wants me to go back to school." He looked down at his bare feet. "But it's not in me. The drive to succeed at all costs skipped me." He shrugged. "I wasn't cut out for this." He waved to the house and all the relatives on the beach. "My main objective is to stay off the radar, especially away from the likes of Susie Q."

"How?" I asked.

"Moving to Oregon. Mom's family has a cabin out there. Guess I'll figure things out from there, but I need to get out of this state. After the holidays, I think." He hopped up and rejoined the dancers.

Fiona attempted to twirl Pat without telegraphing the move, and the two of them tumbled onto the sand. Rory applauded, and Grover licked their faces.

Ham laughed. "Do you think she'll ever settle down?"

"Not likely. Fiona views life like she views her dancing: never settle into any type of pattern. Speaking of which, I never thought you would either." I cocked my head, focusing on the outline of his angular face in the moonlight. His damaged eye was out of view, and I wondered whether he did that subconsciously, even around family. We both sat on a sand dune, partially hidden by beach grass.

Ham sifted sand through his hands, letting the granules fall through his fingers. "Never thought I'd fall in love, or even could fall in love."

"But you did?"

He cupped his hand, staunching the flow of the sand, and looked to his right, where Mei stood with Mother and Uncle Owen.

"I did," he said, his voice light-hearted yet determined.

Remembering an incident during dinner, I laughed.

"What's so funny?" he asked.

"Oh, I was thinking of Shirley." Shirley came from a wealthy family with all the right connections and had married one of our dim-witted cousins. For better or worse, she was dumber than a yellow lab and looked like one. Earlier in the evening, when she'd shaken Mei's hand, she'd said, "You speak English very well."

"Thank you. I was born in New York," Mei responded in a thick New York accent.

"I was surprised Mei didn't smack her right in the kisser. That's a sore subject with her," Ham said.

"How so?"

"Let's just say it's not the first time she's been told she speaks English very well." Ham spoke the last three words slowly, mimicking Shirley. "It's 2015 and people still act like this country is for whites only. Mei's great-great-grandfather immigrated to the West Coast when railroad companies were hiring Chinese laborers to lay track. He was one of the few who escaped, in the hope of leaving racism behind. No one in her family has yet."

We both sat in quiet contemplation, watching the others on the beach. Maya's insistence that we came from different backgrounds infiltrated my mind.

"It's funny," Ham said, "both of our families can trace their American roots to guys who didn't belong, were brought here as cheap labor, and only wanted to lead a normal life. Mei's grandfather ran away because he wanted to have a family. Most Chinese immigrants couldn't marry or have kids back then."

"How was that enforced?"

"Not many who came to work on the railroads or in the mines were women. One year, more than 4,000 men came and only seven women. White Americans feared the 'Yellow Peril,' so they clamped down on the cheap labor. Government officials claimed the women who did arrive were prostitutes, so in 1875 Congress passed the *Page Act,* denying entry to women who were considered 'obnoxious.' Not much has changed in this country."

I nodded, understanding. "Now some want to erect a wall along the Mexican border." I thought of Maya and of how desperately I wanted to walk along the family beach with her at my side. I doubted that would ever happen. I glanced at Mei; maybe it could, though.

Ham shifted his weight in the sand. "Mom doesn't look good."

"She's too thin," I agreed.

"Stress. Things are changing in politics. Having money and family connections aren't always assets anymore. The political landscape is shifting so fast. I have a feeling Mom and Owen won't be in office much longer."

I whipped my head around, sure I cracked a vertebra.

Ham paid no heed. "People are sick of the old political dynasties," he continued. "They want outsiders who promise the world, even if the promises are false. They want politicians who'll do their best to turn back the clock to the good ol' days when a gas station attendant could support a family of four. Sadly, those days are long gone. And Grandmother ..." Ham shrugged, not completing the thought.

I remembered the quote the homeless woman shoved into my hand and recited it. "'The winds and waves are always on the side — '"

Ham finished the quote, "'of the ablest navigators.'" He paused. "How do you know that quote?"

"Oh, some crazy lady in Harvard Square was handing out leaflets with the quote. Not sure how I remembered it." I avoided his eyes.

"It's from an eighteenth century historian. I keep receiving weird emails with quotes by the same historian, such as 'History is little more — '"

I cut him off. "How weird. I've been getting texts from an unknown number. One had that quote. Another was about revenge. I figured Susie was behind it."

"But not now?"

I remembered Fee's insistence that the quotes seemed too intellectual. Susie could quote her hero, Ann Coulter, off the cuff, but a historian who'd been dead for centuries? It was highly unlikely. Even Fiona, a student of history, hadn't recognized the words.

I answered Ham's question with one of my own. "Why would she email you?"

"I know. She's never targeted me, and it seems out of her league. So why are we both receiving them?" He scanned the horizon, shielding his brow with a hand. "This coincidence makes me uneasy." He stood abruptly. "I need to make a call."

"Okay."

Ham stood off to the side and barked, "Tess, I'm going to forward some emails to you. I need you to look into them." He tottered farther into the brush, ruining my chance to eavesdrop on the rest of his commands.

Moments later, he sat down next to me, smiling. It didn't put me at ease.

"Who's Tess?"

Ham cocked his head, studying my face as if he was determining whether he could trust me. "Tess and her partner, Rita, are the types you don't want to meet. Not in person. When you do, it means the shit has seriously hit the fan."

"Partners?"

"Business."

"What business?" My voice cracked, showing my frustration. To my knowledge, only Grandmother had fixers on the payroll, but I was fairly certain Tess and Rita didn't work for her, considering I'd never heard so much as a whisper of their names.

"Trust me, please. I'm not sure the quotes mean anything, but I'm on it just in case. It's probably some crackpot trying to ruffle our feathers. I'll keep you in the loop if you need to be. I promise. And if you receive any more, let me know right away."

"And you'll let me know if you get more?"

His nod lacked any trace of assurance.

Before I had a chance to push, Grover waddled over and collapsed in front of us, panting. His tongue lolled to one side as he rolled around on his back to cool off. Fiona and Pat joined us, breathing just as heavily.

Ham raised a palm, indicating the end of the conversation for now, and I bit my lower lip.

Pat pulled a flask out of his lilac plaid Vineyard Vines shorts, which he'd paired with a mint-green gingham button-up. One of his sleeves was rolled up; the other must have tumbled down with the exertion of keeping up with Fiona's dancing. His outfit would have looked ridiculous on most men, but it suited happy-go-lucky Pat. He took a sip from the flask and handed it to Fiona, who took a lustful slug before wiping her mouth with the back of her hand.

"There you are," Mei said. She sat in front of Ham and leaned back into his waiting arms. When the flask reached her, Mei took a generous swig. Grover made his way over and exposed his belly to her, and Mei enthusiastically rubbed his freckled stomach, all the while calling him handsome.

"Look at that. He doesn't even trust me like that." Fiona's smile confirmed she had accepted Mei into the family fold. If Grover trusted her, Fiona would too.

Mei looked up at Fiona, her black eyes sparkling, and said, "How'd you come up with the name?"

Everyone let out a bark of laughter. Indignant, Fiona tugged the hem of her linen shirt. "He's named after Grover Cleveland, of course."

"Ah, the twenty-second and twenty-fourth president." Mei continued showering Grover with love.

Fiona didn't say anything, but I now imagined she'd walk through fire for Mei. Not many people could spout off the numbers of presidents, let alone knew Cleveland was the only one to serve two non-consecutive terms.

"How'd you two meet?" Pat asked, taking another sip from the flask.

"Work," Ham responded. "Mei's a lobbyist."

Everything clicked in my head. Mei had political clout in DC. Grandmother would allow any one of us to marry a serial killer as long as that person could promise votes. Whenever she met someone, her first thought was, "How is this person helpful?"

"Corporate lobbyist or hired gun?" Fiona asked.

"Corporate. Online privacy for social media's Goliath."

"Can you take down Susie Q for me?" I asked.

"Me, no. But I may know someone who knows someone." She winked.

I snapped my fingers at Pat. "Give this woman more whiskey."

Fiona quizzed Mei about her job, but the last thing I wanted to discuss was politics. I was still reeling over discovering Ham had his own political fixers who could swoop in and save people's asses when they got caught with their hands in the proverbial cookie jar. My brother's determination to treat me like a child grated more than I cared to admit. I looked away, watching the gentle waves roll over the sand. The watery fingers chased a few Carmichael youngsters, who were thrilled to be awake well past their bedtime. They squealed, running after the retreating water, doing their best to not get wet feet. Their parents stood to the side, chatting in small groups.

Rory stood alone, gazing at the moon. I wondered what thoughts roared through his mind.

On the veranda of the big house, I spied Grandmother leaning on her cane with both hands. She quietly observed the Carmichael generations. Even from this distance, though, I could sense her plotting the next move.

CHAPTER
eleven

THE BUGLE BLARED RIGHT ON the dot on Monday morning.

Twenty minutes later, I stood out on the drive, waiting for Pat and Fee and scanning my daily briefing email from the goons.

Pat's eyes were blurry. "Bloody bugle. What family wakes up this way?"

"The Carmichaels," Fiona and I said in unison.

"Come on. We're burning daylight." I unlocked the car doors. Pat's feet seemed glued. "Chop, chop, Irish!"

Fee gave him a shove. He growled.

"I don't know why you're so grumpy," I said. "I, for one, can't wait to get out of here. If I have to spend another day with the Carmichael clan, I'll start pulling my hair out."

"And Ainsley loves her red Carmichael curls," Fiona said.

It was true. I adored them, especially the way a few curls wouldn't fit in a ponytail and bounced around my face when I walked. Sometimes I adjusted my step to optimize the effect. I'd mastered how to cock my head so one lone curl demurely covered one eye. It wasn't solely for sex appeal. It covered a scar near my right eye, from when I'd rammed through a screen door when I was five. Unlike Ham, I'd avoided permanent damage, aside from a small fleck of a scar that most never detected, even those who knew where to look.

The scar was the only imperfection on my face, according to many. For me, it added character. Grandmother once told me we were all made up of scars, visible and invisible. How we dealt with them determined how we performed in life. Embrace and learn from all the cuts, bumps, and bruises along the way, and nothing could stop you.

By five minutes to eight, I was sitting in the classroom, massaging my scar and so lost in thought I didn't notice Maya sit down next to me.

"How was your weekend?" she asked.

At first, I didn't answer, because I didn't think the question was directed to me. The only person I knew in class, aside from Susie, was Maya, and she hardly spoke. Eventually, it finally registered she was talking to me, and she was waiting for a response.

"Joyous family time." I smiled from ear to ear, not meaning a word of it.

She smirked, catching my sarcastic tone.

"You?"

"Joyous work time."

"Trade you."

Shit! Why did I say that? I pictured a newscaster saying, "Well, Phil, it seems Ainsley Carmichael can't stop herself from putting her foot in it. Just take a look at this ..."

Maya laughed. "I don't think the owners could afford the insurance policy for you. Accident-prone people don't last long." She winked. Maya actually winked. At me. And she made a joke. A wink and a joke. Sinatra's song "Fly Me to the Moon" played in my head.

"I'm not accident-prone." I jutted out my bottom lip.

"And the Pope isn't Catholic. How's your hand?"

"Oh, it wasn't bad at all. In a few days all proof of the coffee incident will be gone. You okay?"

"Yep."

Dr. Gingas walked in, immediately bursting into lecture. I wondered whether she actually started the lecture the moment she stepped out of her office, and it was up to us to catch up.

Fifty minutes later, Dr. Gingas goose-stepped out of the classroom without any indication that she'd finished. The woman was insane.

Maya continued taking notes. Curious about her incessant scribbling, I leaned over and peeked, but I couldn't decipher her scrawl. Was she writing in code? Shorthand? Did shorthand still exist? Knowing Maya, it was her own code that only she could understand. She smelled like gardenias, and before I could stop myself, I inhaled her heady, potent, and lustful scent.

"Can I help you?" She threw me a confounding Maya smile, the corners of her mouth tugging upward, forcing two faint dimples to appear on her left cheek.

"I love your perfume," I said in a foolish, lovesick voice.

"I'll get you a bottle for your birthday." She continued writing, but I detected a hint of a smile.

Feeling bold, or drunk on her scent, I responded, "I prefer it on you."

The scratch of the pen's tip came to a screeching halt. I froze.

We were the only two left in the room. Within moments, students in the next class would trickle in. Again the internal newscaster said, "This just in. Ainsley Carmichael has crashed and burned in the love department."

"What am I going to do with you?" She tapped thoughtful fingers on the table.

"What do you want to do to me?" I braced for the worst.

She laughed. "Can I buy you breakfast?"

I stared at her, unable to speak, feeling as if my mouth was full of marshmallows.

Maya finished writing and packed her bag with the efficiency I had come to admire in her. Nothing was done in a rush, yet some-how she gave the impression she was miles ahead of everyone, even if she was the last to finish.

Sitting at a table outside a café on a quaint side street near the university, I nibbled on a cinnamon roll as I waited for Maya. She had opted for a breakfast burrito, even though the wait was much longer. It was a gorgeous sunny day, and we were in the midst of a stunning Indian summer. The trees along the Charles River were beginning to burst with gold, crimson, and orange leaves, contrasting with a deep-azure horizon. Soon, it would be so cold no one would want to be outside unless absolutely necessary.

She appeared victoriously holding a foil-wrapped burrito above her head. God, she was adorable. Maya the Gray was finally letting down her walls, brick by brick, and with each fallen piece I was falling further and further into Maya's rabbit hole.

"You got it!" I checked the time on my cell phone. "And in plenty of time." I still had an hour before my next class. Sighing, I added, "Such a shame we can't sit here all day to soak it in." Stretching my arms above my head, I leaned back in the plastic chair, letting the sun's rays warm my freckled skin.

The chair wobbled, and Maya was quick to put a steadying hand out to prevent me from crashing head over teakettle.

I laughed bashfully. "Thanks."

"No problem. I'm getting used to it."

I crossed my arms. "What does that mean?"

"I can't take my eyes off you or who knows what will happen? You" — she pointed her burrito at me — "are the most accident-prone person I've ever known."

"Is that the only reason you can't take your eyes off me?"

She was about to take a bite, but her eyes locked on mine, and I sat there, transfixed by her gaze, unable to determine the meaning. Finally, she sank her teeth into the potato burrito and chewed with purpose. After washing it down with some water, she said, "That's for me to know and for you to find out."

It was a hopeful answer — playful, even.

CHAPTER
Twelve

THE BUGLE ALARM ON MY phone blared at five the following morning. The night before, Fiona had texted, ordering me to meet her at the boathouse at five thirty to row on the Charles.

That wasn't what pulled me out of bed, however. I enjoyed it, the process of more doing and less thinking. Bend the knees, reach back with the oars, dip the oars, push the legs, pull with the arms, propel yourself farther along the water. I loved the rhythm. Bend, reach, dip, push, and pull. It wasn't often that I could escape thinking about what I said or did in public. In today's world, the threat of appearing on Twitter, YouTube, Facebook, Instagram, Reddit, Snapchat, or any new type of social media was a constant threat. Living under a microscope was exhausting.

I met Fiona outside the boathouse. She was bent over, stretching her arms behind her back. "How goes it with Maya the Gray?" she asked.

I adopted the same stretching position and replied, "Progress has been made."

Fiona bent further. "Good progress?"

"Excellent progress." I stretched my right arm across my chest, and then my left. "What about you and Pat?"

"Confusion," she said. Standing, she avoided my eyes and headed for the water. That was all she would say about Pat. Fiona had to work things out in her head before she would ever explain it to anyone, including me. I liked to talk things over. She preferred mulling things over in private. I was surprised she had even admitted she was confused; that was a minor breakthrough, or it showed her desperation.

On the river, it was just us, each in our own boat, our own sheer exertion propelling us downriver. We never raced each other; that would ruin it. It wasn't about Fiona versus Ainsley. It was about us as individuals.

We had started sculling in high school and competed nationally for our club. The Olympics weren't in our sights, but we'd hoped to race in the Head of the Charles the following year. Fiona had been a lackluster rower until she learned that the club our family had belonged to since its founding in the 1850s didn't allow women to compete until a measly twenty years ago. She had found a new passion: compete in the Head of the Charles or die.

We started, and I focused on my form: bend, reach, dip, push, and pull.

It was a glorious day on the river. The sun inched over the horizon, and I marveled over the pink streaks painting the murky water as I skimmed along the surface. There wasn't much noise, only some birds chattering, the dip of the oars, and the sloshing of the water. The morning air this autumn was fresh, with just enough bite to make me feel alive and free.

These were the moments I cherished, the times when I was simply Ainsley, not Ainsley Carmichael, the daughter of Senator Lillian Carmichael and the future President of the United States.

Fiona picked up her pace. I didn't give chase, preferring to maintain a relaxed tempo. Fee would wait for me, and she would understand, just as I understood her need to go on her own.

Afterward, we sat outside the boathouse, steaming cups of coffee clasped between our hands. "We still on for tonight?" Fee asked.

"Yep, Maya hasn't backed out yet."

"Will she, do you think?" Fiona watched a man on the river. From the way he was pushing himself, it was obvious he was training, and neither of us could tear our eyes away from his scull slicing through the water as if it were flying.

"I don't think so. At least I hope not."

She slowly turned to look at me, and a smile appeared, softening her eyes. "It's good to see you like this."

I put my arm around her shoulder, and she rested her head on mine. Another rower came into view, but his amateur efforts didn't hold our interest.

"All right, then. See you tonight." She strode to her car, her manic energy returned. Without looking back, she lifted a hand in the air and waved good-bye over her shoulder. I remained for a few moments before making my way back to the dorm to get dressed for my internship.

I'd insisted that I pick Maya up at her dorm room. I wasn't trying to invade her privacy; it was a matter of principle. Once, in high school, a friend had honked her horn outside my house to alert me of her presence. Grandmother had been over for dinner that night, and she wouldn't let me leave until my friend, just a friend, walked to the front door and rang the bell.

"Respect. Always respect those in your life. And demand it from those in your life," Grandmother had said that night.

I wanted Maya to know I respected her. Her background, her mother — none of it mattered to me.

And I wanted to know how to reach her since she still hadn't given me her cell number, not that I'd ever seen her with one. Surprisingly, she didn't argue when I'd asked for her address. I took that as a positive sign.

Before I knocked on the door, I let out a rush of air, shook my arms, rolled my neck from side to side, and then lightly rapped on the door.

There was a whoosh of jeans and the shuffle of feet. Maya answered the door, jacket in hand. Had she been sitting on her bed, waiting for me so we could make a fast escape? Was that how they did things in Mattapan? No pleasantries, no how-do-you-dos, just dash?

Not wanting to push her boundaries, I didn't insist on entering her domain. I knew where she lived, and that was enough for the moment.

"You ready?" I asked, needlessly.

"Yup." Her succinct answer was followed by a nervous dip of the head. Was she scared of me or of Fiona?

I motioned for her to walk ahead, but she waited and walked right by my side — another positive sign.

In preparation for the car ride — which would last approximately sixteen minutes, according to my dry run the previous night — I had made a playlist for my iPhone and synced it with my car. It started with Melissa Ferrick's "Will You Be the One." I worried that was beyond obvious, but as Ham liked to say, "Go big or go home."

Maya started tapping her fingers on her leg. She kept her steely grays glued to the side window, taking in everything as the car turned right, veering toward Boston University Bridge. When Melissa's gravelly voice reached down deep to express the ferocity of her emotions, Maya's finger tapping intensified, and she passionately bobbed her head.

So far, everything was going to plan.

To avoid being too blatant, next up was Ani DiFranco's "Untouchable Face." Maya's fingers halted, but she nodded along to the beat as she continued watching the river draw closer.

Leonard Cohen's "I'm Your Man" started. She paused, and for a second I was worried I'd lost her. I'd known when I selected the song that it was a calculated risk. But as his seductive voice pleaded with her, Maya turned and smiled at me. I expected her to immediately look out the side window again, but she didn't. Maya actually leaned her head against the seat and closed her eyes, listening to the soulful words.

"I think my mom used to play this when I was a kid," she said, opening her eyes again.

"I can't remember the first time I heard it. Probably with Fiona."

"You two spend a lot of time together." It was a statement, not a question.

"Always. My family jokes we were Siamese twins in another life."

"Is she always …?" Maya motioned for me to fill in the blank.

"Highly strung. Mostly. Fiona comes across as a tour de force, but she's a sweetheart once you learn she only has two speeds: stop and go. She can sit, stare, not talk for hours, and have a marvelous time, enjoying quiet companionship and contemplation. Or she'll chatter nonstop like a chipmunk on crack."

I didn't add that my cousin also excelled at listening and observing others without being noticed. I wondered whether that was her mission this evening: study Maya in the hope of cracking the secret of who and what Maya was.

"Mad World" started and Maya closed her eyes again. I didn't know why I'd included the song, but its sadness and sense of not fitting in made me think of Maya, and of me, truthfully. It wasn't a romantic song, but I wanted her to know I understood. Well, maybe not understood, but I was willing to listen if she would let me into her world. That was all I wanted: a chance.

We were three minutes from Fiona's when Maya's eyes popped open. "Is this U2?" She listened intently. "Which song?"

"'Dancing Barefoot.'"

"Never heard this one." She turned her left ear to the speaker. "I like it."

She liked it! Score!

As the song ended, I parked outside of Fee's building.

She answered the door with a cigarette dangling from her bottom lip and a wine bottle and corkscrew in her hands. She thrust both into my arms and said, "Pat's completely useless, and you know I always snap that damn thing in half."

Pat popped into view, wiggling his fingers. "I have to preserve these babies for surgery."

"Yet you can rip a beer top off with your teeth." Fiona wasn't teasing. It was one of Pat's skills, and it had come in handy on more than one occasion until Fiona feared he would lose one of his pearly whites and had purchased bottle openers for everyone's key chains.

He noticed Maya. "Hiya! I'm Pat."

Maya put her hand out. The six-four, 200-pound man from Southie swiped it away and wrapped Maya up into a crushing bear hug, briefly hoisting her off the hardwood floor.

Maya paled but handled it much better than I thought she would. I half-expected her to coldcock him.

Pat's eyes were slightly glazed, testimony he'd been dipping into his flask well before we arrived. He was never without it. The reporter in my head announced, "Right in the middle of surgery, Dr. Pat asked his nurse for his flask." The reporter faded out as I pictured the interview with the nurse.

I snapped back to reality, setting my Givenchy tote down so I could open the wine. "It smells delicious in here, Fee."

Maya plucked the bottle from my hand. "Let's start the night off right. No injuries." She proceeded to uncork the bottle.

Pat chuckled. "Boy, does she have your number."

Fiona biffed the back of Pat's head, not to defend my honor, but because she seized every opportunity to take a swipe at him.

Maya expertly uncorked the wine, handing it to Fiona.

"Well, look at that." Fiona held up the cork. "It's in one piece. What's your trick?"

Maya smiled. "Trade secret. If I tell you, I'll have to kill you."

Fiona let out a bark of laughter. "I like you."

Pat motioned for us to take a seat on the couch. I made sure to sit close enough to Maya that our legs touched. "What restaurant did you work at?" Pat asked.

Fee and I exchanged a nervous glance over Pat's assumption,

and I didn't take a breath until Maya rattled off a few names of high-end places, including Nadine's, a family favorite. Fiona's eyes found mine again. How had I not noticed Maya on previous visits to the restaurant?

Pat nodded. "I worked at Nadine's — for a day. I accidentally dumped a platter of raw oysters into the mayor's lap. He laughed and asked whether I was Republican. I told him I was an Independent, and the mayor rebutted with, 'A fence-sitting opportunist. How can I get your vote this year?' I told him whiskey, much to his delight. The manager didn't see the humor, though." Pat rubbed his scruffy chin. "He even kept my tips for the day."

"The manager can be a prick. I've been on the receiving end of a few brutal dressing-downs. Haven't been fired yet, though." Maya gave Pat a chin-up smile.

"Is that where you learned to uncork a ... cork?" I asked.

Fee snorted, quickly covering her mouth, and Pat shook his head, his eyes wide.

Maya laughed and placed a hand on my knee. "My mom taught me. She's been a waitress all her life."

"What else can you uncork?" Fee asked.

Maya squeezed my knee, but she remained mute.

Pat perched on the armrest of the chair and jabbed Fiona in the ribs. "My mom worked in my uncle's diner, off and on, depending whether she was pregnant or nursing. For years I was a short-order cook. I make the best eggs and hash browns, but opening a bottle of wine is not in my DNA." He lifted his meaty hands.

The conversation seemed to put Maya at ease. Maybe knowing she wasn't the only one in the room who knew what it was like to hold down a hospitality job soothed her nerves. Pat had that way with people.

"Pat's poor mother had five boys, all just as ugly and stupid as Irish here." Fiona touched his cheek tenderly, before flicking it.

"How 'bout you, Maya? You got any brothers or sisters?" Pat's expression was all innocence, probably because Fiona had already sworn up and down that she wouldn't divulge any information about Maya to anyone. Not that we had any information. He draped an arm over Fee's shoulders.

"Nope. It's just me and my mom."

I wouldn't say an air of sadness hung around Maya, but she had an air of assured solemnity.

"How did you two meet?" Maya leaned back on the sofa, gesturing toward Pat and Fiona.

Was she deflecting questions about herself?

"Through Fee's brother," Pat said.

"The no-good scoundrel," Fiona muttered.

Pat gave her shoulders a squeeze. "They don't see eye to eye. Ya know, siblings." He shrugged and then plowed on, easing the tension. "Anyway, Rory had mentioned his baby sister played rugby. I'd never met a female rugby player before, so I was instantly taken with Fiona, even before I laid eyes on her."

Fiona huffed. "You make me sound like a freak of nature!"

Pat gazed lovingly down into her eyes, and they both stared at each other for a moment before he continued. "I was enthralled by her no-fear attitude on the field. I started going to all the games."

"He was the team's most loyal fan, besides Ainsley, of course." Fiona's eyes glowed.

"For two years he went to all of her games, wearing a shirt proclaiming: 'Rugby Women Know How to Try,' referring to grounding the ball behind the goal line," I added. "He'd scrawled the words on a plain white Hanes T-shirt in black marker." I leaned back against the sofa, near Maya. She shifted closer.

"Do you still have that shirt?" Fiona peered up at Pat.

"Of course. I'm hoping you come out of retirement." He turned to Maya. "She wrecked her knee last season."

Fiona waved it off. "A minor injury."

"You tore your meniscus. They had to shave some cartilage off your knee." Pat tsked.

"Pffft. I was walking hours after the surgery."

Pat rolled his eyes.

Rustling issued from the bedroom, quickly followed by a shrill bark. "Is Grover here?" I asked.

Fiona sighed. "Pat insisted on bringing him over. I don't know who he likes more, me or my dog."

Pat strutted to the bedroom to free the lovable, demented terrier. "You two make a great package," he shouted over his shoulder.

Fiona excused herself to check on dinner.

Both Maya and I stood as Grover raced out, circling the main room, hunting for food or a toy. When he spied guests, he paused briefly and then barreled toward us, almost bowling Maya over as he jumped on her legs. As greetings went, his was the most enthusiastic.

Maya laughed and squatted on her haunches. "Hello, Grover."

The terrier shamelessly smothered her with sloppy kisses, making her laugh even more.

"You wouldn't believe it, but he's actually a well-trained dog. Just not when it comes to meeting new victims." I leaned down next to them, and Grover welcomed me in the same fashion.

"He loves people. Don't ya, Grover?" Pat squatted to scratch the dog's ear.

"I love dogs. I wasn't allowed to have a pet growing up," Maya said, speaking more to Grover than anyone else. It was clearly love at first sight for both. She retook her seat on the couch, and Grover jumped into her lap. "Aren't you a handsome devil?" She rubbed behind his ears. "I love Bostons. Their coloring makes them look like they're wearing tiny tuxedos."

Fiona returned from the kitchen. "Shall we eat?" She ushered us to the dining area, and I noticed she'd set the table with normal plates, not the usual quirky dishes featuring presidential facts, which she'd purchased in a gift shop in Philly, outside of Independence Hall. However, unable to completely contain her presidential nerdiness, the placemats revealed photos of all forty-four presidents.

I eyed Maya as she took it all in: the placemats, Fiona's apron with Obama's body on it, the figurine of Teddy Roosevelt charging San Juan Hill as the table's centerpiece, and all the other knick-knacks on the counter and corner bookshelf, which contained only three cookbooks because the rest of the space was filled with presidential biographies. Fiona's shrine-like apartment even included the presidents who were most hated. She may have been the only person who used busts of Milliard Fillmore and Warren G. Harding as bookends.

"How do you like the apron, Ainsley? Took me ages to track that one down." Pat grinned. He celebrated Fiona's obsession and was fond of saying, "Gotta love a woman with passion who isn't afraid to show it."

"You've outdone yourself, Pat." I had my fingers crossed that my cousin would learn to appreciate Pat's acceptance of her quirkiness. For years, Fiona's mom had lectured her, "No one will want to settle down with a nutjob. Think about your future. Who in their right mind would want to live in a Graceland for presidents?"

Maya stood behind one of four chairs at the kitchen table. "How did you find all this stuff?"

"When we were kids, Fee's parents started taking us on trips to visit the houses and cities of former presidents. The first was Mount Vernon, where Fiona purchased this." I whisked a plaster head of Washington off one of the shelves. "It's a piggy bank." I rattled it, and Maya laughed when she heard the coins. "This" — I shook George — "morphed into this." I waved to all the memorabilia.

"Last summer we visited Regan's library in California." Pat pointed out the Reagan coffee mug on the granite countertop.

"I take it that's why Grover is named after the president." Maya tapped Cleveland's photo on a placemat while sliding into the seat.

I nodded as I took the seat next to Maya.

A plate piled high with BBQ ribs, corn on the cob, Boston baked beans, steamed vegetables, and corn bread sat in the middle of the table.

"Dig in, folks." Fiona took her seat.

"It all looks wonderful." Pat immediately tore into a rib, ripping half off the bone and smearing sauce over his face.

"Oh, that reminds me." Fiona popped up and snatched plastic bibs from a drawer, tying one around each of our necks. As she finished tying Pat's, I noticed she let her hand linger on his neck.

Maya turned to me with a shy smile. I wondered what she'd envisioned before arriving: china and crystal, I guess. With servants. Black servants.

Maya and I simultaneously reached for the steamed vegetables.

"Oh, no. Not another one." Fiona smiled at me. "Every meal, Ainsley goes straight for the veggies."

"Hush, Fee. That leaves more ribs for me." Pat rubbed his belly, smearing more sauce onto his shirt. "Ribs are my favorite."

Fiona waggled a finger in his face. "Pat, use the bib or a napkin. It'll take me ages to get the stains out of your shirt."

Fiona was doing Pat's laundry? That was news to me. I knew he'd been staying over several nights a week since the start of semester, but I had no idea they were enjoying domestic bliss on this level. No wonder Fiona was on edge.

"Ah, just throw it on the fire. Don't bother with washing it." Pat once again used his T-shirt to clean his hands, and then gripped the silver serving spoon and ladled veggies onto his plate. "I have a million of these shirts." He was wearing a faded Finnegan's café shirt from his uncle's joint.

Maya bit into a rib daintily at first, but then took a more savage bite.

"Good, huh?" Pat nodded and shoved a piece of corn bread into his maw, demolishing it in less than three seconds. He swiped the back of his hand along his chin and mouth. "Where'ya from, Maya? I don't detect much of a Boston accent. A slight bit of a twang, perhaps."

"Wyoming," she said, tearing off a massive portion of rib. I wondered whether she had done that to prevent Pat from probing further into her past.

"I always wanted to go out there and visit a dude ranch. It would be fun to be a cowboy for a few days."

"When I was seven, my mom took me to a dude ranch owned by Buffalo Bill's grandson. He looked just like him with the flowing white hair and long beard." Maya sipped her water. She hadn't touched her wine.

"No kidding?" Pat's eyes widened enviously, and then his gaze wandered to the window, lost in thought.

"What brought you to Massachusetts?" Fiona pushed.

"My mom. She always loved Revolutionary War history, and her passion rubbed off on me. I had this book on Paul Revere that I wore out from thumbing through, looking at the pictures." Her guarded aura faded almost completely. "My great aunt used to live here."

"Did she move?" I asked.

She looked down at her plate. "Oh, she died. Years ago."

I got the message; she didn't want to talk about it. I squeezed her leg under the table as Fee and I exchanged a quizzical look. Chuck hadn't mentioned an aunt.

"Anyone need more wine?" Pat refilled his glass, which had been full two minutes before. "Ainsley?"

"No, thanks. I'm driving tonight."

"What? I changed the sheets in the guest bedroom for you two." Pat flashed a devilish grin.

Fiona flared her *I'm going to kill you* smile, and there was a scuffle of legs under the table.

"Ha!" Pat laughed after a second or two. "I never owned steel-capped boots until I started hanging out with Fiona. She doesn't kick your shins. She stomps on your toes with the intention to pulverize." He ground a fist into his other hand.

Fiona smiled sheepishly.

"My mom was subtler. She used to pinch the skin under my arm and twist it. No one saw." Maya took a bite of corn.

"Like this?" Fiona tried out the new technique on Pat, who squealed.

"Just like that." Maya confirmed.

Pat rubbed his arm. "I wouldn't want to mess around with the women in your family. Tread carefully, Ains."

I sipped iced water, trying to douse the fire reddening my cheeks.

Having Pat present was working for the most part, but he could be a loose cannon.

"Are you the Pat who fixed Ainsley up after the coffee incident?" Maya, her fingers smeared with sauce, pointed her rib toward the now-drunk Irishman.

Pat burped behind his hand before answering. "Yep. I've fixed these two up on a few occasions." He half-covered his mouth again and whispered, "The press, you know." He followed it up with an exaggerated wink. "Fiona's pretty resourceful. If you ever need anyone for anything, she has a connection. Even if you need life support for a ferret."

"It was a guinea pig," Fiona defended John Q, her beloved pet named after John Quincy Adams, the seventh president and son of John Adams, the second commander in chief.

"A guinea pig?" Maya's tone bordered on disbelief, but she eased into her uncomfortable smile, which I found oddly comforting. "How does that work? Oxygen tubes in his exercise ball?"

I tittered.

Fiona harrumphed. "I'll have you know it worked. He lived another year."

"Just like his namesake after he left the White House and got a second chance in the Senate," I threw out there.

"Damn right!" Fiona slapped the tabletop.

Pat's eyes clouded over. "She's got a heart of gold, but don't make her angry," he told Maya. "That's when the Scottish temper flares. The Carmichael women are especially dangerous."

"You make us sound like gangsters, or hit men." I avoided

Maya's eyes.

"And I ain't stretching the truth." Pat's control was gone. "Ever hear of Liam? He was a dawg: prostitutes, drugs …"

The table bounced off the floor, making it obvious that Fiona was desperate to shut Pat up. No one outside the family was supposed to know about Liam. Actually, I was completely taken aback that she had even confided in Pat.

"Would anyone like more ribs?" I leapt out of my seat, afraid Maya would detect the shame in my eyes.

Pat's arm darted into the air like he was in the first grade and dying to answer the teacher's question. Just to make sure I understood, he shouted, "Yessum!"

"More ribs coming up." The dining room table was off to the side of the kitchen, so while I didn't escape the awkwardness, I did manage to divert Pat's attention away from our "missing" uncle.

"Maya, what are the odds I can talk you into making us a cup of joe after dinner?" asked Fiona.

"Fee-own-a Carmichael! Maya's a guest," I whirled around, holding a heaped plate of ribs.

"Shut your trap, Ains. I hear her coffee is the best," Pat said, wearing a whiskey-foozled grin.

Maya blinked, looking like she had no clue what to say or how to act around Fiona or Pat. "Of course."

"Accourse," Pat repeated, now in a drunken slur. "Wild horses couldn't drag me away before sampling Maya's brew."

Fiona didn't say a word, but her ashen face spoke volumes about Pat's slurred speech.

Maya laughed. "Wild horses, huh? Never heard a compliment like that before."

Maya hadn't touched her wine, and I feared she'd run for the hills after Pat's performance. I'd had no idea she was a teetotaler.

"So, Pat, what was it like growing up in Southie?" she asked, putting Fiona and me temporarily at ease.

"Exciting." Pat leaned closer. "Ever hear of Whitey Bulger?"

"Oh, Irish! You didn't know Bulger. He went into hiding

when you were a speck of a boy, and repeatedly watching *The Departed* doesn't make you an expert." Fiona rested her chin on one palm, doing her best not to smile at her drunken fool of a boyfriend.

"Stop your jawin', woman."

"So did you know any mobsters?" Maya asked, amusement making her lips twitch.

He mimed locking his lips and throwing away the key.

"Yeah, right. Our Southie boy hates violence, avoids it at all costs. Just last week he talked down two BU students in the bar." She pinched his cheek.

"Hey, now. I seem to remember taking care of a photographer for you two" — he gestured to Fee and me — "at the Cape this summer."

I came to Pat's defense. "Haven't seen that man since." Maybe he could take care of the mystery quote sender.

"And you won't after the talkin' I gave him. Taking photos of you topless in Truro on Longnook Beach. Not on my watch!"

Maya quirked an eyebrow at me.

I mouthed, "Not me. Fiona." Her foot tapped mine under the table, but I wasn't sure whether she meant that was good or too bad.

Pat turned to Maya, clearly ready to embellish some more, but the fire went out of his eyes and some clarity returned. "Pass me some corn bread, please," he said in a hoity-toity way, causing all of us to laugh.

I suspected Fiona had given his underarm another good twist. Maya was right; it only took a couple of times to learn how to behave.

"You close with ya ma?" Pat asked her.

"I am. You?"

I considered her ability to steer conversations back to Pat quite impressive. She'd make a great politician.

"Yep." He belched. "I'm the youngest of five, and the cutest, so naturally I was spoiled." He tapped his head. "I was also the smartest. Everyone pitched in to pay for medical school. My uncle even held fundraisers at the café. I wanted to be a vet, but everyone decided medical school would be a better investment." He hitched up a sad shoulder.

Maya turned to face me. "You don't talk about your family much. What are they like?"

"Uh …" My throat seized.

"Oh, Ainsley won't tell you much. If you want to learn the good stuff, check out Susie Q's blog." Pat's eyes lit up. "Hey, you were there when she farted, weren't you? How loud was it?"

Maya laughed. "Trust me, that was blown out of proportion."

"From what I heard, Ains blew a hole in her panties." Pat laughed.

I slumped down in my seat.

Maya must have noticed, because she changed the subject. "You have a brother and sister, right?" she asked.

I nodded.

Pat was about to sip his wine but waved it to interrupt. "Don't forget Craig."

"Craig?" Maya asked.

I cleared my throat. "My eldest brother died before I was born."

"Murdered?" Maya's eyes clouded over with concern.

I flinched. "No. Leukemia."

"That's awful." She squeezed my hand. "I'm so sorry."

"It's because of Craig's death and Hammie's accident that Ains is here," Pat blurted.

"What?" Maya blinked.

"She's the Chosen One," Pat whispered behind his hand.

Fiona and I sat frozen as if a line of skeletons had just congaed right out of the Carmichael closet. So much for the Southie boy's ability to keep secrets.

Some recognition returned to Pat's eyes and he stood. "Uh, anyone need more?" He opened the fridge, hunting for something — hopefully common sense.

Fiona perked up in her seat and shared a story about one of her first dates with Pat.

While Fiona chatted about their date, I pondered Maya's question. Why had she thought Craig might have been murdered? Did Susie Q have another crackpot conspiracy theory on her blog? Or was that an automatic Mattapan thought?

In the car on the way back to Maya's dorm, I apologized for Pat. "I'm sorry. I should have warned you about his flask."

She waved me off. "He's pretty funny. Odd, though. Who was the guy he mentioned? Liam?"

"Oh, him. Dad's younger brother decided the Carmichaels were too much to handle." Lying left a nasty taste in my mouth, but what could I say? *We're almost certain Uncle Liam is swimming with the fishes because of Grandmother?* I braced for a question about being the Chosen One.

"I wish I could take Grover home with me. What a sweet dog," Maya said.

The tension behind my eyes dissipated. "You and Pat both. He adores that dog. That's one thing he's always loved about Fiona." I was intrigued she'd asked about Liam but hadn't said anything about the other stuff. Was she trying to respect my privacy? Or was she afraid of opening conversations that might involve tit for tat?

"Grover?"

I laughed. "No, her love of animals."

Maya nodded thoughtfully. I wanted to know what thoughts ran through her beautiful head. "He really loves Fiona."

"Yes, he does. I hope it doesn't ruin him." I hadn't intended to share that much information. "Here we are," I said in a silly singsong voice as I pulled up in front of her dorm.

She didn't bolt from the car like she had last time; instead, Maya the Gray chewed the side of her cheek, like she was mulling something over. Several seconds passed before she said, "Would you like a cup of coffee?" She swallowed. "Another one, I mean?"

"Sure. Is the shop still open?" I turned the keys in the ignition, clutching the gearshift in my right hand, ready to put the car into reverse.

"Upstairs." Maya placed her hand on mine. "I've mastered making coffee in my room."

Her hand stayed on top of mine, and my heartrate shot through the roof. "That would be lovely," I said, my voice cracking.

We walked up three flights of stairs, neither of us speaking. When we entered her room, I was taken aback by its sparseness. My room wasn't extravagant, but Fiona had helped me decorate it a smidgeon to make it homier, even though I spent many a night in her guest bedroom.

In the corner sat a coffee pot — the most expensive item in the room. "I can't live without coffee," Maya explained, filling the machine from a jug of water she'd pulled out of a dented mini-fridge that appeared older than Maya was.

"Is that why you work at La Creperie and not any of the restaurants you mentioned earlier?"

"Partly. I got tired of the clientele. Occasionally, I pick up some shifts at Nadine's," she said with her back turned.

"I can only imagine about the patrons," I said, hoping to relieve the tension.

"How'd you end up at the crepe shop?"

"A few years back, the owner of La Creperie was the manager of one of the places I worked. When she opened her place, she asked me to join the staff. It's not close to here," she said, waving to her room, "but I like the atmosphere."

I enjoyed listening to her soft voice. "Do you miss Matta — your home?"

Would anyone miss Mattapan? *Think before you speak, Ainsley.*

"I miss my mom. We get together once a week for dinner. Been doing that since I moved out three years ago." She smiled shyly. "I like having my own space," she offered. "Even if I have to work twenty hours a day to pay for it."

Pride and determination flickered in her eyes.

While Maya ground the coffee beans, I gazed around the room, spying a worn copy of *Little Women* on her desk. Many of the pages had been dog-eared. A handful of library books, including McCullough's biography on Adams, sat on the desk as well. I picked it up. According to the bookmark, she was more than halfway through. When did she sleep? At one corner of the desk, a photo leaned against the wall. A young Maya and a woman sat astride horses. I squinted to make out the woman, but the photo was too grainy to allow for much detail.

"Is this your mom?" I asked, holding up the frame.

She smiled over her shoulder. "Yep."

"Where was it taken?"

"At the dude ranch in Cody I mentioned earlier."

I put the worn photo back with care. One of the beds was stripped bare. "You don't have a roommate?"

"Luckily, I have the perfect roommate. She's never here."

"Has she been here at all?" I pointed to the bed.

"She pops in to say hi and to see if she missed anything. Her boyfriend is a couple of years older, and she lives with him. Her parents don't know about her living situation." Maya busied herself measuring out milk and sugar. "Thank God for cell phones. I don't have to field calls from her family."

"Ah, lucky you."

She peered at me over her shoulder. "What's your roommate like?"

"Oh, I don't have one." I rushed the pretentious words in an attempt not to be heard. There weren't many single rooms available, and they weren't cheap.

Maya shrugged off my guilt. "That's nice. I know having a roommate is part of the whole college experience, but I'm not much of a people person."

I had to bite my bottom lip to prevent myself from laughing.

She handed me a mug I was certain had originally belonged to La Creperie and motioned for me to sit on her bed. Maya sat on a plastic desk chair. Our knees practically touched, and I couldn't imagine having a roommate in such a confined space. Fiona's cramped two-bedroom apartment seemed like a mansion now.

"What did you mean when you said hopefully loving Fiona wouldn't ruin Pat?"

I had the feeling she wasn't really asking about him, more about relationships in the Carmichael family.

"Fiona doesn't believe in monogamy. She loves Pat, but she also likes to …"

"She seeks experiences."

"Yes! Exactly."

"Like nude sunbathing?"

"Yes. And others."

Maya studied me carefully, as though my expression could tell her all she needed to know. I averted my eyes, staring at the steam rising from the rich concoction.

Maya sipped hers and said over the brim, "I see." She slowly lowered her cup and chewed on her bottom lip. "Do you think they can make it work?"

"I hope they can."

"So you believe love conquers all?"

I nearly swallowed my tongue. "I'd like to believe it does. It's hard to imagine a world without the power of love." Where in the hell had that line come from? I was fairly certain I was the first Carmichael to have ever uttered such a ridiculous phrase away from the microphone, yet at that moment, it didn't feel ridiculous. Was I drinking the love Kool-Aid now?

She continued to study me.

"What do you believe?" I asked.

Maya placed her cup on the desk and steepled her fingers, resting her chin on them. "I haven't put much thought into it, really. But I hope so. It's a nice thought."

Her sad eyes suggested she had thought about it a lot, even if something stopped her from believing wholeheartedly. What had broken her?

I wanted to sweep her into my arms, kiss her pain away. I

wanted to make Maya feel safe. She lifted her cup again and heartily quenched her thirst.

This conversation was drastically different than the ones we had previously about relationships. Both of us were tap-dancing our way around our earlier declarations of cherishing independence and shunning relationships without putting too much on the line.

"Would you like another cup?" She raised her nearly empty one.

"Not yet." I wanted to add, "Maybe in the morning," but I lost my nerve.

She fixed another for herself, and I pretended to look out the window, all the while trying to slow my thundering heart. Her window overlooked the athletic center with the track and field in the center.

"Not much of a view," she said. She was standing right behind me, and I could feel the heat radiating off her body. "But if you lean over a little and look closely, you can glimpse the Charles." I followed her lead, imagining moonlight shimmering on the dark river.

Nodding, I wrapped my arms around my chest and shivered. "Are you cold?"

I'd expected her to offer me a sweatshirt, but to my surprise she enveloped me in her arms and held me close. I melted as Maya peppered my neck with soft kisses. Closing my eyes, I tried not to say anything. I didn't want to blow the moment. Instead, I turned slowly and gazed into her smoldering gray eyes.

I placed a palm on her cheek. "I want to kiss you."

She started to lean in, but I held her face away from mine. "Before I do, I don't want you to run this time."

"I won't. I promise." She wore an aw-shucks grin.

"Are you sure?"

She nodded.

I hesitated. But not for long.

Our lips met, and the kiss was soft at first, gentle. Then she deepened it. Her tongue entered my mouth, and a moan escaped me. When she tugged away from me, my heart lurched into my throat, nearly cutting off all oxygen.

She ran her fingers through my curls. "I'm so sorry about last time. I wanted to tell you right then and there how sorry I was, and to take it back. But you looked so hurt, and I was kicking myself for being such an ass … I didn't know how to fix it."

"Shhh … we can't change that, but we can …" I kissed her. She reciprocated with equal desire. As Maya maneuvered us to the bed and lay me down on the bright aqua comforter, it dawned on me what was about to happen. Panic roiled through my entire body.

"Are you okay?" She must have sensed it.

"Yes. Yes … It's just that …" I shrugged, hoping my body language conveyed what I was too embarrassed to admit: I was a virgin.

"Ainsley." She cupped my cheek. "We don't have to go that far. I could kiss you all night and be perfectly happy."

I smiled, feeling confident. "What if I want more?"

She flicked a curl out of my eyes but didn't respond. Her eyes communicated the truth. Maya wanted to make love to me. It didn't take me long to rip her shirt off.

Before I could kiss her again, she placed a finger on my lips. "Just so you know, I haven't either."

That stunned me. A twenty-one-year-old virgin? She really did enjoy her independence.

She clumsily removed my cardigan, making us both giggle. I made three failed attempts to unclasp her bra. When I finally succeeded, she raised a congratulatory brow.

I nuzzled her nipple, hardening it and bolstering my confidence. Then I rolled Maya onto her back and took her erect nipple into my mouth. She let out an encouraging gasp, her head arching against the pillow at the sensation. Her arms and stomach were a toned milk chocolate, and I let my fingers trail up and over her soft skin.

She pulled my head to hers and we kissed again, sending a deep throbbing down south. I didn't want that to end, but I had the urge to explore her skin with my tongue. Little electric currents singed my fingertips where I trailed my hand down her side. When I reached the top of her jeans, I tried slipping my hand beneath the waistband, but my silver Pandora charm bracelet snagged the top button.

It made her laugh — the most genuine, alluring sound.

"Let me help you out." She carefully freed my bracelet and unbuttoned her jeans. Without speaking, she flicked her gaze to my knit dress. I got the message: she wasn't getting naked alone.

I shucked my dress and panties faster than a sprinter at hearing the starting gun, which made her laugh more, but she didn't mess around in removing her jeans.

My hands shook a little as I started to lower her emerald cotton, lace-trim panties. She lifted her butt, and my eyes feasted on her nakedness. The curve of her hips. Her perky breasts. Maya was the most gorgeous woman I had seen in the flesh. Of course, she was the only woman I had seen naked too, unless you counted locker room encounters, and I didn't. I typically averted my eyes out of fear of appearing on Susie Q's blog embroiled in a lesbian sex scandal.

Still, I'd read more than my fair share of lesbian erotica to know that foreplay was vital in satisfying a woman, so I didn't want to rush things with Maya. I lay on top of her, enjoying the sensation of our naked bodies pressed together. Every nerve tingled with anticipation, and all we had done was kiss and touch. Could we simply kiss all night? Part of me would be ecstatic just with that. The other part of me craved the whole shebang — with the emphasis on bang.

But what if I sucked?

Maya seemed content to continue kissing and groping.

After several moments, she opened her legs and my hip pressed against her crotch. My God, she was wet. I slowly rubbed my hip against her pussy, the fervor in my groin intensifying.

My right hand skated down the side of her body, migrating to the triangle between her thighs. My fingers carefully caressed her tender lips.

She moaned, and I smiled in satisfaction. I'd made Maya the Gray moan in bliss.

My fingers were slick with her wetness, and I stared into her eyes, saying nothing as my finger slowly entered her. She was warm, inviting, slippery. I hadn't expected the slippery part. It made sense, but it still took me by surprise. Hesitantly, I pushed my finger in further, feeling her muscles contract around me. "Oh, Jesus," she exclaimed.

Terrified, I pulled out. Smiling, she guided my finger back inside her. "Please, don't stop. You feel so good." She reassured me, gripping my wrist tight.

I worked up the nerve to pump my finger inside her. Maya's back arched, and our eyes met as if we were sharing the same thoughts and feelings. The connection was surreal yet real.

Her mouth captured mine again, and I groaned.

"You feel so good." She bit my lip playfully.

I looked down at my fingers between her legs and then back to her eyes. "It's amazing, being inside you." My cheeks flushed as she stroked my cheekbone. Then she closed her eyes as I dove in deeper.

I kissed the hollow of her throat, ventured on to a nipple, relishing her gasp when I bit down on one rosy bud. I slid a second finger inside her, her muscles once again welcoming it with contraction.

My tongue trailed down her firm belly, seeking the dark thatch of her pubic hair; when I found it, I nuzzled its softness, inhaling its heady scent.

Maya's moans intensified, but I didn't want her to come before I had the chance of a taste. My eyes fixed on the hood of her clit, and I licked my lips, unsure. Maya watched me, the corners of her mouth curving upward in enigmatic Maya the Gray fashion.

Slowly, my mouth descended. It was greeted with a pungent slickness that made my clit throb. Her intoxicating smell, the urgent gyration of her hips coaxed my tongue to the magic spot. The first flicker of my tongue against her clit elicited the most satisfying groan to ever reach my ears. I continued on with passion, her convulsions matching my enthusiasm.

"Oh, Ainsley … Oh. My. God."

She bolted upright, clutching my head with both of her hands. I wanted so badly to see her face, but I didn't want to quell my efforts either. I sucked her engorged clit into my mouth, and Maya let out a scream, her body trembling before she collapsed back onto the bed, out of breath.

Sensing she was satiated for the moment, I crawled up next to her and rested my face on her breast. She pulled me closer with an arm, craning her neck to kiss the top of my head.

I had found my way, finally, to Maya.

CHAPTER
thirteen

EARLY THE FOLLOWING MORNING, I sat in my car, waiting for a red light. Half-asleep, I rubbed my jaw, noting that my fingers still smelled of Maya, which prompted a satisfied smile. It was like I was able to take a little part of her with me. I let them linger near my nose and continued to inhale. I closed my eyes, remembering being inside her, taking her clit into my mouth. Her moans. The gyration of her hips. Maya's arched back. Her convulsions.

And then her fingers inside me, her tongue tasting and exploring my body, my sex.

A car horn blared, jolting me back to the present.

"Hold your horses," I grumbled, waving to apologize to the impatient motorist.

It was a little after five, and everyone around me was in a rush while I was in a daze, a splendid, morning-after fog I hoped would never lift.

Fiona was already outside her building, stretching in preparation for our run. We exercised together several times a week. When she saw me get out of the car, wearing the dress I'd been in the previous night, a knowing smile spread over her face, but she didn't say anything except, "Grab a pair of shorts and a shirt. I think there's a pair of your Nikes in the hall closet."

Inside, Pat's snores shook the walls. How in the world did she sleep with that racket?

In the bathroom, I changed quickly, and even though I didn't want to, washed my face and hands. Maya's scent slipped down the drain, but the memories remained. Hopefully, we'd make more in the near future.

Fiona gave me a couple of minutes to stretch before loping toward the river. Her long-legged stride reminded me of the impalas I'd seen in Botswana several years back while traveling with Fiona and her mom for Fee's eighteenth birthday. Grace, elegance, and beauty. I usually felt like a warthog next to her, with my stubby, uncoordinated legs.

Not this morning, though. This morning I brimmed with confidence.

My cousin took pity on me, so we only ran four miles rather than our typical six. I suppose she guessed I'd been up most of the night.

When we entered Fiona's kitchen, Pat was standing in front of the fridge, a towel wrapped around his waist as he guzzled OJ right from the container.

"Good morning, ladies. How was your night, Ainsley?" He winked.

"What?" I muttered.

"I noticed your dress from last night hanging in the bathroom." A grin flashed across his face before he left the room.

"For someone doing the walk of shame this morning, you don't look humiliated," Fiona said, and her smugness made me laugh.

She handed me bottled water. "So, do we need to have the lesbian sex talk? Dental dams? Proper cleaning of dildos?" She said it with a straight face, but the energy she expended to keep her excitement in check was practically pooling around her feet.

"I think I'm good," I replied.

"One roll in the hay, and you already think you're God's gift to women," she teased. "How'd you leave it this morning?" She leaned over to search for food in the fridge, plucking two apples from the back and tossing me one.

"She was sound asleep, so I left a note."

Fiona stopped mid-bite. "That was bold." The uncertainty in her eyes suggested she thought it was a mistake.

"W-what?" I stumbled over the word, and my stomach somersaulted three times. "Do you think I blew it?"

Her expression softened. "Time will tell."

That didn't put me at ease. Not at all!

I pulled her arm. "Be serious. How can I fix this?"

"First, don't panic. We don't even know whether there's reason to panic. Most women don't like waking up to a note, but then again, Maya isn't most women. You have that going for you. Second, it's not the first blip you two have experienced — if it was a blip, and I'm not saying it was." She hitched up one shoulder.

"Oh my God! Oh my God!" I waved my arms around like a baby bird trying to get liftoff. "What have I done? She was a virgin … and I just left."

"You must really like her. Usually, you don't overreact," Fiona said with a grin.

A snapping sound behind me made me jump, and I wheeled about to find Pat holding a banana that was more green than yellow. He hated bananas that had turned completely yellow.

"I never thought you'd be a love 'em and leave 'em type of gal." He yanked the peel back and bit into the firm flesh. "I suggest you watch more rom-coms and not so many episodes of *Scandal*, *House of Cards*, and *Veep*. You'd learn a lot about wooing a lady. Rule one: never deflower someone you care about and then bolt at first light." He walked over to Fiona, gave her a peck on the cheek, and said, "Gotta go. Shift at the hospital."

"What do you think?" I asked Fiona.

"He may be on to something. I know gushy films aren't our thing, but it might help. Although *Scandal* revolves around the Olivia and Fitz relationship, I'm not sure it's helping your romantic side flourish, considering." She had one arm over her head, leaning to the side to stretch her back.

I groaned. "Not that. What should I do now?"

"I suggest you go home, put on one of your cutest outfits, and get to class to assess the damage. Bring her a coffee or something. No wait, you make shitty coffee. Go to her shop and pick up coffee there. Have you baked any banana bread lately? You make killer banana bread." She looked around the kitchen in search of a loaf.

"You expect me to win her over with banana bread?" I was beyond exasperated. An hour ago I'd been over the moon. Now I visualized sitting on a meteor plummeting back to Earth.

"It couldn't hurt." Fee shrugged.

"Do I have time?" It was 6:30 a.m. I groaned again. "Shit, I don't." I grabbed my car keys off the kitchen counter. "Bye!"

I hurdled over a random cardboard box that had been carelessly left in the corridor as I ran to the lecture room, Maya's coffee in one hand and my cell phone in the other. I was hoping she'd call or text, even though I suspected she didn't have a phone. Miraculously, I didn't spill a drop. But I had bigger worries.

Who in today's world didn't have a cell phone? *People who didn't want to be found.* I pushed that thought out of my head and prayed for a miracle.

Sliding into my usual seat, I noticed I was one of the first to arrive. The wall clock read 7:40 a.m. Twenty minutes should give me enough time to calm my heart, which at the moment was revving like a race car at the start of the Indy 500.

Three minutes ticked by — I'd been incessantly checking my cell phone and the wall clock for confirmation. My phone buzzed, causing me to nearly jump out of my seat and upset Maya's coffee, but it was only a text from Fiona. It contained a question mark, nothing else. I ignored her.

"Hello, stranger." Maya's silky voice reached me before I had a chance to whip my head around and gauge her mood: sexual afterglow or scorned woman?

I bolted out of my seat, her cup of coffee in my hand. "I got you this." My voice was too loud and shaky.

Right at that moment, two guys bounded in, one pretending to fade back and shoot an imaginary basketball. "Yes, two points!" he shouted, accidentally bumping into Maya, who, in turn, smashed her hip into me. The plastic lid on the to-go cup shot off, and before I could do anything, I was dripping with hot liquid. Again!

"Oh, no." The guy looked sincere. "I'm so sorry." He reached into his backpack and retrieved some loose paper in an attempt to clean me up. Focusing on my Diane von Furstenberg spotted silk blouse, which was now practically see-through, he rubbed notebook paper over my drenched breasts.

"Got it!" Susie Q stood with her phone in hand. "A little early for a wet T-shirt contest, doncha think?" Her malicious wink made me groan. How was it she always popped up at the most inopportune times?

"It's okay. I'm fine." I stepped back, and the guy's friend burst into laughter at my reaction to his buddy pawing my breasts.

The boy turned cherry red. "Uh, I didn't mean ... I'm so sorry." He rushed to his seat, mortified.

Dr. Gingas arrived, appraised my drowned rat appearance, shook her head, and launched straight into her lecture.

Maya scrambled to get her notebook out, and I sat down in a huff, pulling the *Boston Globe* out of my bag and placing it over the coffee spill, my foot firmly on top to soak up the dregs and hopefully dilute the fumes. I slipped on a thin sweater to hide my nipples.

Maya eyed me sidelong and gave me an encouraging smile, which settled me some. Our knees bumped, and neither one of us pulled away.

Halfway through the lecture, I started to shiver. My shirt still wasn't dry, and the thin sweater offered little warmth.

Maya reached into her backpack and pulled out a gray sweatshirt. "Here," she whispered.

Surely that was a sign she wasn't upset about this morning.

If I wasn't already the class clown and if Genghis didn't scare the bejeezus out of me, I would have shot out of my seat and bellowed, "She likes me. She really likes me!" Instead, I communicated my thanks by squeezing her arm. Maya dipped her head.

Eventually the continual scratch of her pen calmed me, and I was able to concentrate on the lecture.

When it was over, Maya stopped writing as soon as Dr. Gingas marched out of the room. "Cup of coffee?"

I rolled my eyes. "I don't know if I'll ever drink another cup of coffee again. How humiliating. And here I was trying to ..."

She raised a finger. Susie Q approached, snapping more photos.

"Let's go outside," I said.

With a knowing smile, Maya led me out of the building. I put my arms out and turned my face to the sun. "Oh, that's better."

Maya had her arms crossed, but the cocky look in her eyes gave her away. "So what were you trying to do?"

I sighed. "What? Oh, with the coffee? I felt like an ass, just leaving this morning, and I wanted to tell you I was sorry."

Maya scratched the side of her head with her pen. "But I got your note."

I wanted to throttle both Fiona and Pat. All the worry for naught, and now I'd be headlining another Susie Q's *Tattler*. What headline would she feature? I was sure wet T-shirt contest would be part of it. Bottlenose loved to shoot from the hip.

"I really enjoyed last night as well," Maya said, referring to a comment I'd made in the note. "Now, let's get some coffee. I need some. I slept through my alarm this morning, for some weird reason, and I nearly missed class."

"Oh, really. Any reason in particular why you were dead to the world?" I nudged her arm with an elbow.

"Nope." She spun around on her heel, like a soldier. I tugged her hand, and together we walked to the student union. Glancing at me coyly out of the corner of her eye, she added, "Maybe there was a reason."

"Hopefully a good reason."

"A fantastic reason."

I looped my arm through hers. "Are you free tonight?" I asked, bursting to make more memories.

"Nope." Her tone suggested I couldn't talk her out of the commitment.

"Doing what?" I tried to sound casual, even though my confidence was crashing down to somewhere near the equator.

"Work and then studying."

"Oh." I hated the obvious disappointment in my response.

"What time should we meet?"

I stopped mid-stride. "What?"

Did she mean she wanted me to pop over for a booty call? A roll in the hay? Oddly, I wasn't insulted. Fee would be so proud.

Maya waved off my indignation. "We made plans to work on our project tonight, remember?" She rested her hand on my shoulder. "I finish work at eight."

"Oh, that!" I almost face-palmed but was able to curb the impulse. Knowing me, I'd give myself a black eye. "I'd forgotten. My place or yours?" I arched one eyebrow, hoping I looked devious and sensual but fearing it made me look comical.

"Yours." She pulled me behind a strategically placed column, and before I knew it, she was kissing me — deeply. Desire rushed through me, my pussy practically flooding my pants.

Maya stepped back, grinning. "I've been wanting to do that all morning."

"How did you spill coffee *again*?" Pat was trying to sound supportive, but his smirk wasn't helping his cause. He reached into the fridge and pulled out a bag of tomatoes.

"Oh, please. If Ainsley becomes president, she'll be the first to spill coffee on the red launch button and start World War III." Fiona squashed a clove of garlic with the flat side of a knife. She was concocting her famous "from scratch" spaghetti sauce.

She reached for another clove, but I stopped her. "Fiona! Not too much, okay?"

She eyeballed me over her shoulder. "Expecting some action tonight. I thought the plan was to work on your group project."

"Group project. Is that code for orgy?" Pat elbowed me in the side.

I rolled my eyes. "We can't study *all* night." I shrugged.

"Garlic is good for you," Pat teased.

"Thanks, Dr. Pat! But it's not good for my breath, and I really want to kiss her again. When she kissed me this morning …" Words failed me. I melted against the countertop, both hands on my heart. How could I describe what I was feeling? Love? Passion? Desire? I didn't know how to define the emotion, but whatever it was, I liked it. I liked it a lot.

Pat put one arm around my shoulder. "Why, Fiona, I do believe our little Ainsley is madly in love." He squeezed my arm, and I rested my head against his barrel chest, letting him kiss the curly top of my head. Pat was like the brother I'd always wanted. Ham loved me, but he was so much older and rarely around.

"This sauce isn't going to make itself." Fiona pointed to us with her knife. "Chop, chop."

We both saluted.

This tradition of us cooking one meal a week together had started when Fiona first moved into the apartment three years ago. Pat weaseled his way in not too long after. Actually, that wasn't fair to Pat. We both enjoyed his company.

"So, when are you going to introduce Maya to the family?" Pat stirred the simmering sauce.

"Haven't thought that far ahead." I avoided Fiona's eyes.

"Fee's been bringing me home for years now."

"Rory brought you home first."

"Not the point. Your grandmother knows we're a couple," Pat explained.

"Shit!" Fiona slipped with her knife.

Dr. Pat rinsed her finger under the water. "Was it the word *couple*?" he teased.

Fiona laughed, fluttering bashful lashes. "Maybe."

He left the kitchen and returned with a Band-Aid. "Just a nick, but we can't let you bleed into the sauce." He kissed the tips of her fingers, and Fee nuzzled against his chest.

My cell vibrated. Something told me I wouldn't like the message, but I had to know. *Wit and valor are qualities that are more easily ascertained than virtue, or the love of wisdom.* Seriously, who thought these quotes instructive?

I stifled a groan and shot an email to Ham, hating that I had to. Who would hack into my phone to retrieve the text: Tess or Rita? The mere thought raised my hackles, but the fear of handling it on my own outweighed the invisible invasion. More than likely, they were already tracking all incoming texts.

I looked at Fee and Pat, who were too wrapped up in each other to notice my anxiety. Watching them, I realized I wanted what they had: open communication about their issues. I wasn't certain their jokes and talks actually helped, but at least they had each other. However, "secrecy" was quickly shooting up my favorite word list, and it didn't take Sigmund Freud to guess Maya cherished it as well.

"Okay." I tapped a pencil against my head. "I think we have our thesis."

Maya sat cross-legged on my bed, a notebook open in her lap. "Do you ever feel like Alcott?"

"I hadn't considered it. Why?"

"I can relate to her some. She worked so hard to pay off her family's debts. The mistakes of those closest to her brought much misery and suffering. Her sense of responsibility was a huge driving force in her success."

"Do you mean — ?"

"No, not my mom. She's the only one who's been there for me."

"What about your aunt?"

"Who?"

"The one who died?" I tried to hide my surprise that she'd forgotten.

"Oh. She died soon after we arrived. I barely knew her." Maya traced one of her fingers with a pen.

At Fiona's she'd given me a different impression, or had I misread the cause of her unease?

"Your father?" I took a stab in the dark.

She let out a frustrated sigh. "I barely know anything about him. Mom says I have his eyes."

"Your eyes were one of the first things I noticed about you."

"Really?" Maya watched me with those magnificent gray irises that spoke directly to my heart.

She started to speak, but faltered.

"What?" I squirmed on the bed next to her.

"It's just … oh I don't know … My parents didn't make the best choices, and I feel like I'm paying for it."

"Do you ever think of contacting your father?"

"No." Her squared shoulders were resolute.

"Are you sure? I know if I had …"

She jumped off my bed and perched on the windowsill, her arms crossed.

"Your family situation is way different. I'm not even sure who my father is or if he wanted me. Mom has only mentioned his name once."

"Really? I'm sorry, Maya. I didn't mean — "

"I know." She cut me off again. "It's just hard to talk about." Her shoulders relaxed a little. "I'm sorry. I didn't mean to snap."

"It's okay. I'm a firm believer in open communication."

Why had I said that?

"I think we should go back to Concord," she blurted, a blatant attempt to change the subject.

"Uh, okay. Why?" Concord no longer conjured warm fuzzy feelings for me.

"We didn't take any pictures, and I think it would be great to put together a montage for the presentation." She looked away. "And ..."

"And?" I motioned for her to continue.

"And I want to erase what happened there last time."

"You mean when you freaked out?" I smirked. This thing between us was still so new. I wanted to be myself, but I didn't want to overdo it. Diplomacy with a dash of humor.

"Yeah, that." She raked a hand through her hair.

"I'm free Saturday."

She looked unsure.

"I can try to make Sunday work," I added.

"It's not that. Saturday's fine." Her crinkled brow implied the opposite.

"What's wrong?" I patted the bed.

She settled next to me but remained frustratingly mute.

"Are you okay?" I rested a hand on her thigh.

"I'm not used to ... this."

"To what?" My heart was spinning in my chest, like an out-of-control Grover had crawled inside and was madly chasing an errant tennis ball.

"Letting people in."

"I know how you feel," I whispered, knowing I sounded scared. "There's a reason Carmichaels spend so much time with family. We get burned a lot."

Her frame sagged with a burden that would have crushed Atlas, and her eyes brimmed with tears. "I just don't want to get hurt," she said, and I wondered whether she wanted to add the word "again." Was that what had broken her, a failed relationship? Or her father's abandonment? Or was it deeper than that?

I feared knowing the whole truth, feared it would taint our relationship, but I still wanted to know everything about Maya the Gray. And I would, eventually. She was too fragile to be pushed all at once.

"I don't want to hurt you, Maya. I want to ..." I lifted her chin and gazed into her eyes. Then I kissed her softly. A tear plopped from her eye, rolling onto our lips and making the kiss taste of salt. She pulled away and wiped her eyes with a sleeve.

"Please, stay the night. We don't have to make love, but I want to be close to you, hold you, let you know I'm here for you, no matter what."

Maya stood. She took two steps away before turning. "You promise not to abandon me if I let you in? No matter what?"

Her words knocked the breath out of my lungs, but I managed, "I promise."

What in the hell had she been through?

I rose from the bed and wrapped her in my arms. "Let me in. Give me a chance."

The tension in her body ebbed away. "I want to, but I'm scared."

"Tell me why."

She shook her head. "I can't. Not yet. I need time."

"I've waited eighteen years to meet someone outside of the family I could trust. I'll give you all the time you need." I buried my head in her neck. "I love the way you smell. It makes me feel like I'm home, safe and sound."

Maya lifted my chin with a finger and planted a lingering kiss on my forehead. Grasping her jaw, I pulled her lips to mine. The intensity of her desire kicked mine into hyperdrive, and I pushed her onto my bed, Maya pulling me on top.

I yanked at the buttons on her chambray shirt, nearly tearing them off as Maya removed my sweater and shirt in one swift movement. My bra followed, and then my jeans. Maya rolled me onto my back, slipping her hand beneath my panties and expertly separating my lips.

"I love how wet you get." She smiled. "How wet you make me."

I lifted my butt to remove my panties. "I don't want your hand to cramp."

"Not that I would notice." She dove in with two fingers.

"This is all I care about. You. Me. Together. Nothing else matters." Her simmering gray eyes pleaded for my agreement.

I agreed.

"Kiss me." Oh boy, did she. The chorus from the Alicia Keys song "Girl on Fire" blared in my brain.

"I love the way you feel," I panted when she finally pulled away for breath.

Maya's fingers glided in and out, slowly, unhurried. "I love how soft your skin is." She rubbed her face in my cleavage, circling a nipple with her nose before nipping it with her teeth.

It made me moan.

Her lips skated down my stomach, never lingering too long, just ensuring they covered all the right spots.

She inched down.

And down.

Farther down.

Bypassing my bud, she caressed my inner thigh, sighing blissfully. Moving to my other thigh, she kissed it gently while her hand pumped ever so slightly — keeping me in the moment but not bursting with lust.

Her tongue landed on my clit, forcing me to gasp. "Oh yes."

Maya circled it, her fingers increasing their steady penetration. My hips bucked, pleading for more, and another finger entered. "Harder."

She enthusiastically complied. It was hard to decipher who was moaning louder; our sounds and bodies melded into one.

"Maya I'm — " I sensed I was about to come right as my body spasmed. Maya didn't let up, and I didn't want her to. Not ever.

Another wave coursed through me. "Jesus!" I screamed. An aftershock overcame me, making my legs quake.

Maya stayed inside me, but stilled her fingers and her tongue.

I gasped for air until I was finally able to say, "I could do this all night."

"I'm game." Maya snaked up my body and kissed me.

I flipped her onto her back. "Only if we take turns." I motioned for her to lift her ass so I could dispense with her jeans and underwear.

"By all means."

Maya's pussy lips glistened with desire, and I traced them gently with a finger.

"I need you. Now," she said.

The words hit me hard, with the sweetest impact.

CHAPTER
fourteen

"MAYA ACTUALLY SAID THAT? NOT to abandon her if she lets you in completely? Which I'm assuming means her past — the one that doesn't exist?" Fiona and I pushed and pirouetted through a herd of Red Sox fans heading in the opposite direction toward Fenway Park. Our destination was Nadine's, one of Boston's oldest and most exclusive restaurants. "What in the hell is she hiding? And please tell me you didn't make that promise?"

I yanked on her arm to get her to stop, and then rested a hand on her shoulder so I could slip off one Christian Louboutin pump. The back of my foot was rubbed raw. "Why do I wear heels? My feet are killing me."

Fiona shook her head. "Because you can't accept that you're a bit on the short side. Besides, Grandmother always insists you look glamorous. The rest of us are chopped liver." She wore sensible black suede flats, which looked stylish and cozy, and didn't make her limp.

I groaned and focused on the Maya problem. "What was I supposed to say? That I plan on running if my granny tells me to, because I don't think I would."

"Especially not in those babies." She gestured to my bloodstained shoes. "Never understood the allure of bloody feet." Fiona put a hand on my shoulder. "Back to the matter at hand, you don't know that for sure. If you learn something truly awful, how can you stay with her? You, of all people, know the political game. Just a whiff of scandal and bye-bye White House."

"Has Pat run out on you? He knows more than most about the skeletons in the Carmichael's closet, even Uncle Liam. That would scare off most." I attempted to put my shoe back on, but it hurt too much. "Do you have a Band-Aid?"

She fished through her black clutch. "You aren't Pat. You do as you're told, and if you're told to run, you run." She snapped her bag closed. "Sorry, I'm not much of a Girl Scout."

I ignored her comment. Weeks ago I would have done as I was told. But now?

"Fine. I'll walk in stockings until I have to look presentable."

"Fingers crossed. Hopefully Susie the Shark doesn't sniff your blood." Fee motioned for me to walk ahead. "I did get a kick out of the wet T-shirt photo, though."

I shot Fiona a look that would have curdled most people's blood, but she laughed it off.

We arrived at Nadine's just as Grandmother was getting out of her Bentley. Her chauffer stood with his hand out, assisting the crone. He made it look effortless, the way he carried most of her weight without revealing he was essentially lifting her out of the back seat. She probably only weighed ninety pounds. Her back slouched slightly, and the cane was a permanent fixture in her right hand. I took the opportunity to examine her face and neck, which were riddled with wrinkles and sagging skin. True to form, Grandmother wore a dress and hat befitting Maggie Smith's character on *Downton Abbey*.

Spying us, she sternly tipped her head; that was her friendly greeting. If angry, she would only glare. Luckily, I had slipped my heels back on moments before.

Fiona kissed her cheek, and I followed suit. "It's lovely to see you," I said.

A tight-lipped nod was her only response.

Fiona offered Grandmother an arm, and I followed them inside. We shed our coats and handed them to one of the hostesses.

Mother and Uncle Owen waited in plush chairs, clutching tumblers of scotch.

"Why, Ainsley, something's different about you," my uncle said. He held my arms out and inspected me from head to toe. "You look so grown-up."

Mom, in a royal-blue power suit that reminded me of Hillary Clinton, eyed my outfit as though my embroidered black crepe dress would confess all.

Fiona hid her know-it-all grin with a palm, and I imagined she was forcing a comment back into the pit of her stomach. She seemed disappointed I hadn't blurted out, "Well, Uncle Owen, I popped my cherry."

The hostess led us through the yellow-marbled restaurant. Most of the tables were semi-private, partitions of frosted glass strategically placed to block any gawkers, but that wasn't enough for Grandmother. She always reserved the private dining room. She settled into her seat and promptly ordered oysters and a French Chablis. I think I was the only Carmichael who hated the raw, bluish-gray, booger-tasting flesh, and I was absolutely convinced that the first person who'd sampled one did so only in a life or death situation.

The family's quarterly dinners were more like board meetings held under crystal chandeliers and gilded ceilings. Tonight's agenda contained the upcoming legislation sponsored by Mom and Uncle Owen, and how many votes they needed. Fee and I weren't silent observers. We were expected to listen and learn, of course, but we would also have to give updates about our lives. Fiona stated her grades and that she'd been asked to cowrite an article with an esteemed professor. When my turn arrived, I drew a complete and total blank.

Luckily, the server arrived with the wine and oysters, and Grandmother sampled the Chablis and gave an approving nod.

Everyone but me tucked into the oysters.

"Go on, Ainsley," encouraged Grandmother.

"I met someone," I said.

Fiona, usually the paragon of self-control around the old lady, dropped her jaw to her chest. No one ever shared personal details unless it was a big deal, like Ham's marriage.

Grandmother stared.

"That's good news." Uncle Owen had always had a soft spot for me. "About time you finally went on a real date."

And then some.

Mother tapped her manicured nails against the base of her wineglass. "That's fine, Ainsley, but remember why you are in school. Look at Fiona — she's coauthoring a paper. You need to think along those lines and not let your hormones get the best of you."

No one else spoke. Grandmother eyed me, deep in thought. The flesh hanging from her neck moved as she swallowed. "Are you going to tell me more, child?"

"I'm doing well in all of my classes."

"I know you are. The girl, tell me about the girl."

"Are you ready to order?"

Thank God! Saved by Nadine's efficiency. I kept my eyes glued to the menu, hoping that by the time everyone finished ordering, the conversation would have moved into less dangerous territory.

Fiona kicked me under the table.

Thinking it was my turn, I directed my gaze to the waitress.

Maya.

She wore a crisp black shirt, black slacks, and a short white apron tied around her waist. She stood with a subservient, stooped posture, arms behind her back, her gaze fixed on mine. What had happened to the dude who was serving us? Something about this bait and switch felt fishy.

"Miss?" she asked.

"Uh …"

Maya didn't blink.

I didn't want to order the lobster, not from Maya. But if I didn't, it would ring alarm bells, force questions. I wanted to avoid any and all questions.

"The broiled Maine Lobster, please."

"Any sides?" Maya's beautiful face was devoid of all emotion.

"The roasted autumn vegetables." I nearly added, "sweetheart."

"Very good." She turned to Fiona. "And you, miss?"

Fiona smacked her lips together, and her eyes darted to me and then back to Maya.

"The pan-roasted halibut, Maya. Thank you."

I cringed, but the rest of our party seemed oblivious to Fiona's mistake.

Maya didn't miss a beat. "Of course, miss. Side?"

"Pommes puree."

She dipped her head slightly, took the other orders with ease, and then disappeared out the side door.

Grandmother dabbed her mouth with a napkin. "Ainsley, you were telling us about the girl you met."

I stared at the door through which Maya had exited.

The room was silent, and I realized they were awaiting my answer.

"Oh, she's a classmate." I turned to Mother. "She's in my history class with Dr. Gingas — now *she's* an interesting character, lectures like a marine drill sergeant."

Fiona practically groaned at my obvious attempt at diversion. For my part, I was abhorred I'd provided a detail that made it easier for the goons to track down Maya. *Stupid, stupid, stupid, Ains.*

Mother smiled without much warmth. Why?

Grandmother cleared her throat and leveled her cold, birdlike eyes on mine.

I smiled as innocently as possible. "Her name is Mara. Mara Channing."

"Mara," repeated Grandmother. "Isn't our waitress named

Mara?" she said it with such a casual air that I almost believed her innocence.

Mother shifted in her seat, but Grandmother stared her down.

Fiona stepped in. "Maya," she corrected. "She's a friend of Pat's. He used to work here."

"Maya, Mara — so close and yet so far," said the calculating old lady. She stared at Fiona and then at me with a conspiratorial air, as if she knew we were playing her for a fool.

My mind whirled, wondering what she knew. Would she know anything? Not yet, at least. Surely. Or had she been watching my every move? Was she the source of the quotes? Should I alert Ham?

"Where is she from?" Grandmother asked.

"Wyoming," I squeaked, and then cleared my throat. *Hold it together, Ainsley. Act normal. Avoid unwanted snooping.*

Grandmother raised an eyebrow. No one in our family had ever been friends with anyone from Dick Cheney territory.

"She and her mother moved to Massachusetts a few years ago."

"Where do they live?"

I never should have mentioned that part. I dug my nails into my legs. "Mattapan," I uttered, washing the word away with a sip of wine. The staff at Nadine's routinely overlooked underage drinking. They had turned the other way since I turned sweet sixteen.

Mother didn't speak. She didn't have to. The snarl in her lip was clear enough. Sure, she wanted people from Mattapan to vote for her, but she didn't want her precious daughter to date one of them. She angrily slurped an oyster. I wanted to shout out that she was a hypocrite, claiming to be a woman of the people.

"I see. What does her mother do?" Grandmother asked.

"She's a waitress," I whispered. Just like Maya at the moment. Would Grandmother circle back to that?

"And?"

I said the first thing that popped into my addled mind. "She's

Puerto Rican, descended from African slaves."

"You managed to find the only black lesbian from Wyoming in all of Massachusetts. Well done, Ainsley," Mother said as she crisply refolded her napkin.

"What does her father do?" Grandmother asked.

"I don't know. Maya hasn't seen him for years."

Grandmother tittered. "Looks like I'm not the only one who can't keep it straight."

"What?"

Fee's eyes widened as if she was trying to communicate telepathically.

"You called her Maya, the name of the waitress." She turned to Fiona. "Isn't that right?"

Fee's tight-lipped smile was loud and clear. She wanted to tell the shrew to shove it, but knew she couldn't.

"Did I?" I squeaked, shifting in my seat. "This wine is going right to my head. I meant Mara hasn't seen her father in years. Silly me." *Stop acting like an amateur!*

No one spoke. None of the marriages in our family were strong ones; they lasted, against all odds, because of the gray-haired woman at the head of the table.

More oysters arrived. On the verge of tears, I excused myself, saying I had to use the restroom.

Fiona crashed through the door seconds later. "That was the most entertaining interrogation I've ever witnessed."

"Not now." I dabbed a tissue under my eyes, careful not to smudge my mascara.

"Look at it this way, she hasn't told you to leave her yet. That's a good sign." Fiona entered a stall. Bodily functions didn't stop her from talking, not even pee splashing into the bowl deterred her. She said, "If you ask me, you've got her blessing for now. The only black lesbian — that was kinda funny, for your mother." Fiona's laugh was drowned out by the sound of the flushing toilet.

She stepped up to the sink to wash her hands, watching my reflection in the mirror. Taking my purse from my shaking hands, she motioned for me to hold still and then applied fresh mascara to my lashes.

"Let's add a little color, too," she said, taking out some blush. "You look like you've seen a ghost. Of course, mine won't be as good as your Elizabeth Arden. Is she on call?"

"Not now, Fee."

She concentrated on the task at hand. Finally, Fiona snapped the compact closed. "You know, next time, maybe you should open with something less alarming, like how you're top of all of your classes, which you are. And then maybe say you have a wonderful 'study buddy' who's been helping you. Ease them into the situation."

I groaned. "Why didn't you prep me earlier?"

"It's not your first rodeo with Grandmother. How was I supposed to know you'd completely lose it, tonight of all nights?"

"I'm not myself these days." For weeks, I'd had Maya on the brain.

"Love and Carmichaels don't really go together. Besides, deep down, I think you want to get caught."

"What do you mean?" I crossed my arms.

"I wouldn't blame you. With the Carmichael quest hanging over your head, you wouldn't be the first to choose self-sabotage."

"That's absurd." I took a step back.

"Is it?" She raised both eyebrows.

"Absolutely." My tone lacked Carmichael conviction.

Fee tilted her head. "That's a shame, because if you are self-sabotaging, I'll call in Pat and he can help you implode before dessert."

I laughed. What a relief to release some of the anxiety roiling in my belly. "That man has had diarrhea of the mouth lately."

"Tell me about it. I nearly died when he told Maya you're the Chosen One."

Some of the tension from earlier seeped back into my mood, and I gulped in air before insisting, "I won't stop seeing her."

Fiona concentrated on fixing my hair and then hers. "We

better get back out there."

"I won't stop seeing her."

"No one has asked you to, darling," she said in a voice that lacked her usual verve. The word "yet" bobbed overhead like a cartoon thought bubble.

Luckily, by the time we returned, the conversation had switched back to politics. For now, I had a reprieve.

Why had I even brought up Maya? And since I had, why didn't I just introduce her? Grandmother's goons were probably already running background checks, and it wouldn't take them long to figure out Maya's real name. Mara Channing. What had I been thinking? And mentioning the class we had together, too? Grandmother would likely get the full report before after-dinner drinks. I wondered what the old lady would say when she found out Maya and her mom didn't even exist until 2003? I was drowning in secrets.

Maya and a fellow waiter arrived with our meals. Neither made eye contact with anyone, as usual. Maya served Fiona and Uncle Owen, keeping her distance from me and Grandmother. Was that intentional? Even those who weren't avid viewers of political talk shows had probably heard of Grandmother and the power she wielded over the Carmichael clan.

I took a deep breath and held it, and then let it escape soundlessly through my mouth. It was a process I had to repeat for the remainder of the meal.

After dinner, I ditched Fiona outside her apartment right after Mother's driver dropped us off, and caught a cab straight back to the restaurant. Wrapping my coat tightly around my body, I staked out a bench across the street.

Around midnight, Maya walked past me. I hadn't seen her leave Nadine's, but staff more than likely had to use the back door.

"Maya!" I called.

She spun, easily spotting me, in my heels, among a sea of drunk and disappointed Red Sox fans.

"This is a pleasant surprise. I didn't expect to see you again tonight." Her smile faded into a frown as she took in my appearance. "Are you okay?"

No, I wasn't. I shouldn't have promised I'd never hurt her. What was I thinking? We hurt everyone; it was the Carmichael way. But that wasn't what bothered me right then and there. After waiting on us all evening, her eyes averted, her head bowed, never once drawing attention to our relationship, how could she still greet me with a smile?

Maya pinned me with a cautious glare. In this light, her eyes reminded me of the sea on a stormy day.

"I'm fine. I just had dinner with my grandmother, as you know, of course." *Way to point out the obvious, Ainsley.*

Maya's shoulders tightened. "Did they suspect?"

"What? No? I don't think so." My eyes ping-ponged every which way other than on Maya's face, unsure whether I was afraid of what I'd see there, or what she would see in my eyes.

"That's a relief." Her posture softened. "When I walked into the room, I nearly fell to the floor."

"A relief? Aren't you mad?" I crossed my arms.

"Mad? About what? We got away with it." She tossed her arms in the air.

"What'd we get away with?"

Maya swallowed as if taking her time to concoct an answer. "Ains, I don't know about you, but the last thing I needed tonight was to lose my job. Dating clientele is strictly forbidden. I don't work here often, but on the nights I do, I make some serious dough — well, for me at least." She shuffled her feet.

I let out a long breath, feeling like I had been swimming underwater for several minutes. "I hadn't looked at it that way. I thought you'd be pissed I didn't introduce you."

"Is that why you rushed back?"

"Yes. I wanted to explain."

"You don't have to explain anything. Being a Carmichael and dealing with your grandmother … well, you know that better than I do."

"Oh boy, do I."

Maya didn't know the half of it. The goons were probably scouring the Web for intel. Now I was worried about Maya's job as well as breaking her heart, and about losing the one person I'd realized I didn't want to live without. Not to mention that Maya would no doubt flip her lid if she learned the goons had invaded her private life. I had to do something to shield her from that, but I was drawing blanks.

"How come you didn't tell me you were working tonight?" I asked.

She laughed. "I didn't know until an hour before the shift started. I got an SOS from Rick. Tonight was my first time working the private room. Imagine my shock when I walked in and saw you."

"What a coincidence." A wave of queasiness flooded my belly, but I willed it away. "Can I walk you home?"

"Yours or mine?" she asked, her tone mischievous. It instantly put me at ease.

"Which do you prefer?"

"I don't care as long as I'm with you. You look beautiful in that dress, but right now, all I want to do is rip it off."

CHAPTER
fifteen

WE LAY IN BED TOGETHER, naked. Maya had one arm wrapped around me, her free hand tracing circles on my stomach.

"What's wrong?" she asked. "You're tense again."

What could I say? That I'd just told my grandmother I was involved with a girl from Mattapan and that I was positive my family's henchmen were right this minute combing through Maya's past, which didn't exist until 2003? Oh, and that I expected a phone call from my mother at any second, telling me to never see Maya again? No. Of course I couldn't say that.

"Just tired."

"Sometimes I think I'm lucky it's just my mom and me. My life is a lot less complicated." She hugged me tightly.

"I have more family members than I know what to do with, but no one really shows an interest in my life, not my real life anyway, only the life I'm allowed to publicly project," I told her. "Everything in my family is orchestrated." I pointed to the dress thrown over the desk chair. "Most of my outfits are bought by a professional. My makeup, same. Lately, I've been feeling like a doll."

"Just lately?" She propped up her head.

"I …" I cupped her cheek. "Someone is showing me there's more to life than boxes to tick on my way to success."

"Who is this person? Sounds like trouble?" She squeezed my nipple.

"The best kind of trouble." I winked.

"Tell me something no one knows about you, not even Fiona." The pad of her thumb circled my breast.

"I've probably read more lesbian romance novels than anyone else on the planet."

"No erotica?" Her eyes widened.

"Of course. I have a secret Kindle I keep in the fireproof safe." I pointed to the metal box on the bottom shelf of my bookcase.

"Scandalous." She scanned the other shelves. "Did Fee help you decorate?" She gestured to Lincoln's image on the middle shelf.

"Some. I admire Lincoln," I tossed out. "This room isn't for me, though. It's in case I have visitors." Everything was neat and tidy, even the family photos, pens and pencils, and silly knick-knacks on the shelves and desk. It was homely, to a point, but still staged.

"Tell me something else." She peppered my neck with kisses.

"No. Your turn. Tell me something no one else knows."

"Let's see … Well, I've never read a lesbian romance in my life."

I elbowed her side.

"Ouch. Okay, how's this? When I was seventeen I tried to brand myself."

"How? With a match or a lighter?"

"No, with a cautery pen. A friend got her hands on one." She shrugged.

"A girlfriend?" I teased.

She shrugged. "We were close for a bit."

"What happened?"

"She moved the summer of our senior year."

"No. I meant did it hurt?"

"Not really. I knew she was moving for a while."

"Not that! The branding."

"Oh, of course it hurt. And I messed it up. Big time."

"How so?"

She showed me her inner arm. "You can't make heads or tails of it."

I gently fingered the scarred flesh. "What's it supposed to be?"

"My initials."

I laughed. "The first letter doesn't look like an M at all."

She pulled her arm away. "I told you I messed up." Anger sparked in her eyes, but they soon softened. "And it got infected."

"Bad?"

"Septicemia bad. I had to spend time in the hospital."

I covered my mouth. "Can septicemia kill you?"

"If it advances to sepsis it can."

"You idiot!" I whacked her arm, knocking her chin off her hand.

"Don't worry. Mom made it clear I should never ever do such a thing again."

"I bet." I thought of how Grandmother would have reacted if I'd tried the same.

"Is everyone afraid of your grandmother?" she asked as if she could read my thoughts.

"I was just thinking what she'd do if I ever did something like that. How'd you know?"

"Your furrowed brow. Everyone seemed tense at dinner, even Fiona."

"Grandmother's a force to be reckoned with."

"Can she be kind?"

"I used to think so, but now I'm not so sure. She expects a lot." *And she's manipulative*, I mentally added, suddenly realizing the quotes might even be from her.

Maya propped her head up with her hand again. "Like what?"

"Success at the highest level."

"Like, president high?" She nodded toward Abe's image.

"Exactly like that."

Maya pulled a face. "Does that mean your mother is going to run? Susie Q will have a field day!"

Susie wasn't the one I feared at that moment.

I pulled Maya's head to my chest. Could she feel my heart hammering? Why did I have to be a Carmichael? Why couldn't I be from a normal family — a family whose only recourse was snide comments, not having an investigator comb through available records to dig up dirt on Maya like she was being vetted for vice president? My grandmother and her connections probably had more reach than those vetting a president's running mate. Hell, my grandmother probably knew who shot JFK.

My eyes popped open at 4:30 a.m. Maya was lying on her back, and my hand trailed her supple skin, teasing her hardening nipples. I kissed her shoulder and she stirred, which had been my intention. Thoughts of last night flooded my mind. Soft kisses. Lingering caresses. Licking. Fingering. My God, I was falling hard for Maya.

Unease still nagged at the recesses of my mind, but waking up with Maya dulled my memories of the night before. All I wanted was to feel her skin against mine.

Then it hit me. Grandmother!

I bolted upright. How could I have forgotten about Grandmother?

I snatched my cell off the bedside table and fired it up. The thirty-second wait took forever, but the absence of alerts shocked me.

No texts. No voice mails. No e-mails. Nothing. Mother — the usual messenger of death — was eerily silent.

Grandmother didn't know anything about Maya. Wait — that was impossible. Chuck had uncovered some of her past, and surely Grandmother's goons were heads above Chuck.

That meant ...

Half-filled with dread and half with hope, I brought up the front page of *The Boston Globe*. There wasn't a death announcement. I googled my Grandmother's name. She *had* to be dead; that was the only explanation for her silence.

There weren't any notices. Nothing. Just a whole lot of nothing. Besides, surely someone in the family would have called by now or sent someone to look for me.

Suddenly, I had never been so frightened in my life.

"Everything okay?" Maya asked, her voice thick with sleep.

I looked over my shoulder at her smiling face. Her hair was mussed from last night's tango in bed, making her look adorable and vulnerable in equal measure.

"Yeah. Everything's fine. Except for one thing."

She sat up. "What's that?"

"You took way too long waking up. I have plans before we head to breakfast."

She cocked an eyebrow. "I'm up now. Let's not waste any more time."

"You haven't heard anything?" Fiona's head popped into view over the coffee table and disappeared just as quickly. I was on her couch, and Fee was on the floor, doing sit-ups.

"Nope. What do you think it means?"

Her head crested the table and then dipped out of sight again. "You got me. It didn't take Chuck long to find out what little there is to know." She finally sat up and guzzled some water. "Maybe Grandmother's losing her touch. She is in her nineties."

I shook my head, and Fiona's scrunched face conveyed her own disbelief.

"No. Something else is going on," I said. "I just don't know what yet."

Fiona was polite enough not to add her two cents. I had enough crazy scenarios running through my brain.

"Why are your panties in a bunch today anyway?" I asked.

My cousin cocked a thin eyebrow.

"Since I've been here, you've jogged on the spot, completed one hundred push-ups, and now 250 sit-ups. What's going on?"

She shrugged. "It's complicated."

"Pat?" I pushed.

Looking away, she nodded. "He's being so open-minded, giving me a pass to do what I want, when I want."

"And you don't want that?"

"Of course it's what I want," snapped my usually cool-as-a-cucumber cousin. "It's ..." She let her sentence die, probably because she didn't know how to explain. Fiona was about action. Doing things, not contemplating emotions.

"Are you afraid he'll take to the lifestyle more than you?"

"I doubt he'll even step outside of the relationship, but he thinks that's what I want."

For as long as I could remember, Fee had preached against monogamy, saying it was virtually impossible to achieve. Pat was giving her a free pass, and she suddenly wanted him to fight to be the only one. Was my cousin becoming the kind of woman she despised? A nester?

"What can we do to get your mind off it?" I asked.

"Eat some bad oysters. That would keep me busy."

"There's always that option. Bit drastic, doncha think? I hate oysters. How about Chinese?"

Her smile answered me. When either of us needed to bury our troubles with binge eating, we headed to our favorite all-you-can-eat Chinese buffet.

"Promise me you won't choke on an egg roll or something. Should we bring Pat, just in case?"

"Why do I ever confide in you?" I groaned.

"Got me. It's not Carmichael-like." Fee smiled.

Maybe that was the reason: I was baby stepping my way to a massive rebellion.

CHAPTER
sixteen

"HOW COME YOU NEVER TALK about your childhood?" I sat across from Maya in La Creperie. She'd finished her shift an hour earlier, and we both had our notebooks open and random stacks of books piled near them on the table. Midterm fever had arrived with a vengeance. I eyed a goofy Frankenstein decoration that hung over Maya's head. When you pulled a string, the arms and legs moved jerkily.

"Not much to tell, really. I didn't have a glamorous life like you." Maya shrugged and continued scribbling on one of her notepads. She had three notebooks laid out, and as hard as I tried, I couldn't figure out her system. Still, she aced every quiz and paper, so whatever her system was, it obviously worked.

"My life isn't glamorous." I scooped a bite of apple and cinnamon crepe into my mouth.

"Says the daughter of a senator with houses in Beacon Hill, Cape Cod, and Washington DC." She looked up from her notebook and winked.

I grunted playfully.

"Your timing is impeccable, though," Maya said with a silly grin.

"What? Why?"

"My mother wants to have you over for dinner."

I didn't respond right away, feeling guilty that I had zero intention of introducing her to my family, aside from Fiona. Not now, at least. Maybe in five years. Or ten. Twenty. If Maya wasn't poor and of mixed race, would I feel so weird about it? I squashed the thought.

"Of course, I told her you were too busy." The unease in her eyes made me feel ten times worse.

I slapped her arm. "Why'd you say that? I'm not too busy, and I would love to meet your mom." I plastered on a fake smile to mask my shame.

"Are you sure?" Maya's face softened.

I gave her my *duh* look. "Tell me when," I said, before taking another bite of crepe.

"S-Sunday after midterms," she stammered.

"Sounds great!" I was overdoing it, but couldn't stop myself. "What can I bring?"

I hated that I was putting on a show. Normally, I could fake it with the best of them, but this was Maya — the girl I was falling for.

"Trust me, you won't need to bring anything. Mom is a tour de force in the kitchen. She'll have enough to feed all of Texas, and then some."

"Does she like roses? Wine? I can't show up empty-handed."

"African violets are her fave, but seriously, you don't have to bring anything. She's not the type to expect anything from anyone."

What would her mother think of me? Even Maya thought I was spoiled.

"Will that be kinda …? Will she like it if I got her an African …?" I didn't know how to ask whether that would be construed as racist. Was it like giving a Chinese person a Chinese teapot as a birthday gift?

Maya's eyes twinkled with merriment. "Are you asking me whether it would be racist to bring my mom African violets?"

"Yes," I whispered, lowering my head, worried someone might overhear.

"You know I'm not just black, right? I'm a regular Heinz 57: African, Hispanic, white, and God knows what else." She looked at her hand. "Of course, many only see the pigment of my skin."

"I don't — "

"You never noticed. Not even after our first night. I noticed your freckled skin." Her grin split her face in half.

"That's not what I meant. I meant I see you as you are."

Her eyes clouded over, but then she forced a snippet of a smile. "Sometimes you overthink things."

Confused by the flicker of fear in her eyes I wanted to move to safer ground. "You write too much." I lamely gestured to her notebooks.

She laughed it off, and I crossed my arms, annoyed.

Maya reached over and uncrossed my arms. "Did you know African violets are linked to motherhood in many cultures? When I was seven, I learned that tidbit and bought Mom her first one for Mother's Day. She's been hooked ever since. Being a mom is her proudest achievement."

"You're lucky." The words slipped out, and I think Maya sensed I hadn't meant to say them aloud. "My mom barely knows I'm alive. I have more contact with her staff."

"What was it like, your childhood?" She stirred a spoon in her coffee.

"Hot and cold. Sometimes I mattered. Most of the time, Mother's career took center stage. Everyone in the family is a political pawn. We have roles to play, and if we break the rules …"

She licked the spoon. "Like dating someone from Mattapan."

I wanted to defend my family, but I didn't want to lie, not outright. "They know I'm seeing someone. It isn't that. Ham, my brother, is engaged to a Chinese–American."

Maya rolled her eyes.

"I didn't mean it like that. I just … They expect big things from me, and well, my past dating experiences — experience — ended in disaster."

"What happened?"

I covered my eyes. "I can't tell you. If you really want to know, it's on Susie Q's blog — the entire humiliating experience."

She tugged my hand from my eyes. "I'd rather hear it from you."

I sucked in a cleansing breath and closed my eyes. "I can't," I said. "Not now."

"Okay, I get it."

I opened my eyes. She wasn't angry. "Thank you."

"So what role does your family have planned for you?" She pushed her chair back and crossed her legs.

"President."

"Student body president?" She scrunched up her face, hiding her beguiling gray eyes from me.

"President of the United States of America," I stated, for the first time to someone outside of the family. The absurdity hit me with the force of an Amtrak train.

"You're joking." She swatted the thought away.

I shook my head. "They've purchased the domain names of all the possible ways to say Ainsley Carmichael for Prez. My fave is the ABCs of the next US president."

"ABCs?"

"My initials: Ainsley Blaire Carmichael."

"Blaire?"

"It's my mother's maiden name."

"Wow, that's heavy. I thought they were grooming you to be senator, which is a big deal. Never thought …" She whistled. "Do you want to be president?" She placed both arms on the table.

"I did when I was a kid."

"But now?" She lowered her head to stare into my eyes.

I chewed on my lower lip. "Now I just want to be Ainsley."

"Tell them that."

"I wish it were that easy. I've been bred for power. Failure is not an option."

Maya nodded, absorbing the information. "Are they okay with you being gay?"

"At first they freaked out, but they ran some focus-group testing and realized it might play to my advantage in thirty years. The fact that I'm girly tested well with straight males."

Maya blinked as if I'd been speaking in tongues. "Please tell me you're kidding."

"They even tested whether I should stay in the closet and never marry, stay in the closet and marry a man, or just come out now. Like I said, everything in our family is orchestrated; everything is plotted."

"But that's insane. Completely insane. It's your life, not theirs."

"I'm starting to learn that." I squeezed her hand. "For years I didn't realize the insanity of being a Carmichael."

"Is that why they call you the Chosen One?" Maya's other hand rested on my thigh under the table.

I nodded. "Craig was supposed to be president. When he died, Ham became the heir apparent — until the accident that damaged his eye. One eye is completely useless and an eyesore to look at."

Maya flinched.

"So they had me."

"Had you? Just for that?"

I sucked my bottom lip into my mouth.

Maya didn't blink or move for several seconds. She started to talk, but then she lowered her eyes and focused on the pen in her hand instead. "I'm sorry. No child should ever feel that way."

"It wasn't all bad. My family is very determined. That's all."

"You can always run away."

"To Walden Pond?" I joked.

"Too many tourists. We'd have to find someplace no one wants to visit."

"We?" I leaned over to kiss her cheek. "I like the sound of that."

"Careful. We aren't alone." She motioned to a guy two tables away, clutching a cell phone in his hand.

"I don't care, Maya. I only care about this." I intertwined my fingers with hers.

Maya picked me up in her mom's car, not wanting me to drive to her hood in the Focus Electric.

"Trust me; that wouldn't be wise," she'd insisted. Not that my little car screamed fancy, because the likes of Susie Q would pitch a fit on their blogs in that case, but it still had the shine of newness.

Personally, I didn't care about the car, but I didn't want to have to call Mother to tell her it had been stolen in Mattapan either, not that everyone there was a thief, of course.

Before getting out of the car, Maya placed her hand on my thigh. "I didn't tell Mom you're a senator's daughter. She won't ask too many personal questions, though, so I don't think …" She squeezed my thigh again, to get her point across, which was to tell the truth but not the whole truth. Luckily, I had been doing that my whole life, and even more so lately.

"But she knows about us?" It seemed foolish I hadn't thought to ask that question earlier.

Maya quirked a sarcastic eyebrow. I was beginning to understand all of her forms of non-verbal communication. This one meant "Don't be stupid; of course she knows. Why else would we be here?"

"Right. Silly question." I opened the car door and balanced the plant so I wouldn't harm it as I got out. It had taken me an entire day to find the right shade of African violet to match Maya's eyes as closely as possible. Eight shops. All of them sold the plant, but I wouldn't settle for the wrong shade, albeit the plant was more blue than gray.

I'd seen enough gritty films about certain Boston neighborhoods to know what type Maya came from. Without being obvious, I scanned her block. The houses were huddled together, some of the porches leaning precariously right or left, making me wonder how they stayed erect. Brown lawns were trampled, bikes strewn about. Some of the yards were littered with trash.

But Maya's house was almost immaculate: a fresh coat of paint and not a scrap of litter. The grass, while not lush, was tidy, and some hedged bushes were planted near the porch. It stood out, but not too much — just like Maya. That made me smile.

Before either one of us stepped onto the porch, the front door swung open.

"There's my baby!" A mammoth of a woman burst through the door, her arms wide open. "Come here!" she instructed, and Maya disappeared into her mother's arms.

"Mom, I'd like you to meet Ainsley." Maya stepped back from her mom's embrace and gestured to me. "Ains, this is my mom, Agnes."

"Ainsley!" She motioned with her arms that it was my turn for a hug, so I handed Maya the plant, fearful it wouldn't survive the crushing embrace. When Maya's mom pulled me into her arms, it was like I was being sucked into a vortex.

"It's so nice to meet you." She tightened her hug. Even Pat didn't give hugs like this, and I had considered him the supreme hugger.

With an arm around my waist, Maya's mom ushered me into her home. The carpet and furniture in the front room weren't new, but everything was spick-and-span with a lived-in feel, not at all like my home. Our home was spotless, and as welcoming as a museum. My dorm room was tidy, but it reflected my personality only as much as was permissible.

A rich scent wafted through the house, and I sniffed.

Her mother smiled. "I'm making Maya's favorite — chicken and dumplings." Mrs. Chandler pinched her daughter's cheek.

Maya reddened, but didn't admonish her mom at all. "Ainsley insisted on bringing you a gift." She sheepishly handed the plant to her mom.

"Oh, it's beautiful. And the color — just like my baby's eyes." She gave me another crushing mom-hug. If she wasn't careful, I might start craving them.

I laughed. "That's why I picked this one. I loved the color." I didn't say because of Maya's eyes, but the look on her mom's face said she understood. I quickly surmised Maya and her mom communicated without actually speaking on a regular basis.

Agnes whisked us into the kitchen, which seemed to be the only other space on the main level. I guessed the bedrooms were upstairs. She carefully placed the gift on the counter, like it was a baby, cooing over it. I squinted to see whether the plant detected her love, too. I couldn't imagine any living thing not feeling loved in this woman's presence.

"Maya, would you be a dear and pour the drinks?" Agnes asked.

Maya opened the fridge and grabbed a pitcher of what I assumed was freshly squeezed lemonade with lemon wedges floating on top. It was late October, but the house was as toasty as a summer afternoon, and lemonade sounded like the perfect drink. I had a feeling it was Maya's favorite beverage, probably since childhood.

I sipped mine. "That's good." I took another swig.

Maya beamed. "Mama's specialty."

Maya's mother buzzed around the kitchen, humming as she put the finishing touches on the meal. It was nice not to have to sit in a sterile room, making polite chitchat before eating. It was less like a cocktail party and more like dinner with family.

"It smells delicious …" I paused. Should I call her Agnes or Mrs. Chandler? I went the safe route and said "Mrs. Chandler" in a deferential voice.

She flipped around and laughed. "Honey, no one calls me that. Please call me Agnes, or I won't know who you're addressing." Her smile and tone were pleasant. It was like I was under some weird mom spell, and nothing could hurt or upset me.

Maya slipped on an apron, and I offered to help only to be shushed by both of them. I was prompted to sit at the table in the corner. A window above the sink overlooked a small yard and the back of another house.

When it was time to eat, I was more than ready. The delicious-smelling steam from my plate promised I was about to taste the best meal of my life. I almost didn't want to dig in, fearing it would be over too soon, but my stomach won. I dipped my fork into the chicken and dumplings, unleashing another wave of fragrant goodness that made my mouth water.

I loaded up a fork and tasted pure heaven, immediately letting out a moan of satisfaction. Both mother and daughter smiled as they tucked into their own meals. For several minutes, no one spoke. When food was this good, conversation was unnecessary.

Halfway through dinner, Agnes could no longer contain herself, and mother and daughter fell easily into conversation. Agnes filled Maya in on all the goings-on in the neighbor-hood — who had been arrested, who was pregnant, who had found a job, and who had been fired. It reminded me of conversations Fee and I had about our scandal-ridden family.

"Can you believe Mrs. Robinson's boy, Ray, will be in jail for Thanksgiving?" Agnes shook her head. I wasn't sure what she found more upsetting: that Ray was in jail or that his momma would be alone for the holiday? I nearly smiled, but controlled myself, knowing it would come across wrong.

"Oh, that reminds me I have to work Thanksgiving morning." Maya scooped in another mouthful.

"Thanksgiving morning!" Agnes's fork clattered onto her empty plate.

"I know." Maya put her hands up in mock surrender. "But it was either that or Christmas morning. Which would you prefer?"

Agnes leveled her eyes on Maya and a torrent of Spanish flew out of her mouth at machine-gun speed. The only word I caught was *Carisa*, and I was fairly certain that was a name.

Maya's body slumped, and her attention flicked briefly to me before settling on her plate.

The fury washed off Agnes's face just as quickly. "What are your plans, Ainsley?"

"For Thanksgiving?"

She nodded.

"Oh, the usual. A quiet meal with my family," I lied.

Maya set her fork down. "Momma always makes sure everyone has a place to spend the holidays. Each year, our home is packed with people I've never met. If there's a person within a thirty-mile radius who'll be alone on a holiday, Momma will hunt them down and drag them here, even if they prefer being alone." Maya's tone was pleasant, but it seemed somewhat forced, considering she was still in the doghouse.

Agnes tutted. "No one should be alone on the holidays. I've finally convinced Florence to join us."

Maya perked up. "Really?"

"Yes. So make fun all you want, Miss Future Community Organizer." Agnes smirked.

"Ainsley volunteers quite a bit."

Agnes turned to me, smiling. "On Thanksgiving?"

I nodded. "Our family volunteers at the shelter each Thanksgiving." I neglected to say our motivation was positive press, a rarity these days for anyone in the family, and that, aside from Fee and me, everyone grumbled about it. Ham used to enjoy it, but he was now glued to his phone, awaiting White House e-mails. My sister had once tried faking the stomach flu to get out of it when we were kids. Then she realized she wouldn't be able to eat all day, and she'd backtracked. "I volunteer regularly," I added.

"Ainsley is helping put together a program to encourage senior citizens to interact more." Maya placed a hand on my thigh under the table and left it there.

"How so?" Agnes rested her elbows on the table.

"We organize outings for those who are able to leave their homes. We're also offering Internet courses, so people can connect online."

"She got Flo a laptop," Maya crowed.

"The program paid for it," I demurred.

"Do you want to be a community organizer like Maya?"

"Oh, I don't know what I want to be yet." I spoke to my lap, avoiding Maya's gaze.

"Don't you worry about that. You're still so young." Agnes hopped up out of her seat, light as a bird, and I marveled how such a large woman moved so nimbly. "Now, I hope you girls saved some room for dessert. I made Maya's favorite."

My stomach was beyond capacity, but saying no wasn't an option; that would be rude.

Before I had a chance to will my stomach to make room, Agnes had three slices of pecan pie sitting on the table. "I hope you don't mind, Ainsley. There's a little bit of bourbon in the pie — not enough to hurt you. Just a smidge for flavor." She smiled a motherly smile.

I remembered Maya forgoing a glass of wine at Fiona's. Alcohol must be taboo in this house or something.

I placed the smallest morsel in my mouth out of politeness. Agnes eyed me like a hawk. My grin and a second, much-larger bite satisfied the momma chef.

Maya had gobbled half of hers by the time I took my third bite. She licked a crumb off her bottom lip, and it made me crave her tongue on me. Immediately, my cheeks burned. How could I think about that in front of her sweet mother?

"Here, let me get you some more lemonade," Agnes said, obviously noticing my flushed cheeks. Before I could respond, she was already at the fridge, pouring a second massive portion.

Maya's crinkled brow let me know she realized something was up. I giggled nervously. For some reason, I tended to giggle when having impure thoughts, which I had confessed to Maya the night before, in a moment of weakness. She winked at me. How odd, having someone completely in tune with my thoughts without me having to spill the beans. Before, I would have found it unsettling, but with Maya, it was reassuring.

Before I wanted the night to end, it was time for Maya to whisk me back to reality. Agnes packed up all the leftovers, including the pie, and shipped us both off with another one of her hugs, which I hoped would last months.

Sitting in a car filled with the aroma of authentic home cooking, my face warmed. "That was fun. Your mom can cook. I've never had such a scrumptious meal in my life."

She tsked skeptically.

I slapped her leg. "I mean it. I can't remember a time when my mother cooked."

"But aren't you used to fancier meals?" Maya asked. "Like lobster?"

"Trust me, if anyone in my family ate that meal, they would be pleading for your mom to cook for them every day." Shit! Had I really just implied my family would want to hire Maya's mom as their cook? *What the eff, Ainsley?* The reporter in my head blared, "Ainsley Carmichael can't keep her foot out of her mouth."

Maya didn't seem insulted. "I guess we'll never know."

"We can try an experiment."

She tilted her head, waiting for me to continue.

"We'll give some to Fiona and Pat, and see what they say."

When Fiona turned her head, Pat dipped his fork into her dumplings. Spying the treacherous act out of the corner of her eye, Fee attempted to swipe his hand away. "Hands off my dumplings, buster!"

"You see." I turned to Maya. "This is the best meal ever."

Pat nodded enthusiastically, unable to speak with his mouth overloaded.

"Did your mom cook for you like this every night?" Fiona asked in a dreamy voice.

Maya laughed. "Not every night. On Sundays she makes a special meal."

Pat forced down a large bite by whacking his chest. "I'm free next Sunday and every Sunday in case you gals ever want company." He flashed his award-winning smile.

"Hey, Irish. I met Maya first. I should get the first invite." Fiona's tone bordered on pleading, which brought a smile to Maya's lips.

"My mom loves to cook for people. It won't be a problem if y'all want to come," she said in a natural Texas drawl — too natural.

Fiona and I momentarily locked eyes.

"You have Sunday dinner every Sunday? Still?" Fiona gulped lemonade. "That must be …" She looked away, leaving the rest unsaid.

Maya studied her profile and then nodded thoughtfully. I sensed she was seeing further into the Carmichael rabbit hole, and it didn't scare me entirely to show her more of my life.

"Yep. We've done it since I can remember." She stood and fished her keys out of her jeans. "I better get the car back to my mom."

I walked her to the car. She started to wave good-bye, but I swatted her hand away, threw my arms around her neck, and kissed her on the lips. "Thanks. This has been a wonderful night."

"Tossing the Carmichael shackles off?" she joked.

"Maybe."

"How does it feel?"

"Normal. This" — I fisted the hair on the back of her head — "is what I want out of life."

Maya rested her forehead against mine. "It's all I want, too."

"Will I see you later?"

She nodded. Her eyes told me I'd be seeing a lot of her later.

"Good. Drive safe." I waited for the car to disappear out of sight before returning inside.

Back in the kitchen, I announced, "I need Chuck."

Fiona stopped mid-bite, her fork hanging an inch from her mouth. "What happened?"

"Who's Chuck?" Pat asked, concern etched into his brow.

"During dinner, I'm fairly certain Maya's mom called her Carisa."

"Fairly certain?" Fee squinted.

"They were speaking Spanish." I waved a hand. "I'm wondering whether that's her real name."

"Could be a term of endearment." Fee blinked excessively.

"Maybe."

"But your gut says differently." Fee rubbed her chin and nodded.

"Something like that. Can you have Chuck widen the search?" I didn't tell her to have him search Texas, but I knew Fiona would understand.

Fiona disappeared from the room, and I took a seat, not wanting to speak.

"Who's Chuck?" Pat asked again with frustration in his tone.

I shrugged. "One of Fiona's friends. I haven't met him."

"Neither have I. You don't meet people like Chuck." Fiona returned and slipped back into her seat. This spy stuff didn't take too long, it seemed. "He'll have a full report by morning."

A full report. It was a risk, but I needed to know, especially if Grandmother's minions were already one step ahead of me. I needed to prepare — it was the Carmichael way.

"Will someone tell me what's going on?" Pat was almost frothing at the mouth.

I looked to Fiona. She knew Pat better than I did. Could he keep it quiet? She must have thought so, because she told him how little we knew about Maya.

"She just popped up in 2003?" Pat shook his head. "Poor kid. There's a story there, but I'm not sure it's one meant for you to find out." He pointed his fork at Fiona and then at me. "It ain't right having Chuck dig around where he's not wanted."

"I know." I blew a red curl out of my eyes. "But I have to know. I really like her, Pat. Hell, I think I'm in love, and you know … with the Web, how much of our lives are actually private anymore?"

"That's just an excuse. It ain't right. Not at all." He pushed his plate away. "The poor girl has no idea what she's up against."

CHAPTER
seventeen

EARLY THE FOLLOWING MORNING, I left Maya in bed, telling her I was meeting Fiona for a run. She didn't suspect I was entering full-fledged panic mode.

"Well?" I said as soon as Fiona stepped outside in running gear.

Fiona eyed me. "Let's run first." Without waiting for my response, she took off; that wasn't good.

I chased after her, faster than normal, but Fee's long legs kept me out of reach. After the third mile, I found Fiona sitting on a secluded bench by the river, waiting.

I slumped next to her and tried to gird my nerves; it wasn't working. I feared I might vomit.

"Agnes isn't Maya's mom. She's her aunt."

The arm on my bullshit meter, the one I'd been ignoring for weeks, flipped all the way to the right, indicating there was more to the story. Did I want to know?

"As you suspected, Maya's real name is Carisa. Carisa Torres."

"What aren't you telling me?"

Fiona let out a long breath, like she was trying to cleanse her soul.

"Maya's mother was murdered."

"Murdered?" I covered my mouth.

Fiona squeezed my leg. "Listen carefully. There were rumors that her mother was the mistress of a business tycoon in Texas." As if sensing my question, she went on. "Maya only lived in Wyoming for a summer, when Agnes worked as a cook at a dude ranch outside of Cody, the year her mom died."

"Who killed her?"

"It's unsolved. The businessman was questioned, but ..."

"But what?"

"He's really powerful."

"Carmichael powerful?"

"My guess, more powerful."

I pulled my knees onto the bench and cradled them. "Who is he?"

"Raymond Eckley."

"The Texas billionaire? Married to the governor of Texas? *That* Raymond Eckley?" I swallowed.

Fee nodded, and I whistled. "He has more money than Bill Gates," I said.

"Actually his wife has all the money, not that he publicizes that when he's throwing his weight around. I thought there were whisperings about a prenup though. Not surprising given the amount of money involved," Fee said.

"Prenup?"

"If he cheats, he's out. Just a rumor, though." She nibbled on a hangnail.

"My daily briefing sheets frequently feature the Eckleys. Isn't that a weird coincidence?"

Fee didn't respond, so I left the thought alone. "How old was Maya when her mom hooked up with him?"

"Unclear, but all signs indicate Maya wasn't yet born." Fee avoided my eyes, now practically gnawing on her finger.

The idea forming in my head was terrifying. "Was Eckley's wife ever questioned?"

"Yes."

"So if Maya is his, she's proof of the affair?"

Fiona rubbed her eyes. "Unfortunately."

"The prenup." I shook my head. "How did Chuck …? Never mind."

Fiona nodded. There was no use asking how Chuck knew so much. People like him didn't elaborate, and who knew how much could be discovered on the dark net.

"Here's the theory according to some crackpot bloggers," Fiona said. "Maya's mom either knew too much about the businessman, or she tried to blackmail him. Once she got popped, Maya's aunt panicked and left the state with Maya. Somehow, after the dude ranch, she bought them new identities. It's not a clear picture — fuzzy at best. And the sources are about as reliable as Susie Q. Another interesting tidbit, none of the bloggers have been heard from since."

"No wonder Maya and Agnes ran, but how? Who helped them?"

"Good question."

"Fuck. So, if Chuck is right, Maya is on the run from her father, who doesn't want his wife to find out he has a child. And Eckley's wife is one of the most powerful politicians in America and has more money than God. This is much more than I thought."

"Exactly. This is the show: the establishment against us, the little guys."

It was the first time anyone had called the Carmichaels the little guys.

"How old was Maya when her mom was murdered?" I asked.

"Seven."

"Shit! Here I was afraid of her dealing with my powerful family, when all along I was in the Eckleys' crosshairs." I hid my face between my knees. "Can it get any worse?"

Fee's silence wasn't comforting.

Was he the one responsible for the quotes? I scanned the

river's surface for answers. Surely, a Texan wouldn't know diddly about a long-dead historian. Most Texans spouted crap about the Alamo when making a point.

"Do you think she knows? Or suspects?" I asked.

"Hard to know. Agnes probably knows, though. Knows enough to run, at least." Fiona turned to face me. "Eckley isn't just big in Texas. He's also big in DC. And he's a Texan. You know Texas has a finger in every presidential election. This is — "

"It's either good or bad," I interrupted. "I haven't decided yet."

"How is it good?" She craned her neck to stare into my eyes.

"I'm still working on that. This type of scandal could be political suicide — Grandmother may not be able to rescue me."

Fiona gripped my shoulder. "I'm not worried about Grandmother. You don't fuck with men like Eckley. He makes Grandmother look feeble."

Could Ham and his fixers handle the Eckleys? But would Ham step in considering who we were dealing with? Or would he worry about committing political suicide? Would his advice be to cut and run? Also, would alerting Ham and his crew set off alarm bells in Eckley's camp? My stomach churned. I leaped to my feet, dashing away to finish our run. I needed to keep moving or go mad.

Fiona didn't object.

My mind flittered to Maya showing me her branding. Was that her way of letting me in some or simply a moment of weakness? Would she ever confess all if I asked? But how could I ask without her knowing how I found out?

Outside the apartment building, I tugged on her arm to prevent her from entering. "How much does Pat know?"

"Nothing, except that we were looking into her past. Chuck knows, of course."

"Do you trust him?"

"He hasn't let me down." The implied *yet* didn't have to be said aloud. Information gathering was a dangerous game.

"Is his name really Chuck?"

"Highly unlikely."

Pat was already dressed and on his way out when we entered. "So are we still on for this Sunday?"

"This Sunday?" I asked.

"Sunday dinner with Maya's mom." He cocked his head, baffled that I'd already forgotten.

"Oh, right. Of course. Why wouldn't we be?" Even I could tell that my voice was uncharacteristically shaky, which was not Carmichael-like. My only thought was Maya, and protecting her at all costs. But how? She'd said it herself: she'd lose her anonymity dating me. Was that what she'd been afraid of that day we'd kissed near Walden Pond? Not the bullshit that we're from different worlds, but that Eckley would find her and finish the job? All along I thought I was being the magnanimous one, but her sacrifice to be with me made my silly presidential ambitions seem petty. Maya's life could potentially be on the line.

Pat's limp smile made my stomach lurch. "I hope the news wasn't that bad. And don't you dare tell me what you found out. People's secrets are just that." He waggled a finger at us as he left.

"It wasn't really that bad, considering," Fiona said, stretching out her calf on one of the kitchen chairs.

Unable to speak, I flashed her a look that said *You've got to be kidding.*

She didn't even bother to glance in my direction. "She's not the first kid to have a questionable mom. And look at how far she's come. The media will eat that shit up."

"I would never splash her history about for political gain!"

"I'm not saying you would. But how can you keep this quiet if you continue to see her? Think, Ains! Everyone in our lives gets vetted, not just by Grandmother's goons, but also by the media. A single picture of you two together could be the game changer. Besides, it might be safer to air her dirty laundry in order to protect her. Right now, Eckley has the advantage."

I collapsed onto a kitchen chair.

"Think, Ains!" she said again. "We need to figure out the endgame. The timer started the moment you two kissed. We just didn't know it."

But had Maya?

Later that night, while I waited at the restaurant for Maya to finish her shift, I pondered Fiona's words. Did we need an endgame, or were we needlessly trying to turn my life into an episode of *House of Cards*?

"You look deep in thought. Everything okay?" Maya set her bag down on the empty chair next to me.

I squeaked, "Just jittery. Too much caffeine today."

She smiled. "I'm not surprised. You've had five cups in the past two hours. Let's get you home."

It was her night to stay at my place. For weeks, we'd been switching back and forth, trying to ensure we both had access to clean clothes. Packing an overnight bag every other day wasn't overly burdensome — not yet, at least. Her roommate, while never around, was still a threat to our domestic bliss. We feared she might fight with her boyfriend and crash into the dorm room at three in the morning, finding us in bed. Yet Maya was adamant about not moving her stuff to my place. Was that a sign she knew the dangers? Was she trying to protect me? Or was it her desire to remain an individual? The more I learned, the more Maya the Gray baffled me.

"Earth to Ainsley. Come in, Ainsley." Maya spoke through cupped hands.

I was sitting in my desk chair, staring into space and probably looking like I'd just seen little green men climbing out of the closet, shouting, "Nanu! Nanu!"

She moved to stand in front of me, and I rested my head against her stomach. "I'm sorry, Maya. I don't feel well."

Squatting down, she placed a tender hand on my forehead, checking my temperature. "Tell me what you need. Aspirin? Sprite?

Hot shower?"

"Lie down with me and hold me."

She carefully tucked a strand of hair off my forehead and behind one ear. "I can do that. Not a problem, beautiful." Her smile brimmed with love and trust.

I bolted off the chair, barely making it to the toilet before spewing the contents of my stomach. Maya rushed in, pulling my hair back just in time for the second wave.

"Shhh …" She pulled me into her arms as I started to sob, rocking me slightly. "Do I need to call Dr. Pat?"

At that moment, I wanted to shout that I loved her, because she understood. She knew I wouldn't go to the ER or the health center. She knew I would go to Pat. But instead of declaring my love, I shook my head and snuggled closer to her chest. "Just hold me, Maya. Hold me and never let me go."

CHAPTER
eighteen

THE FOLLOWING SUNDAY, MAYA INSISTED we bring Grover to
Agnes's place for dinner, which thrilled Pat, of course. He had been
picking Grover up at Fee's mom's and sneaking the terrier into
Fiona's apartment a couple of nights a week, and the two of them
were perfectly suited for each other — both crazy but loveable.

Fiona thought Grover would provide a wonderful distraction,
for me and from me. Half the time, I was on the verge of puking
my guts out; the other half, I spent racking my brain trying to figure
a way out of the Eckley dilemma.

I had wanted to nix the dinner, but Fee was worried that
would trip a distress signal, and who knew who was watching? Her
plan, so far, was to stay the course.

She also quickly dismissed my fear that having dinner with
Agnes would lead Grandmother's goons to Maya's front door.

"Think, Ains. She already knows about Maya anyway. Chuck
is good, but the witch's goons can no doubt run circles around little
Chuckie with their hands tied behind their backs. It's not the time
to act fearful. Be bold. Think JFK during the Cuban Missile Crisis."

Grover barked, pulling my thoughts back to the present.

"My apologies, Grover." Agnes leaned over and patted his

head. "I didn't mean to ignore you."

Agnes took to Grover right away, even making him a plate of hamburger while the rest of us binged on homemade chili. For a moment, I thought she was going to wrap a bib around the dog and sit him at the table with us. Pat was only one step away from that at Fiona's, too, and Grover seemed utterly convinced he was human. The terrier even slept under the covers with his head on a pillow. Who couldn't love him?

While Agnes gave Maya her weekly update about the goings-on in the neighborhood, Pat and Fiona listened half-heartedly, too busy scarfing their meals.

I kept listening for Eckley buzzwords or code words, but there were none. What did I expect? For Agnes to say, *Do you remember Raymond? He e-mailed the other day to say he's watching.*

After the report of who was pregnant, in prison, or going to college, Agnes turned to Fiona and asked, "What are you studying?"

Fiona covered her mouth and mumbled, "History," to the best of her ability.

"Ah, these two lovebirds" — Agnes pointed with a spoon to Maya and then to me — "met in a history class. Are you in it as well?" She scooped up a spoonful of chili.

"No. I go to Harvard."

"She's wicked smart," Pat said, through his own mouthful of food.

"Fiona wants to be like Doris Kearns Goodwin," Maya added.

Agnes nodded appreciatively. "I loved her book *Team of Rivals*. Now I'm reading *Bully Pulpit*. There's so much I never knew about William Howard Taft. And Teddy has always been one of my faves."

"Me too." Fiona held a palm to her chest, and it was hard to miss the excitement coursing through her veins. Not only did Agnes know Fee's favorite historian, she had also read some of her books.

Maya's triumphant grin let me in on her secret that she'd planned the comment, knowing Agnes and Fiona would easily slip into conversation. Maya would make an excellent fixer someday. She was highly intelligent, but even more than that she was cunning. I was learning firsthand that Maya could figure people out with just one look. Like Grandmother, she knew whom to trust, how to work them, and how to control them. In the beginning, I'd wondered how Maya had learned those skills; the Eckley bombshell, though, made me realize she'd had to learn how to survive. I laid a hand on her thigh, and she rested hers on top. Again, I made a silent vow to protect her at all costs, and Agnes. I had to help them both.

"I love to read but could never stomach romance novels or thrillers." Agnes pointed to a small shelf that contained a handful of library books. "For some reason, I can never get enough of American history. I didn't have a chance to go to college like Maya, but I try to keep up."

"Keep up? I can never keep up with you." Maya turned to me. "I swear my mother knows more than Dr. Gingas, and all because of a library card. Ben Franklin would be so proud."

Agnes flushed. Fiona patted her hand and launched into her favorite topic: Teddy Roosevelt.

Pat scraped the bottom of his bowl with some bread, not wanting to miss a drop.

"There's more on the stove." Agnes tilted her head, giving him permission to help himself.

Pat pushed his empty plate back, rose, and retrieved a pan off the stove, serving generous second helpings of chili for all. Agnes, embroiled in scintillating political conversation with Fiona, nodded a thank-you.

I wondered how it was that both Fiona and Pat looked like they belonged here. Agnes seemed thrilled to host us in her home, and Maya glowed with happiness. I finally felt like I belonged to a loving family. I gave Maya's leg a squeeze. Her dazzling smile, though, couldn't erase the fear roiling inside me.

Please, God, don't let Maya's father swoop in and take this away.

CHAPTER
nineteen

MY PRAYERS WENT UNANSWERED.

"Great heavens and earth." Fiona slumped back on the couch two days later, her face as pale as if she had just walked through a minefield and was still unsure whether she was safe. Without saying anything else, she held up her phone, displaying her Twitter feed.

"You have a Twitter account?"

"Of course, but not in my name. Everyone in the family has an account, except you. You're missing the point." She shook the phone in my face, and my world crashed down around me.

Squinting at the screen, I saw a photo of Maya and me kissing. Air whooshed out of my mouth as if I'd been hit, and I snatched the phone out of her hands to examine the photo.

"When was this taken?"

Pat grabbed the phone off me. "Looks like the front of Fiona's apartment. Is this what she was wearing that night you two brought over leftovers?"

It was. I locked eyes on Fiona.

"Don't give me the stink eye. I'm not the one dating a billionaire's daughter."

"Billionaire's daughter?" Pat exclaimed. "That's what you

found out. Maya is a modern-day Little Orphan Annie? And I thought the news was a game changer."

It was, but how could I loop Pat in without putting Maya at risk?

"Hey, wait, there's another photo." Pat handed the phone back to us. It was of Ham and Mei, in bed, and then another one of Pat and Fiona smoking a joint. Next was my mother with a man I didn't recognize, although from the looks of it, they were intimately acquainted.

"Let me guess. My pops is next." Fiona waited, wide-eyed, but the next image was of my sister.

"Kylie?" Fee exclaimed.

"In her judge's robes. Why?" I racked my brain.

We didn't have time to ponder. Fiona's father, my uncle Owen, was next. He wasn't alone, but we knew that was coming.

Someone with the Twitter handle @EdwardGibbon had been stalking every member of our family, snapping photos for weeks, if not months. Was this Eckley's doing? Or Susie Q's? Others? Or were all Carmichael-haters in cahoots?

"Who would do this?" Pat asked.

"Why would anyone do this?" Fiona asked.

"Edward Gibbon? Aren't groups like this usually called 'Anonymous' or something more sinister? This name seems harmless. Nerdy, even," I said, adding my two cents.

"My guess is it's a reference to Edward Gibbon who wrote *The Decline and Fall of the Roman Empire*," Fiona said.

"Meaning the end of the Carmichael dynasty." I stated the obvious, shaking my head. "Ham warned me the end was near."

"Who would pretend to be Edward Gibbon, besides historiographers, of course?" Fee tapped her fingertips on her cheek.

"Why 'of course'?" Pat cocked his head.

"He published in the late 1700s if memory serves me correctly. He's a big deal within academia but not in Twitter world." Fiona pulled a face.

I sat up straight. "Wait. Did he come up with 'Revenge is profitable, gratitude is expensive' line?"

"That sounds familiar." Fee queried her cell.

"Remember I received a text with that quote. I thought Susie sent it after Fart Gate."

"Yep. That was Gibbon." Fiona set her phone aside.

"I need to call Ham."

"Ham? Why Ham?"

"He knows about the quotes. He's been getting them as well."

"Quotes?" She put a hand to her breast. "You've received more and went to Ham and didn't even tell me?"

I didn't get a chance to answer. My phone rang, immediately followed by Fiona's. We knew, without answering, we were being summoned. Time to circle the wagons. Time to get off the grid and retreat to a fortress where photographers and the press couldn't reach us. Neither of us answered our phones. It wasn't necessary.

"We should get going," I said. "We can talk in the car."

Fee nodded. "Pat, go get Maya. We'll meet you there."

"Why?" Pat asked.

"Please, Pat. The poor girl has never had to deal with this before. Media dogs will be crawling all over her like she's Princess Diana back from the dead. Something tells me Maya won't like that and — "

"What about Agnes?" Pat interrupted. This was his first official Carmichael rally around the flag, but he wasn't thinking like an amateur, and thank God for that; my mind was reeling so much I wasn't thinking of the big picture: Maya and Agnes.

"Yes, please get her, too. I can't bear to think …" Fiona gave him a shove to get him going.

"Where does Maya live?" He gripped his car keys like they were a weapon.

"She's at work," I said.

Pat nodded and left.

"Are you sure we should bring Maya into the viper's den?" I asked Fiona once the coast was clear. A vision of Grandmother having one of her goons escort Maya and Agnes out of her house invaded my mind. "What if she tosses them out?"

"It's a risk we have to take. Look, we've never dealt with a man like Eckley. I'm not ashamed to admit we're in over our heads. Grandmother and the goons will know what to do. Ham obviously didn't take care of the problem." Her facial expression softened. "I know you've been itching to declare your independence, but now isn't the time. Think of Maya." She put a hand on each of my shoulders. "She and Agnes need Grandmother in their corner. Besides, Maya is in one of the photos. The old lady will want her off the grid and not chatting with bloggers."

"That's what I'm worried about. Once Grandmother is in their corner, how do we get her out?"

"One problem at a time, Ains. One problem at a time."

Grandmother sat in her plush chair in her "office," aka her bedroom. It wasn't a typical bedroom. It had a bed, of course, but that was on the other side of an elaborate Chinese-silk screen none of us were allowed behind. Fiona had once dared me to peek, but the plan was foiled by Grandmother's assistant, who always popped up like a ninja at inopportune moments. The room also contained a desk, a couch, and several wing chairs. Grandmother, of course, only sat in the largest and most luxurious chair. Dragon-red, it resembled a throne.

"Chuck has been busy."

I stared at her, dumbfounded. How did she know about Chuck?

"Don't stand there with your mouth open, catching flies. There's not much I don't know. Every time Fiona pings Chuck, he alerts my staff." She didn't even have the decency to look conniving; she looked bored, like I should have known all along. And I should have. What an amateur move!

"So when I told you about Maya, you already knew every-thing?" I said, trying to stop my revulsion from registering in my voice.

Grandmother waved me away. "Please, Ainsley. I don't have time for questions you already know the answers to. You used to be bright."

What in the hell did that mean?

She leaned on her cane with both hands. "And you used to be one of my favorites. Hard as nails, you were, always putting the quest first."

Why was she talking like Yoda? Although she was just as wrinkled and frail as the Jedi Master.

Tears formed in my eyes, but I willed them away.

"Do you want to know what I plan to do?" she asked.

Actually, I preferred not knowing a thing, but that wasn't an option. Grandmother always had to be pulling all the strings, and she made damn sure we understood who the puppet master was.

"The way I see it," she said through gritted teeth, clearly frustrated by my zipped trap, "is this *relationship* will run its course in due time, so why not end it now?"

Run its course! She said it like Maya was a dose of the flu.

"I don't have the flu, Grandmother." I resisted the urge to spit the word "Grandmother" with more venom. "I'm not infatuated with Maya. I'm in love with her."

She raised an eyebrow, implying "so what?"

I gave her my best steely-eyed glare.

"And you think you have a future with this girl? You are aware of her mother, of course."

Was the Eckley ball about to drop?

"Do you really think you can be with a girl whose mother was a whore?"

"She wasn't a whore," I spat.

"Mistress, whore, the other woman — none of it will look good. We've cultivated your narrative since before you were born, Ainsley. We've conducted focus tests on so many scenarios. Maya was never in the equation. There are plenty of other girls — respectable girls. I've already got my eye on three potential — "

"You can't force me to love someone else!"

A bark of laughter exploded from her chest, surprising the hell out of me because I didn't think she had that much energy left. "I'm not asking you to love anyone. Marriage and love …" She waved away the connection between the two like she was swatting away a bothersome gnat.

"What made you this way?" I asked.

My grandmother flinched slightly. "Don't be impertinent."

"I'm not. I want to understand. You've been controlling all of our lives for decades now. What gave you that power?"

Her smile suggested an evilness I hadn't considered. "You don't get it. I don't need anyone's permission, and you're ignoring that this family would be nowhere without me."

"Only if we let you."

"What would you do without me? My connections? My money?" Her voice was getting stronger. I was clearly pressing the right buttons, or the wrong ones.

"And if I don't want your connections or your money, what then?" I crossed my arms, not out of defiance, just to still my shaking body.

"Oh, you silly girl! You think you have life all figured out. You're just like your father. He stood there once, telling me he was in love. He did as he was told."

"I'm not my father. I'm not my mother. And I'm sure as hell not you."

"But you are a Carmichael." She stood shakily and ambled toward me, the tap of her cane accompanying each step. Stretching out bony fingers, she gripped my jaw. "You have a decision to make. Maya or me."

I winced, surprised by the strength of her fingers, her nails digging into my flesh.

Then I smiled. She mirrored my smile, sure I was going to make the right choice. "I choose both."

To her credit, Grandmother didn't scream. She stood there, leaning on her cane, with a look in her eyes I'd never seen before. I wish I could say she looked beaten, but that would be a lie. Her wily brain was busily plotting against me, and I almost thumped my chest and said, "Bring it, old woman."

"And how do you think that'll work?"

"Because you need me as much as I need you. I'm the Chosen One, remember? I'm the one you've been grooming."

"As simple as that, you think you can make demands of me?"

"I'd rather we work together. Times are changing, Grandmother. Wake up. People are coming after this family, and if we're not smart, they'll win."

She cackled. "Little Ainsley thinks she's holding the winning hand. When are you going to learn I can make you or break you? I don't work with you or anyone." She dismissed me with a nod of her head. "Think about it."

Fiona stood outside Grandmother's door.

"Have you been out here the whole time?" I straightened my shirt.

She nodded. "How'd it go?"

When she saw my face, she strode over, gave me one of her curt nods, and said, "Well, now. And then there was only us."

I started to protest, saying this was my fight, but her palm in the air made it clear.

My cell rang. Ham. Before I could say hello, my brother said, "I take it I should come over to The Cottage."

"That's sweet of you, but I don't think that would be wise. Grandmother is on the warpath."

"Probably not. But I'm coming anyway. I have to meet this Maya." I could feel the smile in his voice. "Besides, I have some information." He hung up before I could register another complaint.

"Circling the wagons around the new leader," Fiona said to no one in particular.

I didn't like the sound of it. Ham wasn't Grandmother, but he was still power hungry. And if Chuck had been on her payroll the entire time, what did that mean about Tess and Rita?

Ham arrived with more information about the Twitter-bombing of our family. Apparently, a website claiming responsibility had popped up overnight. According to the site, the Carmichaels were filled with dykes (me), heroin addicts (Rory), chinks (Mei), adulterers (Mom and Uncle Owen), druggies (Fiona), and my personal fave, witches. At first, I supposed they meant Grandmother, but the photographer had snapped an image of my sister in her judge's robes and mistaken her for a practicing sorceress. Even my super-serious and uptight sister giggled when she heard that news. She wasn't bothered enough by her Web image to consider flying home.

Edward Gibbon didn't stop with the living Carmichaels, either. A litany of accusations about deceased Carmichaels and questions about Uncle Liam's disappearance had been published on the site as well. Pretty much every Carmichael disgrace had been smeared all over the Web. I cringed at the thought of how many people were viewing the Cassidy video, which was prominently displayed on the home page.

The name of the website was clear: *The Fall of the Carmichael Reign.* Given the amount of dirt they'd dug up, the title wasn't far off the mark. But why now?

My mind skittered to Maya and Eckley.

CHAPTER
twenty

PAT PULLED UP IN FRONT of The Cottage in his beat-up Volvo with a bewildered-looking Agnes and Maya in the back. What would they think of me and of my family now? All they'd wanted was to fly under the radar, and today Maya's photo was smeared all over the Internet. I sighed. Fiona rubbed my back before shoving me out the door to greet them.

"Thanks," I told her over my shoulder, "for keeping it real."

She smiled sheepishly. "Right now, it isn't about you. Remember that."

I dipped my head in shame. She was right, as usual. No feeling sorry for myself. Now that Maya's photo was out there, investigative journalists and bloggers wouldn't let her be. The truth would come out. Maya would never be a nobody again, and it was my fault.

Agnes stepped out of the car first, grinning when her eyes landed on me. "There you are!" She embraced me, and all the tension melted from my body.

Maya, still in her work clothes, was standing next to her, but she gave no indication she was relieved to see me. "Shell-shocked" was the word that came to mind when I stared into her glassy gray eyes.

"It's going to be okay," Agnes reassured us both.

"You aren't mad?" I asked.

Agnes waved the idea away. "You can't control the nutjobs in this world. The only person you are responsible for is you. Remember that, or you'll drive yourself crazy."

Oh, how I wished Grandmother had heard that. She, of course, would have wholeheartedly disagreed.

Out of the corner of my eye, I observed Pat whisk Fiona into a hug, clearly putting their relationship woes aside. She bent her head and snuggled into his chest, relieved to be in his arms. Witnessing the tenderness between the two of them made my heart ache. I could see them always having each other, while Maya and I …

I returned my gaze to Maya, but I was again met with no emotion.

Since 2003, Maya had done everything right. She had avoided the Internet and social media and she didn't have a cell phone — she'd made it her life's mission to go unnoticed. Then I'd entered the picture, and now she'd never be free again.

Fiona grabbed my arm and yanked me out of the kitchen in The Cottage. Ham had transformed the house into the headquarters for damage control. "You have to talk to them."

"I was just talking with Agnes when you manhandled me out of the room." I massaged my arm.

"No, I mean you have to tell Maya and Agnes that you know."

"Know what?" I feigned innocence, but the meaning behind her words hit me like a tsunami. My throat closed, and I gasped for breath.

"If they hear about it from someone else, it won't be good."

"Who here would tell?" I knew the answer, but I couldn't admit it to myself.

Fiona cocked her head and then shook it in disbelief.

"Okay, okay. I'll tell them."

"Now! You need to tell them *now*. I'll send them to you in the library." Before I could stop her, Fiona left. Within moments, Maya and Agnes entered the room where I was nervously flipping the pages of a dictionary on a stand.

Maya looked even more perplexed and angry than she had when she'd arrived, and Agnes … well, she looked like Agnes — full of love. I watched her take in the wall-to-wall books, the fancy library ladders, and plush leather chairs and couches. It was a paradise for booklovers, and it made her eyes widen in amazement.

"Hiya!" I wanted to kick myself for being such an ass. Like that would that make everything all right. *Come on, Ainsley. Pull it together.*

From the look on Maya's face, my hiya had definitely hit the wrong chord.

"Why don't the two of you have a seat?" I motioned to a leather couch. They sat facing me, not speaking. Even Agnes's smile had been replaced with a befuddled frown. Standing behind a couch opposite them, I felt farther away from Maya than I would have if I were talking to her by phone — from Egypt.

"I think it's time I confess something." I let out a puff of air and stared into Maya's eyes. "Do you remember the first time we kissed?"

She turned bright red, and I realized that probably wasn't the best way to start, not in front of Agnes. Now that it was out, though, I had no choice but to keep plugging along.

Agnes seemed amused by my discomfort and Maya's embarrassment, so at least there was one friendly face in the room.

"After we, uh, kissed and you freaked out, well …"

Maya and Agnes stared at me, dumbfounded.

"That was when I started … And then we had dinner with Agnes, and the pieces started to fall into place."

How could I explain this properly? Started what? Unearthing the secret they wanted to protect at all costs? I couldn't say that. *Sugarcoat it some, Ains.*

"I know who you are, Maya. And Agnes, I know about you."

Their expressions told me I hadn't added nearly enough syrup to the intensity of my words.

Maya cleared her throat. "Would you mind telling us what you think you know?"

I blinked, and then fluttered my lashes several more times, thinking.

Maya watched me carefully, and I wondered how much our future depended on how I responded at this moment. *No pressure. No pressure whatsoever.*

"Well, you see, Chuck ..."

Maya and Agnes exchanged a look that suggested I was certifiably crazy. Maybe I was. Maybe that was the true Carmichael curse — being power mad.

I closed my eyes and blurted, "Maya, I love you. I never thought I would find someone like you, and when I did, well, it changed me. You changed me. All of this" — I waved to the room — "none of it matters anymore."

She remained stone-faced.

I had to get to the point or I would lose her — if I hadn't already.

"I know your real name." I looked at Agnes. "And I know you aren't Maya's birth mom."

Both of them exchanged a worried glance before squaring their shoulders.

"I've known for a while now. I'm so sorry."

"Who's Chuck?" asked Maya.

"A hacker," I said, immediately covering my mouth as I heard how that must have sounded to a non-Carmichael.

"You hired a hacker?" Maya jumped off the couch.

"I ..." I slowly backed away.

Maya turned to Agnes. "We need to go."

"You can't," I said.

They both raised their brows.

"I'm not the only one who knows," I blurted without realizing this statement would do nothing to alleviate their fear. "No, I mean ..." I rubbed at my eyes. "This isn't going well. I'm not trying to frighten you. I wanted to be honest."

Maya snorted. "And that's supposed to make me feel better? You spied into things that were none of your business. That's your definition of honesty? Do you remember when you asked me to never dig into your past? Never read Susie Q's blog? I stuck to my promise, and all along you were digging into mine."

"I know, and I'm truly sorry. I thought you were going to use me or something."

Maya staggered backward several steps.

"I know how awful it sounds … It's happened to me before, and after that kiss, I feared the worst. I had to know more about you to protect myself." I added, "For us."

"You stuck your nose into my business to save our relationship? Puh-lease. You're a Carmichael, through and through. I was a fool to think differently." Hardness steeled her eyes.

I stared back, stunned.

"Before or after?" she demanded.

"Before or after what? The kiss?"

"Before you slept with me? Did you know everything?" She crossed her arms.

My cheeks flushed, and Agnes glanced away, giving us some privacy. "Oh, Maya, it's not like that. It really isn't. I didn't know everything until very recently. There wasn't much to find out until I realized your birth name."

She stared at me with the coldest of gray eyes. This conversation couldn't have gone any worse.

Fiona popped her head in. "You've been requested."

I turned to Maya. "Please don't go yet. I'll be back as soon as possible, and we can discuss this."

Fiona cleared her throat.

"I'll be right there!" I snapped. "Grandmother can wait."

Fiona's face whipped back like I'd smacked her. No one had ever insisted Grandmother could wait.

"That's not what I meant," Fiona said. "All three of you have been requested."

"What? Why?" I crossed my arms defiantly, even though resistance was futile. Fiona knew as much as I did, and she wasn't forcing my hand. My last name controlled all of my actions. I'd been stuck in a trap since birth.

Maya stared at Fiona and then turned to Agnes, who shrugged, suggesting the game was up. She didn't lose her smile, but she no longer oozed confidence. Maya refused to meet my eyes.

"Fine, we'll see your grandmother, and then we're leaving." Maya stormed out of the room.

Agnes waited for me. I couldn't tell whether she was being polite or whether she felt sorry for me, but I was betting on the latter.

Mother and Grandmother were alone in the room. I had expected the fixers to be present, but perhaps Grandmother didn't want them to witness our interaction. Or maybe they were too busy fixing the clusterfuck, and they'd get Grandmother's report later.

Tea and cookies sat on a tray near the matriarch, and my grandmother gestured for me to serve. I forced down angry words and focused on my social duty, carefully pouring four cups from the Wedgewood teapot that had been brought over from England three hundred years ago. My mother's great-great-grandmother refused to leave home without her precious teapot and cups. Somehow, they had miraculously survived the perilous trip, and I prayed some of their luck would rub off on me.

Mother declined tea. She was gulping scotch like it was water. In other circumstances, I would have worried how it might look to Agnes and Maya, but today it was the least of my concerns.

"Nice to see you again, Maya," my grandmother said.

I bristled. The old crone still had a sharp memory, and she must have recognized Maya from Nadine's or from the recent photo clogging all social media feeds.

Maya just stared. Agnes sat off to the side, ramrod straight as she stared mutely out the bay window. Considering the whole

Texas situation, she'd probably experienced more than her fair share of intimidating experiences with powerful people. Maya would have been too young at the time, but I doubt she forgot much either, which didn't bode well for me.

I had to make a move, but what? Ham always said, "Go big or go home." *Here goes nothing.*

"Grandmother, Mother, I'd like you to meet my girlfriend, Maya, and her mother, Agnes."

Agnes nodded a greeting but remained tightlipped.

Grandmother laughed. "No introductions are necessary. Agnes, you look well. And Maya, you've grown since the last time I saw you. What was that — fifteen years ago?" She used a silver demitasse spoon to stir a lump of sugar into her tea, each clink against the fine china reverberating like a hammer blow.

"What in the hell are you talking about?" I sputtered.

Seconds ticked by.

Still no one spoke.

Finally, Grandmother told Agnes, "It seems we have a slight issue."

Agnes tipped her head.

"A Texas issue," my grandmother continued.

"Why is that your concern?" Maya snapped.

I admired her bravery. I really did.

"Oh, the jig's up, Maya. You can drop your façade. With your photo smeared all over the Web, kissing my granddaughter, do you really think you can remain hidden?"

Maya opened her mouth, but Agnes patted her niece's thigh, effectively shutting her up before she said something they both might regret. Grandmother flashed them a thin smile that was anything but comforting. "This is not how I foresaw things." She stared at Maya, obviously trying to force the right response.

"What are you saying?" Agnes asked, using an authoritative tone that surprised me.

Grandmother set her cup down and pursed her lips as if carefully weighing her words. The last couple of days had done a number on her. She looked tired, where she never had before. And old. The wrinkles on her forehead and around her eyes had nearly doubled, or had I never bothered to notice?

"I don't want to interfere with your life, but this situation has forced my hand. The way I see it, you have two options. Option one: hope for the best. Option two: let me help you. You'll get new identities, a new home. Just like we did last time."

"Last time?" I warbled.

Grandmother stared at me, shaking her head as if I should know everything instinctively. Then she narrowed her eyes on Maya. "You can try to stay out of the limelight, until … But, times are a-changing. Once something goes up on the Internet, it's always there for someone else to find. It won't be easy to disappear again, but what alternative do you have?" Grandmother stirred her tea again, urging them to face reality. "Plastic surgery is an option, if we have to go that route."

"Plastic surgery?" I shook the thought out of my head. "And what do you mean *last time*?" I asked again.

Maya turned her back to me.

"Will someone please tell me what's going on?" I stomped a foot.

It was as if I were a ghost in the room — one who couldn't be heard.

No one looked at or spoke to me.

Maya and Agnes whispered behind their hands. Maya said something, which prompted Agnes to violently shake her head. Maya didn't respond, although she seemed to hold her ground. Her aunt's shoulders drooped as she whispered again. Maya nodded resolutely. Agnes rubbed at her eye. Was she wiping away a tear?

Agnes cleared her throat. "We choose option two," she said.

"What? No! You can't." I placed a hand on my chest to stop all the air from gushing out of my body.

"Ainsley," Mother said, "it's for the best."

Ignoring her, I spoke directly to Agnes, since Maya refused to meet my eyes. "I love her."

"I know," Agnes responded, her voice soft with understanding.

Everyone else, including Maya, resembled petrified trees: stalwart and immovable.

"There has to be another option," I cried. "There has to be! New identities? Plastic surgery? Do you really want to do that?"

"And what do you propose, Ainsley?" Grandmother asked. "Ride off into the sunset and live happily ever after? Hope this media storm blows over?"

"Fix it!" I shouted. "That's what you do. You're the great Carmichael matriarch! Do what you do best."

"You silly girl. It was reckless of you to continue a relationship once I allowed Chuck to provide some kernels of truth. Do you really think love conquers all?" Grandmother tapped her cane on the floor. "You were reckless with Maya's feelings, knowing what you knew, and you were reckless with her safety. How'd you think she'd stay hidden? And now I have to save Maya and Agnes from you and …" She shook her head.

No one in the room had mentioned Eckley, but his presence loomed over our heads.

However, I couldn't focus on that. "I was reckless?" I waggled my finger at her. "What about your role in all of this? How did you even get involved fifteen years ago?"

"That doesn't concern you, now does it? You're the one who's so focused on the future, your future with Maya. How funny that you want to know how we all got here. Young people just don't understand!"

"Of course it concerns me! It concerns me, Maya, and Agnes." I paced.

"Sit down, Ainsley!" my grandmother commanded with a wobbly lilt in her words.

My mother swirled her scotch, desperate to be in control of something — anything.

I studied her. "You knew all along, didn't you, Mother?"

She stared at her glass.

"At Nadine's, both of you knew. It must have been a wonderful game for you two. Whose idea was it? To have Maya called in at the last second? We never have two servers, but you probably arranged for Maya to appear when she did to test my mettle, or to trap me. You've been following every second of her life. You probably knew we'd meet in class." I rubbed my forehead. "Everything is starting to fall into place. I knew something fishy was going on at Nadine's." I wiped my sweaty palms on my jeans.

"That may be the case. But you were too busy putting your foot in it and not thinking. Face it. You aren't ready to play with the grown-ups." Grandmother tapped her cane.

"Play? This isn't a game. This is my life. Their lives." I waved to Maya and Agnes.

Grandmother's controlling smile suggested none of us mattered.

I turned to Maya. "I snooped out of love. These two" — I pointed to Grandmother and Mother — "only do things to control people. They only think about one thing: How is this person helpful? If you trust them, you'll never be free. You'll always be their pawns."

Maya looked to Grandmother and Mother, and Agnes whispered behind her hand.

I returned to that night at Nadine's. "Calling Maya in at the last second," I muttered to no one in particular. "That was probably your doing, wasn't it, Grandmother? Just one way to torture me. The great puppeteer! The fucking mind game." I about-faced to Maya. "Can't you see what's going on? The manipulation?" I stared hard, trying to convey my meaning: *Think like Louisa May Alcott, who chose autonomy over the easy life.*

Grandmother cleared her throat but failed to speak, which answered everything.

My mind whirled, trying to unscramble all the pieces into the real narrative, not the created one. "I never stopped to think why so many daily briefings included information on the Eckleys. But you wanted me to know, on some level, the effort you've gone to — for me. For my future. But why did you get involved in their lives in the first place?" I tapped my fingertips together. "Political capital? To have Eckley cornered and gain access to his billions? You swooped in, saved Agnes and Maya, and then kept them in your back pocket all these years. They were collateral in case you needed them. If I didn't know you, I'd think that was ludicrous. Who could be so determined? So conniving? So cruel? Who would plot that far in advance? But that's the Carmichael way: always focus on the long game. Hell, I wouldn't rule out that you were complicit in the death of Maya's mom. Or that you've doctored evidence to set up Eckley, to keep him in line, and possibly his wife, the governor of Texas. The options are limitless, but you're always working to cover your bases, aren't you? That's what I am. An option. The Chosen One. And that's what Maya is."

Maya's gray eyes soaked up every accusation I made. Then she leapt up and charged the old woman. Agnes, who was one step ahead, interceded, holding her back.

"Let me go!" Maya shouted.

I stood helplessly as she stormed out of the room. No one, not even Grandmother, would make eye contact with me.

"I hope you two are happy! I'm finally seeing everything — the good, the bad, and the ugly. So ugly I'm ashamed to have the last name Carmichael."

CHAPTER
twenty-one

AGNES AND I STUMBLED ONTO the veranda, where Grover made a beeline toward her.

Pat laughed. "I think he's hoping for more of your home cooking."

"I'd be more than happy to oblige if I had access to a kitchen. Cooking soothes me. It helps me think." Agnes scratched behind Grover's ear, and he kicked out his back leg in time with the scratching.

"Can we go?" Maya appeared around the corner.

Fiona shook her head. "That wouldn't be advisable. Word has it your neighborhood is crawling with press, and so is Pat's. We can go back to The Cottage, where it's less … stressful."

That settled it. Our party moved to the small house, but Maya kept as much distance as possible from me. Agnes kept flashing me supportive looks that suggested I give Maya time. She might not be Maya's real mom, but she always would be in my mind. Any woman who would risk so much deserved the title.

Agnes raided the fridge, pantry, and freezers in the garage and hauled in enough food to feed the whole Carmichael clan. Right then, Ham and Mei joined us, quickly followed by Rory. Not much was said, but the mood was lightening, although Maya continued to scowl.

Soon enough, Maya slipped out of the side door in the kitchen, with Grover in tow. Agnes, noticing as I had, sidled up to me.

"Go talk to her." She nodded in the direction Maya had taken.

I shook my head. "I'm the last person she wants to talk to." My eyes misted over.

"That may be true, but you're the only one who can reach her right now. She's mad, yes, but she's more embarrassed than anything." Agnes rubbed my shoulder.

"About what? I'm the one who should be embarrassed. My family ..." A sob swallowed the rest of my words.

"Ever since Maya was a little girl, she's only wanted to be normal. Not her mother's daughter, not ..." Agnes looked at me to see whether I caught her meaning.

I did.

"If you can't do it for Maya, do it for me." Agnes whispered.

I half laughed, half sniffled. "That's not fair."

"I know, but it's the right thing to do."

Dammit, she was right.

I found Maya and Grover down by the water. She was chucking Grover's ball as far as she could, and the terrier gleefully barreled back and forth, oblivious to Maya's hunched shoulders and miserable mood.

She reached back to heave the ball again and spied me. She froze in place, and I froze mid-step as Grover yipped at our feet, frustrated she wasn't throwing his ball. Turning to the beach again, she threw the ball, but with much less force.

"Hi," I said.

"Hi." Her tone was frigid, and I imagined myself standing in the middle of Antarctica.

"Can we talk?"

Grover returned, panting. He flopped onto his back and rolled around madly, making happy grunting sounds. He needed a rest.

"It seems I'm under your family's thumb for the rest of my life, so we can do whatever you want." She stared at the water and hooked her thumbs through the belt loops on her jeans.

"Please, Maya. Don't …" I put my hand on her back, but she shrugged it off.

"Don't what? State the obvious? I'm at your mercy. I should be thankful, I guess, that you were kind enough to look past who and what I am. A bastard." Slowly, she turned to face me. "Thanks for that. Thanks for all of this." She waved a hand pathetically through the air.

I wished she hadn't used the word bastard. I didn't see her that way. None of that mattered to me.

"Oh, right. Carmichaels talk around things instead of confronting simple facts. My mother was a dancer — 'stripper' would be the Susie Q word. Eckley liked what he saw. He made her his own. That's the way of the rich." She glared at me. "I wasn't in the equation, of course, but no matter how hard you try to plan, shit happens. If you learn one thing from this, Ainsley, I hope that's it. You can't plan for everything. The long game always evolves and more than likely it's the little guys that get trampled." She stomped off, and Grover snorted in my direction and chased after her.

Screw it. I trailed after her, too. "Maya, wait!"

As expected, she didn't heed my words. I sprinted and got in front of her. With both hands on her shoulders, I said, "What is it you want me to say?"

Maya ground her teeth.

"I'm sorry. I'm sorry I dug into your past. I'm sorry your name got out. I'm sorry I ruined your life. And I'm sorry you met me! Is that what you want me to say? That everything is my fault? My fault because I'm a Carmichael?"

She remained speechless, but the tension in her shoulders eased a little.

"If that's what you want me to say, then I'm sorry, but I'm not going to say I'm sorry I met you."

Maya blinked rapidly.

"None of this is my fault. And it's not yours either. Everything that's been going on is out of our control. It has been since day one. You didn't choose your parents, and I didn't choose my family. Those were the cards we were dealt."

More tension slid from her body.

"What we can choose is up to us. Do you want to go around being your mother's daughter, or do you just want to be Maya? Or Carisa? I don't know about you, but I'm sick and tired of being Ainsley Carmichael. I want to be just Ainsley. I want people to know me for who I am, not who others want me to be — *demand* me to be."

Grover barked right on cue, as if he was saying *damn right*. Or possibly *throw my ball*, which Maya did. He zipped off, and Maya followed him with her eyes.

"I know this has been hard on you. Not just today. All of it. And then finding out that I knew …" I let out a bark of mirthless laughter. "I'm sure that didn't feel good at all. But ask yourself something: Are you angry with me for knowing, or are you angry that you never got the chance to tell me?"

"I'm angry you broke your promise to me. You of all people. I trusted you, and I don't trust anyone but Agnes." Her face darkened with rage.

I took a step back and studied a retreating wave. "I know," I whispered.

"I kept my word." She had to dig the dagger deeper into my heart.

"I never doubted you. Do you want to know why I made you promise not to read Susie Q's blog?"

She remained speechless.

"Because I didn't want you to see this." I whipped my iPhone out of my back jeans pocket. "When I was sixteen, I fell for a friend."

Maya stiffened.

"She was gay," I explained, "but what I didn't know was that she was on Susie Q's bankroll." I fiddled with the phone. "They concocted an elaborate plan to humiliate me."

I hit play on the video.

Cassidy and I were sitting on her bed, confessing how much we liked each other. It was obvious we were going to kiss. When I leaned in, Cassidy put a finger on my lips. "Wait," she said. "I want this to be special. Close your eyes."

Unable to watch what was about to happen, to relive that day, I closed my eyes on the beach, too.

A rustling sound came over the video, and I heard my sixteen-year-old voice ask, "What are you doing?"

"Don't you trust me?" Cassidy giggled.

My younger self chirped, "With my heart."

I cringed at how pathetic I sounded.

Maya's sharp intake of breath alerted me it was about to happen.

The betrayal.

Cassidy's voice on the video said, "Okay, keep your eyes closed, but I'm ready."

And then the shriek, followed by an ear-piercing squeal.

"This just in folks. Carmichaels will do anything for a vote." Then Susie Q's laughter.

I hadn't ever actually watched the video, but I'd relived it a million times since then in my head.

I hadn't kissed Cassidy that day; I'd kissed a piglet.

"In less than twelve hours, everyone at school had seen the video. It went viral on YouTube. For the next year, everyone at school called me Piglet." I wiped my eyes with a sleeve.

Maya nodded as if she was starting to understand, but she didn't attempt to reassure me.

"At the time, I thought Cassidy had gone to brush her teeth or something," I explained. "I later learned Susie Q had been waiting downstairs with the animal. The entire thing was a setup. It had been from day one."

Maya blackened the screen on my phone and handed it back to me.

"After that, I threw myself into the Carmichael quest. I vowed I'd never let another person into my life, vowed never to trust. Then I met you. When you stormed off after our first kiss, I panicked. I thought …"

"That I worked for Susie." She filled in the blanks.

"That's why I started digging. It wasn't right, but that's why. I'd known Cassidy since grade school. She'd been my best friend."

Maya busied herself with digging the toe of her shoe into the wet sand.

"No matter how hard I try to shake off my last name, everything circles back to the political shenanigans pulling all the strings since the first Carmichael set foot on American soil. You aren't alone in feeling manipulated. Our pasts our different, but we both ended up here. Me, I'm tired of the game. How about you?" I wrapped my arms tightly across my chest.

Maya shaded her eyes, rubbing her brow. Maybe she needed time to absorb the information. I spun on my heel and marched back to the house.

Grover let out a yip that positively meant *good riddance*. It took everything I had not to turn around to see Maya's expression, to gain some insight. But the fear of what I might see kept me moving forward.

"Be careful." I shouted over my shoulder. "The press pack is right over that ridge." To emphasize my point, a news helicopter buzzed overhead.

Agnes waited for me on the porch. She still wore her apron, and from the looks of it, the crew was making progress on creating a delicious home-cooked meal. She wiped her hands on her apron before pulling me into a hug.

I wished I could cry, really have a meltdown, and feel better. Instead, all of my emotions brimmed under the surface. Carmichaels didn't cry.

Agnes pulled back, peered into my face, and sighed. "Let me go talk to her."

Maya had worked her way back to The Cottage, near the veranda, but she was taking a stand by not coming inside. Agnes joined her, and they sat on a rock with Grover at their feet, standing guard.

CHAPTER
twenty-two

TEN MINUTES LATER, I WATCHED them walk, arm in arm, back to the deck.

"I'm going to make some tea and check on Pat in the kitchen. That boy can cook." Agnes smiled bashfully and left me alone with Maya.

Maya refused to look in my direction. I took off my sweater and handed it to her. At first she didn't budge, but after a while, she reluctantly took it. Agnes appeared, saw Maya wearing my sweater, smiled, and handed me a Whitlock sweatshirt. It was massive on me, but comforting. I tipped my head in thanks, and she left us again, without speaking.

Maya slumped into one of the wicker chairs. "What else do you know about me?" she barked, but her tone didn't have much bite left.

"What do you mean?"

She lifted her head. "You know about my mom. What else did Chuck find?"

Oh, that. Right.

I sat in the chair to her right and tucked my knees to my chest. The temperature was drastically plummeting now that the clouds had dissipated overhead. "Honestly, I don't know that much. I know you're intelligent, kind, loving, and you make the best coffee." I laughed nervously. "I think your favorite color is black." I paused, not knowing how to continue. "You don't open up much, Maya. It's one of the things I admire about you, but it also drives me crazy."

"You don't open up much either." Her smile sagged. "Maybe that's one of the things I fell for — a kindred spirit."

Agnes appeared with two steaming teacups, handing one to each of us before she turned and fled.

Neither of us spoke. I held the cup under my chin for warmth. "Green."

I turned to Maya. "What?"

"My favorite color is green."

A smile forced its way onto my face. "Green. I never would have guessed. You never wear green."

She shrugged. "It was one of the first things I noticed when we moved here. Everything was so green. Back home, everything was brown. Hopeless and bleak. Here everything always seems alive, even in the dead of winter."

I nodded my understanding and gave her arm a squeeze.

"I know your favorite book is *Little Women*."

Maya nodded. "And you like David McCullough," she said.

The tension started to leave my body. At least she was speaking to me again without looking like she was about to spit in my face.

Ham approached, smiling. "Hi, Maya. I'm Ham."

Maya shook his hand.

"It's a pleasure meeting you. Ains has never brought a girl home before."

Maya smiled awkwardly, which made my brother laugh. "Of course, given the circumstances, you might not be impressed by that. But you should be. I've been worried for years about my little sister. I never thought she'd find ..." He pointed to Maya to finish his train of thought.

His genuine smile softened Maya's grimace.

"Would you mind if I borrowed Ainsley for a moment?" he asked.

Maya shook her head. Part of me felt guilty for her "deer in headlights" look; the other part was frustrated. Opening up about Cassidy wasn't easy, but Maya hadn't said a word about it. Why?

"You're welcome to join us." I placed a hand on her shoulder.

"I should check on Mom," she said with a weak smile.

"If you change your mind, we'll be in the office next to the library." I leveled my eyes on her grays. "You have a say in this if you want."

Fiona, Mei, and two women I didn't recognize, sat in folding chairs at a long, makeshift table piled with overstuffed manila folders. On one wall hung the photos from online. While Agnes and Pat prepared a feast for the army, this was how the rest of us dealt with stress — working our way out of the mess. The office had become the unofficial war room. Operation Save the Carmichael Family had begun.

Pictures of the suspects hung on a wall on the far side of the room. Raymond Eckley's mug was dead center, next to his wife, and with strings to possible helpers, including Susie Q. I walked to his photo, trying to identify any resemblance to Maya. I traced the outline of his eyes. "They have the same eyes," I muttered.

"Who?" One of the fixers I hadn't met yet joined me. Was she Tess or Rita?

I swiveled to Fiona.

"Haven't said a word," she said, putting her palms up.

"About what?" asked the other fixer.

I raised my eyebrows at Ham.

"Ains, remember the two women I said you never wanted to meet?"

I nodded. "The ones who have been reading my text messages."

Ham sniffed, absorbing my indignation. "This" — he waved to the board — "has forced all of our hands. Meet Rita George."

He pointed to the reedy woman standing next to me. "And Tess Deaver." He nodded to the portly woman at the table.

Neither resembled Olivia Pope from *Scandal* in any way, shape, or form. My confidence in them, and in Ham, nearly shattered.

"You can trust them with your life," Ham continued.

I wavered, deciding whether I had a third option after already burning the grandmother bridge. Not seeing one, I said, "I'm not worried about my life." That got the room's attention.

Ham crossed his arms and leaned against the doorjamb. "Maya?" he mumbled, nodding.

My non-answer was the only way to answer.

Mei sucked in a deep breath and said, "Fuck. What are we missing?" Her blurry eyes suggested she, along with Ham and his fixers, had been racking her brain well before the storm unfurled.

"I think we have to fill them in," Fiona said.

I gritted my teeth but didn't make an objection.

"Only if everyone promises never to utter a word of this outside of this room." I locked eyes on everyone, and each gave a succinct nod. Then I filled them in on what I knew.

After I finished, Ham's face reddened. "You should have called me right away. All of this may have been avoided." He pounded his hand on the suspect wall.

"Ham!" Fee shouted.

I stabbed my finger in his direction. "I told you about the quotes — all Edward Gibbon quotes, I might add. That was a clue. Where did those lead?"

He sucked in air. "Once you found out about Maya and Eckley, I should have been your first call. You're in way over your head."

"Because you're the big shot now? Working in the White House qualifies you for the gig?" I mimed whoop-dee-do with my hands.

"Did it ever cross your mind that Eckley could have been sending the quotes?"

"Of course it did, but I dismissed him."

His eyes widened. "Why?"

"Because I thought a Texan would reference the Alamo."

He staggered back a step, shaking his head. "You think you're so clever. At first, you're sure it's Susie. Then, you write off Eckley because you think all Texans are rednecks. You need to learn that even though you're clever, others are better manipulators. God, you're such a child." He scoffed.

"I am not!"

"Then stop acting like one," he roared, taking a step closer and jabbing a finger in my face.

Mei inserted herself between us. "Don't let him get to you. He's angry with himself, not you. We sensed something was going to happen, but we never suspected everyone was in the crosshairs." She flipped around to confront Ham. "You know this isn't her fault. No one in this room is to blame. Big picture, Ham. Big picture." She patted his scruffy cheek. "Whoever is responsible wants this. They want us to tear into each other instead of banding together to fight."

Ham stepped back, massaging his temple. "I'm sorry, Ains. I didn't mean it."

"Maybe we should take a moment. To regroup," Fee suggested.

"No," I said. "I want to nail whoever did this. This isn't just about the Carmichaels. It's also about the people we love." I ran my finger over Maya's image on the board.

Ham placed his hand on Mei's shoulder, his eyes flickering with determination.

Rita fished a close-up of Maya from a pile on the makeshift table. Holding it up to Eckley's, she said, "They do have the same eyes, but …"

"You need proof?" Ham asked, back in control of his emotions.

"It'd help." She shrugged.

I turned to Ham. "How much do you want to bet that Grandmother has everyone's DNA? Always the long game."

"I'll work on that." Ham didn't bother showing disgust. He knew how she worked — probably better than I did, considering his own damage-control team. I had so much to learn.

I plucked the printout from Tess's hand. It was of Maya standing outside Nadine's the night of the dinner. Her face was lit up, and she was waving — to me, if I remembered correctly. Would she ever again light up like that in my presence?

Rita stepped out of the room, and I overheard her barking commands into her cell.

"Eckley's involvement in the Twitter bomb makes sense, but how does Maya fit in? Why would he take the chance of exposing his daughter? Or, more to the point, of exposing his relationship with Maya's mom?" Tess scribbled something in a leather journal. I wondered how many high-powered secrets it held.

"Maybe he didn't realize," Mei said. "Maya was just a kid when her mother was killed."

"I was seven."

Everyone in the room circled around to stare at the gray-eyed girl standing with one foot in the doorway.

"I only met him once that I remember, but at the time I didn't know who he was. He was never interested in being a father."

Rita stood behind Maya, absorbing every word.

"She always said I had his eyes." Maya approached the picture on the wall. "But I never cared. For me, my father was a fairy tale." She crossed her arms, cocked her head, and studied his photo as if she were in a museum or art gallery.

"He never contacted you — ?"

"No. And I never tried to get in touch."

"After — so you knew who he was?" Rita's kind voice softened the blow.

"Years ago. Mo — Agnes confessed all."

"And you never reached out? Not even for money?" Rita's smile was dubious and difficult to read. "You're a billionaire's daughter living in Mattapan, and you never thought to ask for money?"

Rita and Tess had done their homework. I'd never mentioned Mattapan to them. It was amazing how much info people of this caliber could turn up in a few short hours. Or terrifying.

"No." Maya stiffened. "Agnes is my only parent — the only parent I need. And the only one I want. Ever."

Rita turned to Ham. "We can use this."

"Use what? Maya?" I flipped to Eckley's photo again. "I'm not comfortable with that. What if …?"

"How can you use it?" Maya asked. "Is he the one responsible for this?" She motioned to the wall of Twitter photos.

"We suspect his wife is. Not sure about his involvement." Rita spoke to Maya as an equal, unlike Grandmother, which was a refreshing change. However, the implication that Eckley's wife was involved in the attacks on my family wasn't comforting at all. "She's planning a run for the presidency, and she's not shy about taking out potential opponents, including your mother."

"Mom's never hinted about a run," I said.

"But she's a Carmichael, and there are always murmurings." Rita shrugged. "Governor Eckley plans for everything."

"President? This is all about politics?" Maya spoke to no one in particular. Her face crumbled. "What would I have to do?"

"Sign a contract saying you'll never acknowledge him and never ask for money," Rita said.

"In exchange for what?" I asked.

"Silence and safety. Eckley won't want his wife to know." Tess dug out some legal papers, spread them on the table, and tapped a section. "According to the prenup — "

"So there *is* a prenup! And you have a copy." Fee peered over Tess's shoulder.

"The contract would have to insist that neither of you would ever acknowledge your connection to the other. Make a permanent break."

Maya sat in a chair next to the window that overlooked the ocean. She stared at the water, lost in thought.

"Wait a minute," Ham interjected. "She should get something

out of him, a one-time payment, at least, after everything."

Mei and Fiona both nodded.

Maya shook her head, but she didn't turn from the window. "Even if he offered me a dime, I'd tell him where to shove it."

"Think, Maya," Fiona said. "I know you hate him. Hell, we all hate him, and none of us has your reason, but this could change — "

"Change what? Bring my mom back?" She whipped her head around.

Everyone looked away, except me. I moved closer. Kneeling down, I took her hands in mine.

She didn't pull away.

"What about a fund to help people like Florence? You wouldn't even have to take the credit. It could be anonymous, but you could make a difference with money like that, help women like your mom, or like Flo." I watched her shoulders sag, and she turned her face to wipe away a tear.

"Who's Florence?" Rita studied the Twitter photos.

"She's not up there," I said. "Maya wants to be a community organizer."

Rita pounced on the idea. "We could arrange that, I'm sure. From what I understand, Eckley would lose everything, even his dog, which he loves more than anything, if his wife finds out about any indiscretion."

"But if he's not involved in this" — Mei motioned to the folders on the table — "how will he get his wife to stop?"

"This." Rita unearthed a file from her bag and spread photos on the table. "Governor Eckley has been canoodling with this man for years."

Mei leaned over to study the photo. "Is that — ?"

"Yep. The Texan running for senator." Rita tapped the photo. "This is how Eckley convinces his wife to back down. And this" — she pointed to Maya — "is how we protect Maya. Mutual-ly assured destruction for husband and wife, but they won't know it. Eckley won't want his wife to find out about Maya, so he'll force the governor, who wants to run for president on family values, to back down lest he expose her own affair. We'll deal with them separately, of course, but they'll shut up. Both have too much to lose."

"How'd you know about the affair?" Ham asked.

Rita's shrug made one thing clear: it was best not to ask questions. How many of our secrets did she have in her back pocket?

Fee let out a deep breath. "That's brilliant. Sick, but brilliant."

I glanced at Maya, who nodded. She then stood and left the room, without uttering a word.

"This is an ugly world," I said.

"And it'll only get uglier," Mei responded as Ham rested a hand on her shoulder.

I found Maya in the library, gazing out the window. Lights from the TV crews over the ridge could be seen off to the far right. She faced left, watching the ocean.

"Hi," I said, approaching her shyly.

She didn't turn around. "Do you know what I hated the most growing up?" she said.

I perched on the window ledge next to her. "What?"

Maya crossed her arms. "Feeling like everything was my fault. If I hadn't been born, my mom would probably be alive."

I blinked away tears.

"You have your own burden," she went on, finally facing me. "Pat wasn't kidding when he said your parents had you after Craig's death and Ham's injury, was he?"

"No. He wasn't kidding." I looked away, ashamed.

"Ham's eye isn't that bad. I was expecting much worse."

"For years, he's been told the opposite."

"So much baggage, even before we were born." Maya sighed. "Earlier, when I was talking to Mom, I realized you've only introduced me to Fiona and Pat. In class, you don't talk to anyone but me." She stared out the window again. "You're just as alone as I am, if not more. You've lived your life in front of the world, yet you have so few connections. What was it like?"

I wasn't expecting her to ask me a question, and my voice came out thick with emotion when I answered. "It's all I've ever known."

"Is it all you want?"

I followed her eyes, her focus on the moonlight shimmering over the rolling water. At night, from the safety of the library, it looked beautiful, peaceful. But the thought of being out there alone was terrifying.

I shook my head.

Maybe she sensed my fear, because she added, "Sometimes you have to be alone to learn how strong you can be."

I tapped a finger against the glass. "I feel like I'm adrift in the dark out there, and I can't find the lighthouse to bring me home."

Maya mulled over my words. "I'm really sorry about … the video. I had no idea." She massaged her eyelids.

I snorted. "That was the idea. I didn't want you to know how much of a loser I am."

She smiled sadly, and I thought she was going to reply that she knew. Instead, she said, "I never thought of you that way. I still don't."

"How do you feel about me, then? About us?"

Maya took my hand in hers. "I'm still working that out in my head."

I stared down at my Nikes.

Turning, Maya craned her neck and lifted my chin with one finger. "The way I see it, it's good that I'm still thinking about it. Usually, I make snap judgments, but you have this way about you."

Perhaps I knew what she meant, because I felt the same about her. Everything had been against us from the beginning, and on some level I think I sensed that. But I couldn't walk away. The day I met Maya, my life changed.

"Do you see that?" Maya pointed out the window.

"What?" I squinted, half expecting to see Susie Q belly crawling up the beach.

"That." Maya tapped the glass.

"The spiderweb?" Grandmother must really be losing her marbles to not have noticed that.

"No. A handkerchief left by a fairy."

"Wh — ?" I started to argue. Then I remembered our conversation at Walden Pond. "Well, look at that." I leaned my forehead against the cool glass. "It's beautiful."

"It is." The two words were filled with emotion.

I turned my face to Maya, my forehead against the pane creating a muted screeching sound. But Maya wasn't staring at the web; she was gazing at me.

Maybe I could believe in fairies. Hell, before I met Maya, I hadn't even believed in love. Not for me, anyway. With Maya by my side, I realized I could believe in anything. I reached for her hand, and she laced her fingers through mine.

Fee popped her head around the library door. "You two ready for dinner?"

The three of us found Ham, Mei, Rory, Pat, and Agnes in the dining room, where ten empty chairs were positioned around the table.

"Where are Rita and Tess?" I asked.

"Heading to Texas," Ham said.

"Does that mean — ?" Agnes was unable to finish her question.

"It means you and Maya don't have to worry about a thing."

"We can stay?" Agnes probed.

"Absolutely. And if you ever have any problems, just give me a call." Ham passed Agnes a business card.

She gasped. "You work in the White House?"

Ham winked, and then motioned for Maya and me to sit. "I'm famished, and I'm not sure my manners will hold out much longer. Agnes, Pat, this smells delicious."

"I can't take the credit. It was all Agnes." Pat tucked a napkin into his shirt.

A smorgasbord of fried chicken, deviled eggs, cornbread, Jambalaya, creamed corn, baby back ribs, dinner rolls, and other side dishes I didn't even know existed covered the table.

Fee pointed at a plate. "Are those fried green tomatoes?"

"They sure are." Agnes grinned. "Ever had one?"

Everyone but Maya shook their heads.

Rory bit into one. "You're hired."

"Rory!" Fiona and I shouted.

Ham rolled his eyes. "You'll have to forgive my cousin. He's been living on cafeteria-style food."

"Ham!" Mei said.

Rory laughed. "It's true. In and out of rehab since I was sixteen. Unlike the rest of the clan, I'm rough around the edges."

Fee stiffened in her seat, but then she glanced at her brother and her posture softened — a small miracle.

"I'm glad you approve." Agnes smiled at him. "I love cooking for people. You're always welcome at our house, all of you." She gazed around the table.

"Does that mean the Sunday dinners will continue?" Pat asked.

"Of course. And now that I've discovered you know your way around the kitchen, Pat, you should come over early. I'll show you all I know. Maya only enjoys making coffee." Agnes winked at her.

"I'll make sure he's there bright and early." Fiona bit into a drumstick.

"Would Mrs. Carmichael ...?" Agnes blushed. "I mean would Lillian and Ainsley like to join us for dinner? There's plenty for everyone."

I sucked in my breath at hearing Agnes say those names.

"Mom, Ainsley is sitting next to you." Maya patted her hand as if Agnes were a dementia patient.

"She means my grandmother," I explained.

Maya's jaw dropped. "You're named after your grand-mother?"

I nodded.

"So you really are the Chosen One," she muttered.

"I was," I replied in little more than a murmur. "Now, I'm just Ainsley."

"Agnes, to answer your question, Mother and Grandmother have left the estate." Ham reached for a rib.

"Where'd they go?" Fiona asked.

"Back to Boston."

"Do they know?" I jerked my head in Maya's direction.

"They're aware that everything has been taken care of."

"Golly, Ham, this is a first." Fiona looked shell-shocked, but it was hard to determine whether she was happy or scared about the power shift. Ham had always craved power, but could he handle it? Only time would tell whether Ham would turn out like Grandmother.

"It's best for all of us if we act as if everything is normal. That means you two" — he pointed to me and Maya — "go back to school on Monday."

Maya's shoulders slumped.

"I'll be right by your side," I whispered in her ear, taking her hand in mine.

She squeezed my hand. "You better stop me from punching Susie Q's lights out, then."

I giggled. "Oh, I wish."

Around ten, everyone dispersed to their rooms to settle in for the night.

After saying goodnight to Agnes, Maya and I walked to my bedroom.

"I know you probably want to talk, but it's been a long day. Do you mind if we go to bed?" Maya asked.

I nodded meekly.

In bed, I clutched Maya like it was the last time I would ever hold her in my arms.

"Is it weird?" she asked.

"Jesus!" I put a hand to my chest. "I thought you were asleep. Is *what* weird?"

"Having me in your bed, here?" She had her back to me, but I sensed she was grinning.

"Oddly, it's not, even though I know it should be. Does that make sense?" I rolled onto my back.

"It makes Ainsley sense." She flipped over and brushed a red curl off my cheek.

"What does that mean?"

She shrugged.

"Can I ask one question?"

Maya feigned a dramatic sigh and puffed out her cheeks. "If you must."

"That brand on your arm, it's your real initials, isn't it? CT, for Carisa Torres. That's why Agnes got so upset."

She sucked her bottom lip into her mouth and nodded.

"Promise me we'll talk more in the morning?" I ran a finger down her nose.

"I promise." She yawned, nestling her head down into the pillow.

An odd silence invaded the room, but outside, the wind stirred the trees, scraping branches against the side of the old house. When I was small, I'd been convinced the house was haunted. Tonight, I'd learned about the family's real phantoms. Was it possible to shake them off? I sighed, leaving the question for now. The real question was whether I could go forward — with Maya.

CHAPTER
twenty-three

THE NEXT MORNING, I AWOKE alone.

I hadn't expected Maya to slip out during the night, but maybe I should have.

The kitchen was silent. It was half past six, and for the first time in my family's recent history, no bugler announced the new day on the Carmichael compound.

I hummed as I prepared the coffee pot.

"Don't tell me we have to live with your shitty coffee this morning." Fee wore one of Pat's shirts, and her hair was a complete wreck.

"Afraid so."

"Does that mean what I think it means?"

I chewed at the corner of my lip.

"She may come around, with time." Fee gave me a one-armed squeeze.

"Maybe."

Fiona slid six slices of bread into the toaster.

"Is Agnes gone too?" she asked.

"I'm assuming so."

Pat yawned in the doorway, more bedraggled than Fiona. "Where's Grover? Outside?"

We both shrugged, and Pat frowned.

"Maybe he slipped into Ham and Mei's room," I said.

"Nope."

We turned to find Ham and his fiancée, looking only slightly more put together than the rest of us.

"The doggie door is locked." Fee pointed to it.

Pat wiggled the door handle. "But the door isn't locked. Has anyone come or gone?" He didn't wait for an answer, shoving the door wide open. "Grover," he called, growing increasingly frantic when the dog didn't appear.

The only answer was a whip of wind coming off the Atlantic. A storm was brewing on the horizon.

We quickly broke into search parties. Pat and Fiona headed for the grounds around the big house. Ham and Mei set out for the tennis court area. And I had my sights on the dunes, where he'd played fetch with Maya the previous evening.

I cupped my mouth with both hands. "Grover!"

Not a sound, only the wind.

I pushed on, cresting a slight hill and praying the news cameras were gone. Some miracle brought forth the first big storm of the season, scaring off the press. In another hour or so, flakes would be flying and the waves crashing.

"Grover!" I called, straining my ears when they picked up a small bark off in the distance. I called his name again and cupped my ear. Sure enough, I heard a bark. "I'm coming, Grover!" I yelled, running toward the water.

A tennis ball whirred by my head.

Tennis ball?

Grover zoomed after it, yapping.

The dog's enthusiastic bark was followed by laughter.

Could it be?

The terrier dropped the ball at my feet. "Come here," I said, and he jumped up and licked my face. "You scared us, little man."

Grover yipped in reply.

I chucked the ball in the direction it had come from, and he took off after it like a bandit. I followed, hoping beyond hope.

Each step brought me closer to the truth, and I held my breath.

Laughter carried on the wind as the dog ran into the grass, and I arrived in time to witness Maya scoop Grover into her arms. She turned back toward the house, waving for me to follow.

And I did.

"Are you ready for coffee?" she asked when we reached the house, a squirming Grover still in her arms.

A tear trickled down my cheek. "You're still here."

A broad smile mirrored the happiness in her eyes. "Of course! Who knows what would happen if I left you all alone."

I pulled her into my arms, squashing Grover, not that he minded a group hug.

"I love you, Maya the Gray," I said and then kissed her.

"The Gray?" She cocked her head and quirked one eyebrow.

I didn't answer. I was too busy kissing her. And I didn't have any intention of stopping.

AUTHOR'S NOTE

Thank you for reading *The Chosen One*. If you enjoyed the novel, please consider leaving a review on Goodreads or Amazon. No matter how long or short, I would very much appreciate your feedback.

You can follow me, T. B. Markinson, on Twitter at @50YearProject, on Facebook, or email me at tbmarkinson@gmail.com. I would love to know your thoughts.

ABOUT THE AUTHOR

TB Markinson is an American writer living in England. When she isn't writing, she's traveling the world, watching sports on the telly, reading, or visiting pubs — not necessarily in that order. She has also written *A Clueless Woman*, *A Woman Lost*, *A Woman Ignored*, *Marionette*, *Confessions from a Coffee Shop*, *Claudia Must Die*, *Girl Love Happens*, and *The Miracle Girl*. For a full listing of all her published works, please visit her Amazon Page.

34243533R00137

Printed in Great Britain
by Amazon